MAKE HASTE SLOWLY

SHORT CREEK MYSTERIES

Book One Make Haste Slowly

MAKE HASTE SLOWLY

BOOK ONE
SHORT CREEK MYSTERIES

By
Amy Rognlie

Make Haste Slowly
Published by Mountain Brook Ink
White Salmon, WA U.S.A.

ISBN 978-1943959-33-4

The Team: Miralee Ferrell, Nikki Wright, Cindy Jackson
Cover Design: Indie Cover Design, Lynnette Bonner Designer

Mountain Brook Ink is an inspirational publisher offering fiction you can believe in.

Printed in the U.S.A. 2017

"We all of us need to be toppled off the throne of self, my dear," he said. "Perched up there the tears of others are never upon our own cheek."

—Elizabeth Goudge, *The White Witch*

Dedication

Dedicated to the memory of my two earthly fathers,

Thomas Lee Burns
(1942-1970)
and
Salvatore "Sam" Spano
(1938-2015)

I can't wait to see you again. Thank you both for your unwavering love for God and for providing me with a solid foundation for my faith and my life.
You loved me well.

Acknowledgments

Thank you to Danny Rognlie, Jan Spano, Vicki Burtchell and Autumn McMurray for reading my manuscript, giving helpful feedback and cheering me on the entire way.

Thank you to my husband, Greg Rognlie, for the endless supply of chocolate and encouraging words.

Thank you to my students (you know who you are) for your excitement and enthusiastic encouragement that spurs me on to continue both writing and teaching writing.

Thank you to my Heavenly Father, who is the Giver of all good things.

CHAPTER ONE

It all started on July 1st, exactly four days before my thirty-sixth birthday. I wasn't expecting anything out of the ordinary, especially since I'd moved into town a few months earlier—who knew it was my birthday? But here it was, an oversized gift bag on the back doorstep of my florist shop.

The pugs strained at their leashes, but I held them firmly. No telling what that bag contained. And I had to be cautious, especially since I could see that a hand was still clutching the package.

Edging closer, I was momentarily relieved to discover that an arm and a body belonged to the gift-bearing hand. I jumped and stumbled back. A person was lying under the crepe myrtle tree next to my porch. A man. Middle-aged, maybe.

Dear God.

I glanced toward the small church next door, but I wouldn't get any help from that direction. Mona would never be there this early, for sure, and I didn't see the reverend's white pickup yet, either.

I could call 911, but what if I was overreacting? What if it was simply a bum who had found a quiet place to rest? I peeked again at the...body, and decided I wasn't overreacting. My knees were about to give way, and I definitely needed my inhaler.

Punching in 911, I retreated to wait in my van. It didn't take long.

Three hours later I sat on my steps, this time relating the morning's events to my best friend, Mona. Mona's ever-present cloud of perfume hovered around us in the humid morning, and the pugs, Purl and Intarsia, lounged nearby in the shade of the pecan tree, their eyelids drooping.

Mona settled her ample self on the step next to me. "I can't believe you didn't call me, Callie."

"I did call you."

Mona snorted. "Yeah, after all the excitement was over. Who was it? Was he *dead*?"

I understood Mona's angst. After all, it's not every day that one finds a body next to one's porch—especially in this town. Nothing exciting ever happens in Short Creek, Texas.

"It wasn't anyone I recognized. All I remember is he had brownish-gray hair that was trimmed close around his neck and ears, like he had recently gotten a haircut." How had I remembered that? I shuddered. "Sheriff Earl and a deputy got here first. But they made me go into the shop while they searched for his ID and stuff. Todd and his crew didn't seem to know him either."

If the volunteer fire department squad didn't know the guy, then no one would. Todd Whitney and his men knew everyone.

Mona mulled that over for a minute. "What about the bag? What was in it? Did you keep it?"

"Nope. They had the bomb-sniffing dogs out here and the whole bit. I guess they decided it wasn't explosive, so Todd took it to the station and said they'd release it to me after they had a chance to look at it."

I pictured the large gift bag. Bright yellow with race cars—not exactly my style. But still, it had looked benign enough. Who knew what it might hold? Was it important enough that someone would die trying to get it to me? Or was the stranger's death only an unusual coincidence? I couldn't make sense of it.

"Let's forget about it for a little while." I stood and stretched my legs, careful not to look at the flattened spot of grass under the tree. "I don't know about you, but I need a cup of tea."

Mona glanced at her watch. "I've got to get to work. The phone will be ringing off the hook, and you know the boss."

I grinned, picturing Mona's "boss." Blond, single, and thirty-something, Reverend Houston Gregory made for the most interesting parson I'd ever known. I attended one of the other churches in town, though, so Handsome Houston and I were acquainted more as neighbors than anything.

Mona shoved a brown paper lunch bag into my hand,

ending my visions of Houston Gregory. "Put this in your fridge for me. The one at the church is broken. I'll be over at noon." She headed toward the hedge that separated the church's parking lot from mine, then turned to give me a stern look.

"Don't open the mystery bag without me!"

I sighed. In the last few hours, my life had once again gotten way more complicated than I would have ever wished for. I wrestled open the door of my shop, C. Willikers, and unhooked the girls from their leashes. It was already ten o'clock in the morning, and I hadn't even tidied up the store yet from last night's successful *Knit, Sip and Gab* session.

The landline was ringing, the plants needed watering, and the dogs were staring at me. *Why hadn't I opened the blinds yet so they could sleep in the square of sunshine?* they were likely wondering. Pugs need their after-waking-in-the-morning nap, after all. Giving in to the two pairs of brown and beseeching eyes, I obediently opened the blinds.

The sun flooded in through the large bay window, illuminating the dust on the bookshelves. Had I forgotten to dust again? I glanced at the little plaque that Mona had given me the other day—a large, wooly sheep with the words, "You can touch the dust, but please don't write in it."

I sighed again. Owning my florist/book/knitting shop was turning out to be a much bigger deal than I had imagined. After what I'd been through the last few years, I was basically looking for peace. Forget peace. I'd settle for *normalcy*. So when Aunt Dot suggested I purchase her house and move here to Short Creek, I took her up on it.

I'd always thought it would be fun to own a yarn store or a florist shop. Or both at once. I had pictured myself sitting serenely, surrounded by shelves and shelves of gorgeous yarn, knitting up a storm while I chatted with other likewise serene knitters. Plants and flowers bloomed around us in glorious profusion, while birds sang outside the window, and—

"Ha!" I said out loud. The dogs jumped, then stared at me again.

Life in general, it seemed, hadn't turned out quite how I thought it would. Take my name, for example. One would think that a woman like me would have a lovely, romantic name like Sophia or Charlotte. I would have even settled for Anastasia or Jacqueline. But instead, I got Calendula. Calendula! Of course, such a name needs to be shortened to something a little more livable, so Callie it is.

I guess it fits me, in a way, since I'm not exactly a supermodel. I have never been able to figure out what to do with my stick-straight, mud-brown hair, so I let it be what it is—straight and brown. At least I'm not too tall or too short, though I could stand to lose a few pounds. And I tried wearing contact lenses, but they weren't worth the pain. I'll stick with my glasses, thank you very much. Besides, they help hide the little wrinkles that are forming around my thirty-something eyes—and the pugs don't care what I look like.

But now this! What if the stranger lying under my crepe myrtle was a...a murderer or something? Or maybe he had come to warn me of imminent danger. My heart started to pound.

"Stop it, Callie!" I whopped the feather duster against the counter.

Cut it out, now. I had read my share of Nancy Drew mysteries, so I knew how these things worked. The corpse would turn out to be the little old man from down the street, who just happened to have a heart attack under my tree. No mystery; no foul play. The real mystery was what was in the bag. And that probably wouldn't turn out to be much of a mystery either. And maybe the bag wasn't even meant for me. Maybe—

The landline rang again, and I decided I'd better answer it this time. The dust would have to wait. I tripped over the dogs as I grabbed for the phone.

"Good morning, C. Will—"

"Hey, Willie. Sheriff Earl Markham down here at the city offices."

Had he called me Willie? I pulled the phone slightly away from my ear. Sheriff Earl was not a quiet man, especially when he was wound up about something.

"Sheriff Earl. I'm glad you called—"

"Y'all can come down and get this package whenever ya want, 'cept don't come down at suppertime."

See? Exactly as I thought. The gift bag was no big deal.

I pulled into the gravel parking lot of the city offices a minute later. In Short Creek, everything was a minute away.

I poked my head into the receptionist's office. "Hello?"

No one appeared, so I wandered through the office into the volunteer fire department. Maybe Todd, the department captain, was still on duty. I knew him from church, sort of. Really, I only knew his name, but—

"Got yer stuff right here, Miss Willie." Sheriff Earl shuffled in through the door, a box in his hands. "This here box was inside the bag. Careful, though. Not real sturdy. Bottom might fall out on ya."

"It's Callie."

"Say again?"

"My name is Callie, not Willie." I took the open box from him and glanced down inside. I couldn't tell what was in there, because the contents were hidden by the gift bag that laid on top. From the looks of it, Sheriff Earl and his boys had opened the bag with about as much care as a German Shepherd tearing into a new bone.

"Sorry, ma'am." He pushed his glasses up farther on his nose. "Guess I got yer name mixed up with the name of your store. Kind of the same, ain't they?"

I met his suddenly intense gaze with a bland smile. "Well, they both have two of the letter 'l' in the middle."

Right.

But he couldn't know the story behind the names, could he?

"I'll need ya to set down right here and tell me everything that happened this morning." He motioned to a battered office chair.

"Again?" I felt sick to my stomach. "I already told you all I know."

"Well, now, we gotta rule out all the possibilities, ma'am."

If I didn't know better, I'd think this backwater, bowlegged sheriff was calling me a suspect. It was going to be a long day.

I drove the six blocks back to the shop after Earl's interrogation, more shaken than I'd like to admit. How did finding a body under one's tree make one a murder suspect? *God, have mercy.* I half-groaned, half-prayed. I didn't have the strength to go through something like this again. It felt like history was repeating itself. I thought I had put all of that behind me but—

He had somehow found out about the case. That's the only way he could have known the connection between my name and the name of my store. When I moved down here to Texas, I decided to make a clean break of things, which is why I had gone back to using my maiden name. I didn't have anything to hide, exactly. Simply wanted a new start to be a new start. But I didn't want to forget completely, so that's why I named the store "C. Willikers," since that was my name for almost a decade.

But somehow, the weasely little sheriff had learned information about me.

Callie Willie.

My husband, Kev, had teasingly called me that until eventually, it had gotten shortened to Willie. Even some of my friends used the silly name. But no one here knew that.

Or rather, no one here *should* know that.

Why would a sheriff in Short Creek, Texas have a reason to know about my past?

And why would he practically *tell* me he knew about it?

I had to get a grip. Focus my mind on something else. I blew out my breath.

The mystery gift, now a plain brown box devoid of its garish bag, stared at me from the passenger seat. I really, really wanted another peek inside, but I had promised Mona that I wouldn't open it without her.

Mona has been my best friend since I moved to Short Creek a few months ago. The fact that she is twenty years older than me and married doesn't seem to matter. Mona is a spunky gal, as my Aunt Dot would say, and she attached herself to me the minute I arrived in town. Literally.

The little town of Short Creek, Texas, still surrounded by corn fields and horse pastures, is a far cry from the suburbs of Columbus, Ohio. I had been shocked at how much lower the housing prices were here. Back home, I had barely been able to pay my mortgage on my decent school social worker salary. And despite being only eight miles from the nearest city, Short Creek had managed to retain its small-town feel. It currently boasted four churches, two schools, two gas stations, a post office, a donut shop—because no self-respecting town in Texas could even be *called* a town without a donut shop—a dollar store, a barbeque joint, and one traffic light.

I had safely driven a large U-Haul all the way from Columbus, Ohio, alone, only to be rear-ended by Mona as I arrived in Short Creek. We've been friends ever since.

I pulled up in front of my shop and sat there, letting the air conditioning run while I gathered myself. Mona stuck her head out of the side door of the church, waving and grinning as if I'd arrived from starring in a TV show or something. I knew she'd be over to inspect the contents of the mystery gift before I could even open my van door.

Sure enough, by the time I reached the door of the shop, she was bustling across the church parking lot as fast as her short legs could carry her. Houston, the pastor, trailed behind her, appearing more rattled than his usual unflappable self.

I wedged the box under one arm and held the door open with my foot.

"Callie!" Houston looked me over, as if appraising my mental state. "Mona told me about your…uh… excitement this morning."

I raised my eyebrows. "I guess you could call it that."

"Are you okay? That must have been such a shock." He used the voice I assumed he usually reserved for ministering to desperately ill parishioners. "I imagine it was difficult to—"

"Well, open the box! I'm dying to know what's in there!" Mona burst out.

I groaned. "You didn't say that."

"What?"

Houston's eyes met mine above Mona's head. We both knew from past experience that it wasn't worth explaining. Or rather, trying to explain.

I plunked the box down on the large counter where I had been happily creating the altar flower arrangement for the Dorsey wedding...until today, that is.

Mona's large, red, Texas-shaped earrings quivered with her excitement as we gathered around the box.

"Okay, here goes!"

I lifted the lid from the box, and we all stared at its contents.

Houston broke the silence. "Looks like someone sent you the leftovers from his garage sale," he said, his tone grave.

I had to agree. The hodgepodge of used vases, old glassware, and a few well-used books meant nothing to me. And someone had *died* for this?

Mona snatched the box. "There's gotta be something else in here," she mumbled, throwing aside the crumpled pieces of newspaper that had been used as packing material. "Nothing." She dug around some more, then flipped through the books. A piece of paper fluttered to the ground. "Ah ha!" She snatched it up and waved it in the air as if she held a winning lottery ticket. "Some sort of secret message!"

She thrust the paper into my hand. "It says 'For C.W.' at the top. I assume that means you."

I smoothed the paper open on the counter so my friends could see.

Once again, we all stared blankly.

"It's a drawing of an anchor...with a dolphin wrapped around the anchor. And some letters and numbers written under it." Mona's brow furrowed. "What kind of clue is that?"

Houston cleared his throat. "Callie's garage-sale admirer is a sailor?" he drawled.

Mona snickered. "Yeah, one who loves dolphins."

"I know what it means," I said.

I *did* know. But I didn't know why. I mean, I didn't know why or how it was connected with the contents of the box. Or crepe myrtle man. Or me.

My friends both stared at me as the pugs had done earlier.

I traced the drawing with my finger. "The anchor with a dolphin is a symbol for the maxim, *Festina lente*. It means—"

"Oh, I know!" Mona said. "It's Italian for 'Fast for Lent.' Get it? Like *fast*--ina for a *la Lent*-e?" She swooped her hand in the air, presumably in imitation of someone Italian.

Houston choked on his iced tea. "Then it's a message from *God*, not from a sailor." He stared at me in mock horror. "Wow, Callie! What did you *do*?"

"Ha, ha. Very funny, you guys." I rolled my eyes. "*Festina lente* is Latin for 'Make haste slowly.' It's an oxymoron."

"That must be better than a regular moron." Mona stage-whispered behind her hand to Houston, clearly knowing she was pushing it with me.

I should have known she wouldn't have been able to let that one pass. "Well, if you're not interested—"

Mona patted my hand. "We are, Callie. But you looked so serious, and—"

I exhaled loudly. "This *is* serious, Mona! A guy is dead and apparently I'm supposed to know what to do about it."

Houston clunked his iced tea cup down on the table. "Callie's right. We need to take this seriously."

"Thank you, Reverend." I rewarded him with a smile. "So the adage itself and this symbol of the anchor with a dolphin around it has been used for centuries. Since Roman times, at least."

Mona wrinkled her forehead. "But what does it *mean*?"

"The general idea is that one should proceed with caution. Or at least preparation. Caesar Augustus used this idea of 'making haste slowly' with his soldiers. He said...um..., let me think." I could almost remember it. "Oh, I know. He said something like 'Better a safe commander than a bold commander.'"

Silence.

I looked from Mona to Houston and back again. "He sometimes also used an image of a crab and a butterfly to illustrate the idea," I added helpfully, in case they didn't get it.

More silence.

Mona tapped her fingernail on the top of her Diet Dr. Pepper can. "How did you know all of that, Callie?"

I shrugged. "My bachelor's degree was in classical literature."

"And so...?" Houston peered at me.

I shrugged again. "I studied Latin. Shakespeare. Aristotle. Gobs of history. You know, the works."

"I watched *Macbeth* once on PBS," Mona piped up. "I thought it was the weirdest thing I had ever seen."

I squeezed my eyes closed for a second. It would take more hours than I had in a week to explain Shakespeare to Mona. And anyway, weren't we supposed to be figuring out what had happened this morning?

I opened my eyes. "History class is over for the day, children." I shooed them both out of the back door into the blazing mid-afternoon Texas heat. "I have work to do. Call me if you think of anything that would explain the box."

CHAPTER TWO

Neither of them called. But Mona texted once to let me know that she hadn't thought of anything, with about eight exclamation marks at the end. Then she texted again to let me know that her grandkids were headed over to their house and Rob was out of town and she hoped she would survive the evening with all five of them at once by herself and would I please pray. Six exclamation marks and three smiley faces. Mona texted like she talked. On and on without a breath in between.

I shook my head. I am definitely a praying woman, but I'm not so sure that Mona's action-packed evening with the grans ranks very high on my prayer list. On the other hand, today's events certainly demanded to be handled with way more wisdom and insight than I could ever possess.

I had relied many times on the Scripture verse which says if anyone lacks wisdom, to ask of God and He would give it to him...her.

"Well, I could sure use divine insight here, Lord," I prayed as I drove home the few blocks from the store. I couldn't make heads or tails of what had happened today. I prayed for crepe myrtle man's family. I prayed for the sheriff. I prayed for myself, that God would watch over me and protect me. I hadn't admitted it earlier, but I was feeling a little creeped out by all of this. What if there was a murderer on the loose still? Who would be his next target?

I scooped the newspaper off of my driveway and laid it on the seat of the rocking chair on my tiny front porch so I would remember to take it in the house with me. I still couldn't believe I could afford Aunt Dot's lovely old Victorian cottage, with a little money left to spare at the end of the month. Just the memories this house held for me were worth far more than that.

The tiny house still needed work, but the wood floors, odd little nooks and crannies, and two small bedrooms were perfect for me. The kitchen was not large, but it was bright and sunny enough that the African violets were thriving on the windowsill. My hand-crocheted lace valence was the crowning touch.

It was nearly seven o'clock in the evening, but it was still ninety degrees out and my plants were feeling it. Had I watered this morning? My brain still felt a little—

"Callie! What was all that ruckus at y'all's place this mornin' with the sheriff and all?" My neighbor, Sherm, hobbled over to the small fence that divided our yards.

I groaned. Sherm Nelson was nosier than a...a pug sniffing out treats. And almost deaf.

"Nothing much, Sherm," I yelled. "An unexpected birthday gift is all."

I turned on the hose. Maybe if I looked busy, he would stop asking questions. I watered the hot-pink bougainvillea that bloomed in the hanging pot by the door, then moved to the lantana. I had fallen in love with lantana when I moved down here, and the ones near the porch were exceeding my expectations. My current favorite was the Dallas Red variety, and if the number of butterflies that visited it on a regular basis was any indication, it was a popular variety with them too. I had even seen a hummingbird or two hover over its brilliant red, yellow and orange blossoms, then dart quickly away.

"Seems like y'all wouldn't need the sheriff over a happy hitch," he yelled back, hooking his thumb in his overalls. "Musta been some weddin'."

What?

I had no idea what he was talking about, so I smiled and waved, hoping he'd take the hint.

He waved back, but he wasn't giving up. "Whose was it?" he bellowed.

Whose what?

I laid the hose in the flower bed. The purple heart was looking a little scraggly this time of year. When I had planted it in the spring, I had been enchanted by its dark, violet-purple leaves and delicate lavender flowers, but if it didn't perk up soon, it would wind up in the compost bin.

Sherm still hovered near the fence. I ignored him as I deadheaded the marigolds. Finally, it dawned on me that he thought I had said "summer hitch" when I said "birthday gift." I can be a little slow on the uptake sometimes. And he knew I was a florist, so...I guess it made sense in a weird kind of way.

I ambled over to him. "Sherm, I said it was a birthday gift. Nothing to do with a wedding."

He squinted at me. "A Thursday wish?"

"A present. A birthday gift," I shouted. I raised my eyebrows at him and smiled encouragingly.

"Is that right? The sheriff had him a birthday this mornin'?" His face lit up. "All that fuss for a party?"

Something like that.

"Not a party, Sherm. Only a gift." At least I hope that's what it was. Just a gift. But somehow, I had the feeling that it was much more than that. I turned off the hose and headed in, the pugs panting along after me.

After checking to make sure I had locked the front door behind me, I fed the dogs, fixed myself a tuna salad sandwich, and sank into a chair with the newspaper. It would be good to get my mind off the situation for a few minutes. The paper still felt warm after lying out all day in the sun, and as I unfurled it from its plastic cocoon, its familiar papery-inky smell comforted me. My eyes moved first, as always, to the Bible verse of the day on the front page of the local *Short Creek Star*. I liked that a newspaper would still print Scripture, even in this day and age.

I had moved to a smaller community on purpose, and that's partly why I subscribed to the newspaper instead of grabbing the headlines online when I had a spare minute. I wanted to read about the little details of the community that would help me feel like I was starting to belong here.

I loved the *Star's* features on historic buildings in the area, particularly the old churches. I especially enjoyed the "This day in history ten, twenty and thirty years ago" section, and the "Pastor's Corner" section. However, I was not so much a fan of the weekly advice column, written by a woman named Joyce, who specialized in dispensing inane "advice" in response to equally inane questions sent in by her fans. Yeesh. I usually skipped that section. But I did often skim the obits, the birth announcements, and even the help-wanted ads. And I *always* did the crossword puzzle and the cryptograms. Uncle Garth would have been proud

I rose and put my dishes in the sink, surprised by the sudden fatigue that gripped me. It was exhausting to find a body under one's tree, apparently. Bedtime couldn't come soon enough.

An hour later I sat in bed, one of Aunt Dot's crocheted afghans across my lap, reading the Psalms until I finally felt comforted enough to turn out the light and try to sleep. I closed my eyes against the images of the man's body lying on the ground, refusing to let my thoughts go there. That was something I was learning, at least, in the aftermath of these last few difficult years. How to purposely focus my brain on something good or beautiful, instead of obsessing over something I couldn't control anyway.

I awoke at dawn, much to my dismay. Sleep would not return, no matter how long I kept my eyes closed, hoping. Nope. Not going to happen.

I grabbed my Bible off my nightstand, and headed to my favorite morning prayer spot. My sunny little office, where I kept my journal, several commentaries, about six versions of the Bible, and my Book of Common Prayer was my own private sanctuary. Over these last tumultuous years of my life, I had learned to cling to God and His Word for dear life. Spending time daily helped me to stay focused; to remember Who was in control.

I finally shuffled out to the kitchen to put the tea kettle on and stood staring at the contents of the box, which I had brought home from the shop with me last night. I had lined the contents up on my kitchen counter: A vase that looked like it had come from the dollar store. Another, larger vase that still had the green, Styrofoam stuff inside of it from a long-ago flower arrangement. A used coffee mug that said, "Don't Mess with Texas" on it. Another mug that clearly proclaimed it had come from a cheap souvenir shop in Colorado. An ordinary-looking kitchen spoon. A few old books...and the *festina lente* symbol, hand-drawn on a plain white piece of paper. Underneath it was written "PSIS58611."

What in the world? And why did it say "To C.W." when everyone here in Short Creek knew me as Callie Erickson? Maybe the person was confusing my name with my store's name.

The tea kettle whistled, and I mindlessly poured the water over my tea bag. Plain black English Breakfast this morning. Earl Grey was for wintertime. I sloshed in more half and half than necessary.

Make haste slowly.

Okay. What was I supposed to be slowly hastening toward? Sometimes I felt like I had been hastening constantly for the last few years of my life—but not very slowly or intentionally. It was only in this last year or so, since I had moved down here, that I was learning to breathe again.

Festina lente. I stared at the symbol again. It almost looked like someone had doodled it, then scribbled the letters and numbers underneath. If only there was more information to go on. A letter. Or an address or—the newspaper!

"Why didn't we think of that yesterday?" I moaned out loud.

Had I thrown away all of that crumpled newspaper from the box here, or at the shop? I remembered Mona flinging it around when she was pawing through the box, but had I stuffed it back in the box? I couldn't remember.

I jerked open the cupboard under the sink, relieved to find the newspapers near the top of my trash can. I fished all of the wadded balls out and laid them on the kitchen table, then carefully smoothed them out one by one. One page had a large soggy spot from my used tea bag, but otherwise, they were completely fine.

I turned to grab my mug of tea, and nearly tripped over the pugs who were huddled together in their little bed, snoring to beat the band. It was too early to be up and about on a Tuesday morning.

Settling into my usual chair at the kitchen table, from where I could watch the hummingbirds flitting around the feeder, I scanned the wrinkled pages before me. Hmm. Looked like random pages from past issues of the *Star.* A write-up about the drought...a huge article detailing the remodeling project at the high school...the funnies page with the crossword puzzle...the weekly police report...the police report? That might be informative.

I glanced at the date at the top of the page, and sucked in my breath. It couldn't be...but it was. It was the same day, five years ago, that Kev had been killed in the car wreck. I hadn't revisited that day in my mind for a long time, but suddenly there it was, full force.

Since the very beginning, our six-year marriage hadn't been fabulous, but it hadn't been awful either. It just kind of...was. And so when Kev was diagnosed with an unusually aggressive form of ALS at the unheard-of age of twenty-seven, neither of us dealt with it—or each other—very well. But we were committed to our relationship, and we somehow made it work, sort of.

Living in Ohio, Kev had had the best of care available at Cleveland Clinic. For over two years, I drove him back and forth...and back and forth...as the docs tried one thing after another. Our hopes would flare, then dim. Flare, and then dim. Weariness overtook me, along with a terrible hopelessness. I knew God could heal Kev, but apparently, He had a different plan to which I was not privy.

By those last few months, I was beginning to separate from Kev emotionally and I felt constantly guilty about it. Oh, I put on a good show of caring for him. I dutifully doled out meds, adjusted the wheelchair, fed him his meals...but my heart wasn't in it. I loved him as a person, but our marriage had held so little emotional support even in its best days, there was nothing to build on when faced with such a crisis. I felt trapped. Lonely. I had built up a wall around my heart to protect it from the inevitable. My husband was going to die, and I would be alone. *When* it would happen was the only variable.

Kev's brother had offered to take him to his weekly appointment with the specialist that day, and I gratefully accepted. Being a 24/7 caretaker was a little more than I could handle some days. Most days.

I gave Kev a quick peck on the cheek as Gary loaded him into the van, and they were off.

The call came half an hour later.

The guys had been in a terrible accident.

Kev was dead; his brother in critical condition. My world, as I knew it, had imploded. The "if onlys" became enough to drive me bananas. If only we had seen that other specialist. If only I had been more patient with him. If only I had driven him to his appointment that day, and not selfishly wanted a day off. If only I had given him a hug when he left. If only I had told him I loved him one more time. If only...

Now, five years later and in my own cozy kitchen in small-town Central Texas, I shook my head and took a sip of lukewarm tea. I had come a long way since that day, thanks be to God. Both emotionally and physically. And spiritually. I had learned, as the grief books say, how to "look back without staring."

After Kev died, I'd had to regroup. To examine all I ever thought I had known about God, His word, and His promises. I slogged my way through that first year of intense pain, buoyed up by my friends in my women's Bible study group, and my Aunt Dot, of course. After many months, I came to realize that I was not only grieving the loss of my husband, I was grieving the loss of what *should* have been. What *could* have been in our relationship, even before Kev's illness.

I read books...I prayed...I cried. I dug in my flower beds, and planted bushes and vegetables like a gardening maniac for months. Digging, planting, weeding. Digging, planting, weeding. And somehow, slowly, as I knelt on the ground, my hands in the dirt, the sun on my back, day after day, the Holy Spirit began to heal my heart. It didn't come all at once. It came in little bits.

Like the morning I wandered into the prayer garden at nearby St. Andrew's church. The autumn air was crisp, the maple leaves beginning to turn their lovely crimson. My heart had healed enough by then that I could make it through the day without crying. But now I was faced with a new dilemma.

I had to find a job. All the life insurance money had gone to pay for medical bills and for the extra debt that had piled up when I was forced to quit my job as a school social worker and nurse Kev fulltime that last year. There weren't many good jobs open right now in Columbus, and besides, I'd definitely need to make more than what I had been paid before. I would either need to go to work for CPS, or get out of social work altogether and finish my ELC director licensing process that I had started before Kevin's illness.

Neither option sounded appealing. My heart felt...fragile. Beat-up. I wasn't sure I could bear to open myself up again to the pain that came with my chosen field. At this point, working as a cashier at the grocery store seemed like a viable option. Go to work, scan groceries, smile impersonally at customers, go home. I could probably handle that.

I shuffled through golden, early-fallen aspen leaves to sit on the lone bench. The prayer garden was beautiful this time of year. Despite the chilly evenings that had signalled the leaves to turn and fall, the manicured grass was still green, and gold and purple mums bloomed with abandon in the well-kept flower beds. A few bright pink roses peeked out here and there amidst their spotted, yellowing leaves. Sometimes, in places like this, I could feel peace beginning to seep back into my heart.

The fountain had not yet been turned off for the winter, and I watched as a robin hopped tentatively toward the cool mist. He flicked his head back and forth between me and the fountain, then risked another hop closer to the tantalizing pool of water in the bowl.

Exactly like me, I thought ruefully. *Dancing around anxiously, but not ready to plunge in.*

Really? Was that what had been wrong with me for these past couple of days? Was I...*afraid*?

As an optimistic, glass-half-full kind of girl, fear had been a somewhat unknown quantity in my life up until Kev's diagnosis. It still snuck up on me at times and caught me off guard.

But I had finally learned what to do with fear—fear that had the power to suck me under and hold me down until I was gasping for air. I took a deep breath. "Jesus, I trust you," I whispered.

"Jesus, I trust you." Louder this time and with more conviction. "Jesus, I trust you. I believe I *will* see the good of the Lord in the land of the living." That verse from Psalm 27 had become a lifeline, and saying it out loud now somehow caused faith to rise up in my heart. *I* will *see God's goodness again. I will be whole again. I will laugh again. I will hope again. In* this *life—not just when I get to Heaven.*

I brushed at the moisture under my eyes, and glanced toward Mr. Robin, who, his thirst apparently slaked, was poised to dart away. Under his little bird feet, engraved in the granite face of the fountain, I saw the words I had missed earlier:

> *All shall be well, and all manner of things shall be well.*
> *Julian of Norwich, 1342-1416 AD*

I blew out my pent-up breath. It would be well. Ultimately, Jesus would make all things right. I didn't know how...didn't know what it would look like. But my task right now was to trust. To lean. To put one foot in front of the other in the light I had already been given. I could do that.

My phone dinged, yanking me out of the past. I pulled it out of the pocket of my robe, grateful for the distraction. It was Mona, who had, apparently, survived the night with the grandchildren and lived to tell about it. And tell about it, she would. I braced myself mentally for the onslaught of photos and accompanying captions that would be proliferated through social media for the foreseeable future.

Mercifully, she hadn't texted me any photos yet. However, she was wondering if I had any news about "our mystery," as she had begun to call it, and was I still planning to go to the women's fellowship lunch today at the taqueria and if so would I please come pick her up because Rob was *still* out of town and she hated to drive places alone and besides, her foot was hurting from when the oldest gran dropped the croquet ball on it last night and she wouldn't be able to eat much anyway because did I forget she was on her low-carb diet? And the only thing she'd be able to order there was the taco salad. Five exclamation points; frowny face, frowny face.

Dang it! I'd forgotten about the women's lunch, and I was exhausted from merely reading Mona's breathless text. But maybe it would be good for me to go.

I called Mona. "Where are we meeting for lunch?"

"The taqueria in Temple. The one on 31st." She sounded liked she'd been running.

Ugh. I pictured the tiny, hole-in-the-wall Mexican restaurant. I loved Mexican food, and theoretically, I wasn't opposed to hole-in-the-wall places. But I hadn't even heard of the word "taqueria" until I moved to Texas. And in my limited experience of the taquerias I'd tried since I'd lived here, there was perhaps a reason that I hadn't heard of them before.

"Who picked that place?"

"I don't know—hold on a minute."

I could hear yapping in the background, then a thud. I grinned. Sounded like Bubbles was locked outside again.

"If it's not the phone ringing, it's the silly dog yapping his head off. I think Lonnie picked the restaurant this time. You can't back out on me now, Callie."

I might. "I was planning to visit Aunt Dot out at Willowbough this afternoon."

"I want to go see Dot too!"

I gave in. If I stayed with something safe, like chips and salsa, I'd probably manage to make it through the taqueria experience. Then we could stop at Sonic and grab Dot her favorite cherry limeade on the way to see her at the senior adult community.

But then I had to get back to work on those flowers. The wedding was tomorrow evening, and all I had done were the altar arrangements and the centerpieces for the tables.

CHAPTER THREE

We peeked into Aunt Dot's room to find her typing furiously on a laptop. From what I could see on her screen, the font was about 48 point. Her lunch tray sat nearby, still laden with a bowl of potato salad and piece of chocolate cake.

"What is she doing?" Mona crowded behind me, trying to see over my shoulder.

The nurse brushed past us into the room. "I think Miss Dot is a-writin' a book."

My aunt turned, and her face lit up at the sight of us. "Come here, darlin'," she called to me. "I was hoping you'd come today!"

I leaned down to give Dot a hug, inhaling her comforting scent. She was my great-aunt—my grandmother's sister. She captured both of my hands as I withdrew from her embrace. Her skin was cool and soft, her nails unpolished but beautifully shaped. Her silver hair was combed neatly away from her face, highlighting her still-lovely hazel eyes and ready smile.

She squeezed my hands tightly, and I could feel her wedding ring pressing into my fingers. Platinum with tiny diamond chips, the ring had never been off her finger since she and Uncle Garth were married over sixty years ago. The thought of it made my heart ache, as always, for the briefest moment. Uncle Garth had been gone for at least ten years, yet she still wore her ring. Their relationship had been the kind I could only dream about.

I disengaged my hands gently, and handed her the limeade. "You remember my friend, Mona, don't you, Aunt Dot?"

Aunt Dot beamed, fishing the maraschino cherry out of her drink with the plastic spork from her lunch tray. "Of course, I do. Now you sit on down and make yourselves at home. My, your toenails are very sparkly today, Mona," she said, popping the cherry into her mouth.

I hadn't noticed. How, I'm not sure, because when I looked at my friend's toes now, I could see that they were painted in red, white and blue stripes...accented with rhinestones. And they matched the rhinestones on her t-shirt, which I had also, apparently, failed to notice. I guess I was used to Mona being sparkly all the time.

"Yes, ma'am. It *is* almost the 4th of July." Mona wiggled her toes so I could see them better.

I was not exactly sure of the significance of celebrating our nation's Independence Day with one's toenails, but if it made Mona happy, who was I to argue? Besides, the patriotic colors matched the ugly bruise, presumably from the croquet-ball-dropping incident, on her left foot.

"So, what are you typing, Aunt Dot?" I couldn't recall ever seeing my aunt use a computer before.

She straightened in her chair. "Well." She grinned at me, and for an instant, I could see the little girl she must have been, shining in her eyes and her impish smile. "It's a secret."

A secret? Well, Aunt Dot always did have a penchant for secrets, but she usually got so excited about her new "secret" that it didn't stay secret for very long.

"You know I don't do anything without praying about it, honey." She was looking at me as if I wasn't listening very well. "And the Lord told me to do it."

Do what? I guess I *wasn't* listening very well. I was suddenly feeling a little muddled what with yesterday's events, Aunt Dot's secrets, and the wedding flowers weighing on my mind.

I glanced at Mona, who was more subdued than normal. Was her foot hurting her that much? I tried to get her attention, but she was staring intently at the stack of letters lying on Dot's bedside table.

Aunt Dot liked to write letters and cards, and she had a thriving pen pal ministry to prison inmates. At last count, I think she said she was writing to thirteen inmates across the country. She was always thinking up new ways to encourage them—Scriptures, jokes, Bible study materials, crossword puzzles. Though she herself was paralyzed from the waist down from a botched neck surgery several years ago, she still had a heart to serve God by loving others. It was one of the things I had always admired about her.

Mona turned to me then, wide-eyed. She gestured to the

bedside table with a jerk of her head, but I didn't see anything unusual. Of course, I'm not the most observant person in the world, either. I frowned at Mona and tuned back into Aunt Dot, pretending not to see my friend surreptitiously pull out her phone and take a picture of Aunt Dot's table. What was Mona up to?

"That sweet young man, Brandon—do you know him, Callie?" Aunt Dot was asking.

I shook my head. There was a middle-aged man at church named Brand or Rand or something like that. Was he a tech guy? I didn't know. He certainly wasn't young, though I suppose "young" was a relative term when one was Aunt Dot's age.

"Brandon comes and teaches us how to do technology. You know, computer things." She sighed. "He seems a little nervous sometimes, but he's such a dear man. And handsome, too."

If I didn't know better, I might think my elderly aunt had a crush on Brandon the computer dude. I suppressed a giggle, not daring to look at Mona.

"Next time he comes, I'll give him your phone number, Callie. You need to meet him."

Oh, no. Memories of the last time Aunt Dot had found me the man of her dreams was enough to give me a panic attack on the spot. The poor guy had not been my type at all.

"I'm not looking for a boyfriend right now." *Not now. Or ever.*

Mona snickered.

"I know, honey. But one of these days, God's going to bring another man into your life. I'm simply trying to help Him out a little." Aunt Dot gave me a guileless grin, then leaned in confidentially. "Most of the other folks in here use the computers to play *games*," she whispered. "But Harry, down the hall, you know?"

Not really, but I nodded anyway.

"Harry does all of that social stuff. Like he chats with people on eBay."

I knew what she meant. I nodded again, an encouraging smile on my face.

"And he even sells stuff on...on...what is it called? Face-twitter? Bookface?"

I ignored Mona's sudden choking fit.

"Facebook," I said.

"Oh, yes. That's it. I never can remember." She closed the laptop and laid it to the side. "How is your mother, dear?" she asked.

I had known the question was coming—because it always did—but that didn't make me like it any more than I did any other time. My parents were on the mission field in Zambia, of all places. House parents at a boarding school that served ex-pat families, missionary families and the local population. Mail took months to arrive there, if it ever did arrive at all. But I rarely sent any mail, anyway. We weren't close like that. In fact, we weren't close at all.

"She's fine," I said, hoping it was true. "The last I saw on Facebook, she and Dad were leading some sort of teacher training thing at their school. But you know how it is there. The internet access is spotty, so I don't hear from her too often."

Aunt Dot's eyes bored into mine. "Don't wait too long, Callie."

She knew that I knew what she meant. I squirmed, feeling the heat rise to my face. It wasn't that there was a problem, exactly, between my parents and me. More like a...wall. One that I either didn't know how to break down or didn't care to. Some days I wasn't sure which.

It wasn't even a deep, dark secret. It was simply the emotional distance, the unresolved little hurts that had piled up between us for so long. The hell that we all lived through during my older brother's struggle with addiction had left wreckage in its wake. After he finally left the house for the last time, or was taken, rather—in a police car—things seemed to settle down. But nothing was ever the same. My parents were exhausted and grieved, and even at the best of times disagreed over how to deal with my brother's ongoing crises.

I had always been a good girl, so I was left to cope with the difficulties of high school and, well, growing up. I know my parents did the best they could. They took me to church; sent me to a private Christian school. Dad provided well for us. Mom cooked dinner every night and took me shopping for a prom dress. But they weren't...present. It was as if they were so emotionally drained from dealing with my sibling, that I was an afterthought. By the time I married Kev, my brother had been in and out of jail for years and was on his way to prison. My parents moved to Zambia a month after my wedding. Almost as if they couldn't get away fast enough.

Mona had recovered from her sudden coughing spell. "Did you know that your niece is a detective now?" she asked Aunt Dot.

I rolled my eyes, but at least Mona had rescued me from drowning in morose thoughts about my parents.

"What? Isn't the florist shop going well, dear? I didn't think you were going to go back to law enforcement, Callie!" Aunt Dot looked stricken.

Being a social worker was hardly law enforcement, but it probably all seemed the same to an eighty-something lady.

"The store is going fine, Aunt Dot." I frowned at Mona. "What Mona means is that I've had some...unusual happenings in the last day or so."

"She found a dead body under her crepe myrtle tree!" Mona burst out, apparently unable to contain herself any longer.

Aunt Dot's hand went to her throat. "Callie." Her eyes were huge. "Are you okay, dear? Why didn't you tell me sooner? Here we've been drinking cherry limeade and talking about Twitterface and a person has been murdered in your *yard*? In *Short Creek*?"

I patted her knee. "Mona said he was *dead*, not murdered, Auntie." I glared at Mona again.

"Oh, dear. Dead is bad enough." She took my hand again, squeezing it tightly, as if I were her little girl. "Are you okay? That must have been a terrible experience."

It was, actually. And amazing that I had been able to sleep at all last night. An image of the man's face rose in my thoughts, but I pushed it away.

"I'm fine. But part of the problem is that no one knows who the man is...was. Or why he was in my yard at the shop."

"Oh, Callie." She went pale.

Maybe we shouldn't have told her about it.

"And he brought Callie a package, too." Mona tapped her nails on the arm of her chair. "It was filled with weird stuff."

"Yes, I was about to show her the pictures." I reached for my phone, then froze.

Wait a minute. Something Mona had said...

I turned to stare at her. "Mona, maybe we assumed that the man brought the package. What if he didn't?"

Mona fiddled with her earring. Red, white, and blue, with dangly rhinestones. She squinted at me. "You mean it could be two separate things? Like he died by the porch and someone else put the package in his hand to make it look like he was the one delivering the package?"

"So, if that's the case, then did the person who actually delivered the package kill the man?" Aunt Dot's eyes widened in horror.

I shrugged. "Maybe the guy was dead first. And someone kind of...put him there." No, that wasn't plausible, either. And I couldn't believe we were sitting around Aunt Dot's room discussing something like this. Usually we talked about gardening. Or knitting. Or Aunt Dot's latest news from around Willowbough. Or what Pastor Brian had preached about on Sunday.

"So...let's say the guy was alive when he arrived in your backyard." Mona fingered her earring again. "Maybe he saw a different person deliver the package, and he thought it seemed suspicious and was trying to get it before you did to protect you from it."

"But I didn't know him. How would he know me? Or maybe he was a nice normal guy trying to do a good deed and got killed for it?"

Too many questions, and no answers. I slumped down in my chair.

CHAPTER FOUR

"Isn't Sheriff Earl going to let you know when they get the autopsy results?" Aunt Dot asked. "You'd think that's the least he could do, with you having to go through such an ordeal in your very own yard," she muttered.

Mona rolled her eyes. "Earl? He's not going to spill the beans. We'll have to talk to Lonnie."

I nodded. "Earl will tell Rick, and Rick will tell Lonnie. I bet she'll tell me."

"Honey, Lonnie Holloway couldn't keep a secret if her life depended on it." Aunt Dot chuckled. "When I had that girl in second grade, I knew who to talk to if I wanted to find out what *really* happened on the playground. I can't believe she ended up being married to the town mayor!"

Sometimes I forgot that my aunt had lived here in Short Creek her entire life. I met Lonnie after I moved down here, but I viewed her, as Anne Shirley of Green Gables would say, as a "kindred spirit." The Lonnie I knew must have come a long way since second grade, because she sure wasn't the type of person to betray anyone's confidence. In fact, she seemed to me to be the perfect role model of a godly wife and mother, and was the leader of our early-morning Friday prayer group. Lonnie, Celia, Karen, and I made up the main group, with a few others who joined us when they could.

I think Lonnie would probably be able to give me inside information on something this important, especially since she knew me well enough to know that I wasn't going to be posting it all over social media or discussing it with everyone in the world.

Mona cleared her throat and glanced at the clock.

"I hope you get a lot of...typing...done, Aunt Dot." I stood. "I'll come by again soon, once I get the Dorsey wedding done, okay?"

"Well, I think you should email me and let me know if you hear any news." Her eyes twinkled like they did when she had a secret.

Email her?

"You do email now?"

"Yes, ma'am." She gave me a sassy smile. "I told you, Brandon's been teaching us all kinds of technology stuff. Tomorrow we're going to learn how to organize our inboxes! I'm so excited!"

Mona grabbed my arm the minute we got out into the hall. "Callie! There was one of those anchor dolphin thingies on one of those envelopes!" she hissed.

"What?"

"One of those, you know, Latin things. Like was in the gift bag." She raised her eyebrows at my apparent dimwittedness. "The mystery box? You know, yesterday?"

The *festina lente* symbol?

"Really?"

Her flag-striped nails tapping furiously, she pulled up the picture on her phone. "Look! It's partly covered by the envelope on top of it, but you can still kind of see it."

She was right.

I sucked in my breath. Had one of Dot's prison inmate friends gotten hold of my information and was trying to send me some kind of message? But why? And if so, how would a prison inmate be able to send me a box of stuff?

I felt a headache coming on. "I have got to finish those flower arrangements today, or I'm sunk," I said. "Maybe we'll have more answers once I can talk to Lonnie."

As it turned out, I didn't even need to talk to Lonnie. Houston popped into the shop as I tied the last bow on the bridesmaids' bouquets. The bouquets were the most awful things I'd ever seen, but they were exactly like the photo the bride had shown me on Pinterest. Tightly-packed round balls of orange-hued roses, with fake Monarch butterflies fluttering ridiculously above the flowers. Yeesh. I was afraid to see what the bridesmaids' dresses looked like.

"You still working?" Houston called as the screen door banged behind him. "Oops, sorry." He turned around to make sure it had closed all the way.

I need to get that thing fixed. It screeched every time someone opened it.

"Just finishing up." I stood and stretched my back. How long had I been hunched over? And why was Houston wearing white athletic socks with his black dress pants?

"What time is it?"

He draped his handsome self over one of the stools behind my counter. "It's eight. And I have good news and bad news for you."

I felt my heart rate accelerate instantly, and I hated it. For years, nothing much had rattled me. But since everything I had gone through with Kev and then those last super-stressful years before I moved down here, it seemed I was overly sensitive to anxiety.

I took a deep breath. At least Houston had said good news *and* bad news. And he didn't have on his funeral-preaching face. In fact, now that I looked closer, there appeared to be a twinkle lurking in those blue eyes.

"Your corpse is not dead." He paused dramatically. "And his name is Roger."

"What?"

"The guy wasn't dead, Callie." He took a swig of his ever-present iced tea.

I sank down on the stool next to him. "Is that the good news or the bad news?"

He laughed. "That's the good news. The bad news is that your friend Roger had absolutely nothing to do with the mysterious gift. So you still have a mystery on your hands."

The man was *not* dead?

I felt my face flush hot as it always did when I was nervous or embarrassed. I was glad the man was alive, of course, but by now half the town would know that I had said I found a dead guy in my yard.

I thought yesterday was complicated.

"How did you find all of this out?" I asked faintly, hoping it wasn't already all over social media. Did Houston even do social media? I guess I hadn't ever thought about it.

"Well, I was at the hospital and he had requested a visit. Of course, at the time, I didn't know he was your corpse."

I rolled my eyes at him. I would never live this down, that was for sure. Plus, I had forgotten that besides pastoring First Church, Houston was a volunteer chaplain at the hospital in Temple.

"He's homeless." Houston's face sobered. "A trucker had picked him up somewhere in Dallas, and got him as far as Short Creek. He said he was trying to make his way down to Houston where his sister or somebody lives."

"But why—" I pictured the man again, lying still as death under my tree.

"He was extremely dehydrated, and he is also diabetic. Sounds like his blood sugar had gone way out of control from not eating much for a couple of days."

I nodded.

"He had been walking past your yard late last night and says he saw the package on your porch. By then, he was desperate, and hoped maybe there would be something in the bag he could eat."

Wow.

"So...he just *looked* dead?"

Houston shrugged. "I understand he was pretty close to meeting his Maker by the time you spotted him. The EMTs were able to at least keep him going until they got him to the hospital." He looked at me curiously. "Did Todd *tell* you he was dead?"

I replayed my short conversation with Todd Whitney, the captain of the volunteer fire department here in Short Creek. I wasn't well acquainted with Todd, but we attended the same church, Short Creek Community Church. In fact, I had enjoyed hearing him speak when he had filled in for Pastor Brian during our adult Sunday school class last week. I could tell he had an extensive knowledge of the Bible.

"Callie?"

"Um...no, not really, I guess. After I first saw the guy's body, I didn't want to go into the store. Just in case, you know? So I waited in my van until Sheriff Earl and the deputy arrived. Then I walked with them up to the...up to him, then right away they told me to go into the shop. I didn't want to watch anyway; you know?"

He nodded.

"But then, Todd knocked on the door to let me know they were loading him up and Earl would be around to question me later. I glanced over toward the ambulance, and the guy was completely covered with a sheet." I shuddered. "I guess I don't know much about these things, but I assumed if he was covered..."

"A reasonable assumption," Houston said easily.

A reasonable assumption, I mused later on my way home from the store. But yet...I hadn't been able to put my finger on it when I had been talking to Houston, but something didn't feel right about this whole thing. It seemed too—silly. Too implausible. A homeless man is walking past my backyard, he happens to see a package right when he needs a snack...seems to be dead, but he actually isn't...

But he was. Dead, I mean. He had to have been. I remembered the ants crawling over his face, the unnatural bloating—the ants!

I called Houston. I felt a little weird about calling him. He and I were friends; but we weren't really friends, like call-you-up-and-chat-about-things friends. But I had to know.

He answered on the second ring. "Hello?"

"Houston, it's me, Callie."

"Callie! Are you okay?"

"Yes, I'm fine," I said.

Why did he sound so concerned about me? We had seen each other ten minutes ago.

"Uh, how did the guy look when you saw him in the hospital?

There was a long pause. "You mean the homeless guy? Maybe a little pale."

"That's all?"

Houston exhaled loudly. "What else do you want to know? He was a normal, scraggly homeless guy."

A *normal* homeless guy? Somehow, "normal" and "homeless" didn't go together in my brain. My brother, Jason, had sometimes been homeless as he struggled with addiction. During that time, I had found myself scanning the side of the road, the ditches, the street corners for his face whenever I drove through the streets of Columbus. Was he alive? Did he have enough to eat? Why wouldn't he get help?

Everyone who was homeless was someone's brother. Or son. Or mother. If it wasn't enough to deal with that in my own family, I had experienced the same heartbreak plenty of times as a school social worker. Poverty, addiction, mental illness...abuse... homelessness...it was all tied together.

I dragged myself back to the present. "So he didn't have any...marks...or anything on his face?"

"Nope, none that I could see."

I could hear rattling and crunching, as if he was eating something out of a bag. "I thought you were doing the low-carb thing with Mona." If he were my own pastor, I would never have teased him like that. But Houston was, well, Houston.

He growled, and I could picture his sandy eyebrows scrunching together. I grinned.

"Did you call me at ten o'clock at night to interrogate me? Or did you have another reason?" he asked. I heard the bag rattle again.

"I'm sorry, Houston. But I think we need to talk about our mystery man again tomorrow if you have a minute." For one thing, the man I had found beneath my crepe myrtle tree was not scraggly. Far from it.

CHAPTER FIVE

My friends at prayer group surprised me this morning with homemade cinnamon rolls for breakfast, since my birthday was in a couple of days. It was often a stretch for me to get up in time to be at Lonnie's by six a.m. every Wednesday, but it was worth it. We took turns hosting the group; usually someone would host it for a month or two and then we'd switch to someone else's house. I especially loved it when we met at Lonnie's magazine-page-perfect home. It wasn't only that her home was beautiful. It was the peace that I sensed there the minute I walked in the door, as if the Holy Spirit was very near.

The one thing I didn't love about Lonnie Holloway was her cat. Fluffers adored me, it seemed, and wanted to rub her gorgeous long coat against me any time she could. I'm sure she was a nice enough cat, but I am so dreadfully allergic to cats that I start sneezing simply looking at Fluffers.

Fortunately, Fluffers was nowhere in sight this morning. It was only Lonnie, me, and Celia. Karen and her husband had left with their church home group for a short-term mission trip last week sometime—maybe Sunday? I couldn't remember. Anyway, she would be gone another week or two. I knew she had been feeling a little anxious being halfway across the world in Uganda with no cell phone service or internet, but at least her twins—two sets of them—were staying with their grandparents.

This morning, we met in Lonnie's garden right as the sun began to rise. A small fountain bubbled gently amidst the wisteria, and the stepping stones were still wet with dew as we began by candlelight. Sitting in the fragrant silence, we quieted our hearts and minds before God.

We lifted up our usual prayer requests—healing and comfort for Lonnie's dad, who was dying of cancer. Wisdom and strength for Celia whose teenaged daughter was making bad choices. Protection and peace for my brother Jason in prison. Divine guidance for me with "the gift" situation and ongoing investigation. We moved on to pray for Karen and her husband and the success of the mission trip. And then we prayed for the grandparents. Hard.

After prayer, I drove the short distance from Lonnie's house to C. Willikers. As always, I admired the rose arbor and the overflowing pots of lime-green sweet potato vine that welcomed visitors to the quaint old building. It was about time to change the window display, though. I liked to change it often; sometimes featuring yarn, sometimes books, sometimes plants, but usually all three at once.

This morning I had brought one of the books from The Gift to put in the window display. Once I had looked at it closer, I realized it was a fairly nice antique copy of *Pilgrim's Progress*. Or at least, it looked antique to me. I have always loved old books, thinking of all the hands that had held that book before me...my imagination conjuring up the life stories behind an inscription or an old-fashioned name written in elegant handwriting, dated a hundred years or more before I was born. I especially loved old hymnals, and often got a chuckle out of the years-old notations made by long-gone organists or choir directors.

Often the aged books themselves were not worth much, I was learning, but for those of us who loved all things written, old books were irresistible, tangible links to by-gone times; to other worlds. I set *Pilgrim's Progress* on a stand in the window next to a basket of vintage spools of thread and a half-worked lace shawl, still on the knitting needles. An enormous asparagus fern and aluminum buckets full of fresh-cut daisies and black-eyed Susans made a beautiful summer window display, I thought, stepping outside briefly to see it from the street view.

Someone honked and waved, and I waved back automatically. It was Houston, no doubt heading out for his morning doughnut. I sighed. I wasn't a doughnut person, but a cup of tea and spending a few minutes working on the baby blanket I was knitting sounded like what I needed after yesterday's events.

I ambled toward the front door, fully cognizant of the fact

that I was putting off talking to the sheriff. He had said he'd call me if they needed to talk to me again. So far, he hadn't called, but things weren't adding up in my brain. I felt like I needed to talk to him about what I'd seen Monday morning. I'd swing past the city offices and try to talk to Earl, then head back to the shop and put the finishing touches on the wedding flowers before I had to deliver them to the Methodist church at two this afternoon. Then after that, I had decided, I was going to the hospital to see crepe myrtle man for myself.

But first, tea. While my electric kettle heated up, I grabbed my Bible and my flowered stationery. It had been too long since I had written to my brother, Jason. I usually tried to send him at least a card every week, even if I didn't get a chance to write a longer letter. Now that I had moved halfway across the country, I couldn't visit him very often.

I could not imagine what it must be like to be in prison, but he seemed to be doing okay. He wrote me occasionally, always thanking me for my letters but never responding to my inquiries about his soul. The same when I talked to him on the phone every once in a while. We would chat about things for a few minutes, but whenever I mentioned God, the line went silent. I had learned to refrain from telling him things he already knew, and mostly I prayed for him that God would draw him back to Himself.

I sat in my favorite rocker near the front display window. From here, I could see the cardinals and the sparrows taking turns at the birdbath. I had been delighted to see cardinals when I moved here, since they had been some of my favorite birds when I lived in Ohio. I loved their little "tip, tip, tip" noises that would alert me to their presence in my new yard. At my house, I had one of those feeders that was attached to my kitchen window, so I was constantly entertained with the many species of birds. I had been enjoying learning the names of the ones that were new to me, and always kept a pair of binoculars handy on the kitchen table.

I described the scene for Jason, knowing he loved birdwatching as much or more than I did. I chatted about the shop and about seeing Aunt Dot yesterday. I told him about how hot it was down here and asked how his GED classes were going, then hesitated. It didn't seem wise to tell him about the crazy things that had happened in my life in the last couple of days. Maybe when it was all over, I would tell him the whole story.

I could have walked to the city offices, since my shop was only a few blocks away, but it was already about one hundred degrees outside and I didn't want to get all sweaty. I pulled up in front of the city offices/volunteer fire department, amused to see that the "ACCEPTING BRISKET DONATIONS" sign was again out front of the aging metal building. When I had first moved to Short Creek, I had puzzled over that sign for months. Were the firefighters especially hungry? If so, they had a pretty specific request. *Brisket? Why not hot dogs? Or pizza?* Maybe it was a joke.

It was not until that fall, when they changed the sign to announce the annual BBQ fundraiser, that it dawned on me why they were asking for brisket donations. I guess I could have asked before then, but I had had enough on my mind at the time that it hadn't been more than a casual wondering. In some small way, I realized this morning, I was starting to feel more like a part of this community, now that I understood the mystery of the brisket sign and was, apparently, on a first-name basis with the sheriff.

I popped my head into the receptionist's tiny office. "Tina?"

The stale little office smelled like cigarette smoke and the decade's worth of paperwork still stuffed in the aging file cabinets that crowded the room. A huge "Lorena Leopards—State Champions 2001" banner dominated the back wall, surrounded by about twenty framed high school basketball team photos. Probably Sheriff Earl's sons, I thought.

Tina, the secretary, was nowhere to be seen. She had probably stepped out for lunch, but I could hear the sheriff's gravelly voice from somewhere down the short hallway.

Should I walk back there? I wanted answers.

I spotted a pad of sticky-notes on Tina's desk, and decided I'd leave Tina a note to call me to schedule an appointment to see Earl. I reached for the pad, then froze. Why was my name written across the top of that file folder?

I glanced toward the hallway. Would it be wrong to pick the folder up and—

Sheriff Earl blustered into the room, one of the EMT guys at his side. "And that nosy woman from Ohio—"

"Hello, Sheriff." I gave him a sweet smile.

He glared at me.

"I was hoping you could give me an update on the investigation of the murder on my property."

"Can't ya listen to the news?" He spat into his Styrofoam cup. "It wasn't a murder, ma'am. Homeless dude named Roger got in a little trouble."

Really. Why was I finding it difficult to believe this man?

"Well, have you been able to determine the circumstances surrounding the, uh, event? It's a bit unnerving to have something like this happen right in the middle of town."

He shrugged and shot a sly glance toward the EMT. "Me and Vic, here, are on it, ma'am. Takes some time, ya know?"

Clearly, I wasn't going to get anything else from him today. I turned and walked to the door.

"Don't worry, Miss Willie. You're perfectly safe."

Willie, again, instead of Callie. The man was mocking me, and there wasn't a thing I could do about it. Yet.

In a rare display of bad temper, I stomped on the gas pedal and whipped out of the gravel parking lot, determined to put the whole weird thing out of my mind, at least for now. The "body" was Roger, and he was recovering well. And the gift bag was probably someone's idea of a practical joke for my birthday, which was now only two days away. And I had a wedding to do.

I backed my minivan up to the church as close as I could so the flowers would be exposed to the humid heat for no longer than a minute or two. The church secretary had said she'd leave the side door unlocked for me and to come right in.

Juggling my purse and the box of orange boutonnieres in one hand, I pulled open the heavy glass door with the other. A welcome whoosh of air conditioning met me as I braced the door open with my foot. With my other foot, I tried in vain to reach the large rock that was apparently used for a doorstop.

This isn't working. With a sigh, I shoved my purse and the flowers on top of a small table, then turned to wedge the door open, this time with both hands and feet free.

Odd. Somehow, the door had closed behind me, and the doorstop rock was nowhere to be seen. The slightest prickle of apprehension warned me a second before something hard connected with my head.

I came to slowly. My head felt like it was about to explode, and my eyes didn't want to open. Why was I lying on the floor? The carpet felt scratchy under my cheek, and there seemed to be an odd silence around me. I forced myself to slit my eyes open to see where I was. Oh, thank God. Still in the side foyer of the Methodist church.

But was I alone?

I lay there for long minutes, my entire body rigid, my pulse beating in my ears, my neck. I could hear nothing but my own breathing.

Finally, I made the barest movement with my hand; chanced a quick peek around.

Nothing.

With effort, I pulled myself to a sitting position against the wall. When my head stopped whirling again, I opened my eyes, fully this time.

I was definitely alone.

The contents of my purse were strewn around me; my delivery van still idling outside of the glass door. I reached a tentative hand up to my head, and felt a bump that must have been about the size of a bowling ball. When I pulled my fingers away, they were sticky with blood, but there wasn't much of it, thank God.

What just happened? I tried to think, but my mind felt muddled. *Jesus.* I couldn't think of anything else. Just His name. *Jesus, help me.*

"Callie!" Mona's horrified voice jerked me out of my stupor. "What happened to you?"

I tried to focus my eyes on my friend. "I'm not...sure." Where were my glasses?

Mona poked furiously at her phone screen, then plunked down on the floor next to me and wrapped her plump arms around me tightly. Her perfume nearly knocked me out again.

"The EMTs are on their way." She pulled away from me and looked into my eyes. "You need to stay awake, Callie. Where are you hurt? Can you tell me what happened?"

I started to shake my head, but almost blacked out again. "A rock," I croaked.

"The lock?" Mona glanced at the door, then back at me. "It's not locked, Callie."

"No, a rock," I said. I could hear my own words coming out of my mouth as if from a distance, but I couldn't seem to keep my thoughts straight. "It smelled weird."

She peered at me and shook her head. Her earrings jingled, and I stared at them. They looked like sunbursts. Or flowers. *Flowers!*

"I have to get the flowers," I murmured. "The flowers for the rocks. The wedding rocks. The flowers..."

Mona looked panicked. "Maybe you should stop talking after all, honey. Here, let me wipe the blood off your fingers."

The volunteer firefighters came to my rescue for the second time in three days. A little while later, I was feeling a mite better with an icepack on my head and some extra-strength Tylenol on board.

I looked up at the guys from where I still sat on the floor. "I guess I owe y'all some brisket."

Y'all? I must have been woozier than I thought I was.

Captain Todd Whitney grinned at me, and I somehow noticed that his eyes were actually dark blue, not brown as I had supposed.

"Now you're talkin'." He reached to help me up. "Earl'll need to question you again, of course. Let's get you loaded up."

What?

"We have to take you to the hospital, Callie." He held his hand up to forestall my objections. "You took quite a knock on the head, and I suspect you have a concussion. Any nausea?"

Well, now that he mentioned it...

I shuddered as the guys rolled a sheet-draped gurney into the foyer. It was probably the same one that the...the body—

When I came to again, I was in the back of the ambulance. The only other time I had been in this end of an ambulance was when Marleigh...oh, no. I couldn't go there right now. I squeezed my eyes closed against the sounds, the smells, the images—

"Hang in there, ma'am. We'll be there in a minute." One of the younger EMTs sat pressed up next to my side in the small space, his eyes on the monitor above my head. He patted my hand soothingly.

Jesus. Jesus, help me. I couldn't relive that day. Not now. Not after I had come so far...had overcome so much...

Fighting against the panic rising in my chest, I focused on the tattoo on the guy's forearm. I could only see a small part of it where his sleeve had pulled up slightly. I couldn't tell what it was exactly. Of course, I was probably looking at it upside down, and besides, my brain still felt fuzzy. I thought it was a...a snake with words intertwined, maybe? Or perhaps a dragon? The image blurred, and I closed my eyes wearily.

I somehow managed to make it to the hospital without completely losing it. Mona met me at the door, clutching my purse.

"I unloaded all of your flowers, Callie." She kept stride with the gurney as I was wheeled into a cubicle in the ER. "The bride arrived right after you left in the ambulance, so she didn't even know anything happened, and the wedding coordinator—

what's her name? Evelyn? said she would take it from there and not to worry about a thing, okay?

I started to nod, then thought better of it. I hadn't intended to stay for the wedding anyway. "Thanks, Mona. Did you grab my phone, too?"

"Earl wouldn't let me touch anything until he took pictures." She rolled her eyes. "Then I gathered up everything I could find. Your phone was all the way under that little table. And here are your glasses."

The Tylenol must be helping. "What happened?" I asked Mona.

"Somebody clobbered you a good one. That's what happened." Sheriff Earl ambled into the room. He came to a stop by my bedside and hitched his pants up. "Found a big ol' rock out there by your van."

The doorstop rock. I remembered now. *But why—*

He squinted at me. "Seems like you got something someone else wants."

What?

"I took a picture of it." He shoved his phone into my face. "Here. See?"

I looked at his phone screen. The doorstop rock, lying on the pavement by my van. A piece of paper under the rock. I enlarged the picture so I could read the words written on the paper: "GIVE IT BACK."

I passed the phone to Mona, too dumbfounded to speak. *Give what back? To whom?*

Mona stared at it, her face turning as red as the blouse she was wearing. She whirled on the sheriff. "Earl, I sure hope y'all catch whoever did this to Callie. You need to spend every waking minute until this...this person is caught. I can't believe something like this happened in Short Creek! And right after the dead guy in her yard, too! If you have to go back to the ironing board and get extra detectives in from somewhere, y'all need to—"

"I already told your friend here, Mona, that guy doesn't have anything to do with this!" Earl's face was even redder than Mona's.

Go back to the ironing board? I groaned. Earl would need to do more than go back to the drawing board to solve this mystery. And he most certainly had *not* told me anything about the dead body that I didn't already know. I closed my eyes, my head throbbing. I couldn't deal with this right now. Maybe things would make more sense tomorrow.

But they didn't. Make sense, that is. Nothing had been stolen from my purse. Not my phone, not my debit card. Not even the twenty-three dollars I had in cash. Nothing.

And I certainly hadn't taken anything from anyone, so how could I give it back? And did this skull-cracking incident have something to do with The Gift and Roger, the crepe myrtle man? I *had* been at the hospital yesterday, but not to see him as I had planned. I would have to go back as soon as I felt better and try to talk to him in person. After all, I was the "nosy woman from Ohio." I might as well live up to that, since I certainly wasn't going to get any answers from the sheriff.

My head started to throb just thinking about it. I hauled Purl up into my lap as I sat at the kitchen table. She settled in with a sigh, folding her legs up under her plump little body. I stroked her soft head as Intarsia stared at me forlornly from her pug bed.

A female cardinal lighted on my window feeder, and I admired her reddish-brown feathers and comical little Mohawk. The females were more timid than the males, so I didn't see them as often. I grabbed my binoculars and trained them on her, hoping to study her markings more clearly. Instead, I got an up-close view of Sherm's side yard, where a bikini-clad young woman lay stretched out on a rickety chaise lounge.

"Yikes," I muttered. *Who is that?*

Usually, my view consisted of Sherm's chain-link fence and air-conditioning unit, which I was hoping my newly-planted Confederate Jasmine would soon hide. So it was a bit of a shock to see—*Oh, Sherm's granddaughter.* Of course. He mentioned her proudly almost every time we had a conversation. Nicole, I think he said her name was. She was beautiful, there was no doubt about that. Her black hair was long and silky-straight, and her legs would make any man drool. But I couldn't get past the tattoos. That, and the fact that she was pregnant. Very pregnant.

I laid the binoculars down on the table and turned back to my cup of tea. Definitely none of my business. I guess this is what happens when one sits around at home on a Thursday morning, but as Aunt Dot would say, my "get up and go got up and went." I sighed. It had been a long time since I felt so…shaky.

But I couldn't sit at home all day stewing about things. Lonnie had texted me last night to see if I'd do the flowers for her daughter's wedding. She and Jenna would be coming into the shop tomorrow at 11:00 for us to go over ideas and prices, so I might as well start thinking about doing another wedding. I sure hope Jenna had better taste than this last bride.

I didn't know Jenna very well. She had been away at college when I moved here, so I had only met her when she came home at Christmas break. She was home for the summer now, and had been singing with the praise and worship team at church. She seemed to be a lovely person, exactly like her mother.

The wedding was set for September, which was autumn elsewhere in the country, but not in Central Texas. I wondered idly what kind of flowers Jenna would choose. She seemed like a classic roses-and-baby's-breath kind of girl. But if it were my wedding, I'd choose something with sunflowers and—my wedding? What was I thinking? Someone knocked on the front door, but before I could scooch Purl off of my lap, Mona popped her head in.

"Anybody home?" she called.

"Come on in, Mona," I said. "I'm in the kitchen, but watch out for the bump!"

I loved this old house with all its lumps and scars, where

Aunt Dot and Uncle Garth had lived for as long as I could remember. After Uncle Garth died, Aunt Dot had paid to keep it in good repair, but most everything was outdated. I had all kinds of ideas for remodeling, but so far, I had spent most of my time and energy on getting C. Willikers up and running.

Mona stepped carefully over the odd bulge between the kitchen linoleum and the hardwood floor of the tiny living room, the smell of lasagna preceding her.

"You need to get that fixed, Callie. That's about the fifth time I've almost fallen on my face."

"I know. It's on my to-do list," I eyed the insulated bag she carried.

"I brought you lunch. I'll get Rob over here to look at the floor next time he's home." She set the bag on the table, then scooped up Intarsia and cuddled her like a baby. "How are you today, sweetie?" she crooned.

"She's better than I am, that's for sure," I said. "I still can't believe someone chucked a rock at my head!"

Mona put the dog down and came to inspect my head. "The lump doesn't look as big this morning, at least." She planted her fist on her ample hip. "Are you keeping ice on it? I told Rob about it, and he couldn't believe it! Especially since I had already told him what happened on Monday."

"Do you want a cup of tea?" I asked, ignoring her question about ice. I was tired of holding an ice pack on my head. "When does Rob get back?"

Rob was an over-the-road trucker, so he was often gone for two or three weeks at a time. Mona was used to it, but I knew by now that when he was home, Mona was practically glued to his side. I didn't blame her.

She plopped into the chair across from me, picking black pug hair off the front of her blouse, which I thought greatly resembled a Native American weaving of some sort. But at least her toenails matched it. Purple, green and black.

"No, thanks. I've already had enough caffeine today. He's still out for another week or so. Arkansas, I think." She wrinkled her nose. "He was telling me last night about this training that he's going to do, Callie. You know how we've been praying at church about human trafficking here in Texas?"

I nodded. A few months ago, we'd had a guest speaker at Short Creek Community Church, who was with Traffick911, an organization dedicated to raising awareness of human trafficking and providing services to those rescued. I, along with everyone else, had been appalled to realize that the "Texas Triangle," as it is called, was one of the major areas of human trafficking in the United States. And our little town of Short Creek was right in the middle of that triangle—from Dallas/Ft. Worth, to San Antonio, to Houston. As a church, we had made a commitment to pray about this heartbreaking situation, and to learn what we could do to help.

"Rob found out about an organization called 'Truckers Against Trafficking.' He's going to do the training for it." Mona beamed.

I smiled at her obvious admiration of her husband. Mona had had a disastrous first marriage, but after surrendering to Christ sometime in her thirties, she had met Rob at a church function. And according to her, Rob had hung the moon. And quite possibly several of the stars, as well.

"I'll pray for him," I promised.

And I would. I consciously tried not to promise I would pray for people unless I actually planned to do so. I disliked that a shallow "I'll pray for you," had become the standard Christian response to hearing someone else's woes. To me, after being on the receiving end of prayers quite often in the last few years, I took it very seriously.

There had been days in my life when about all I could muster was to say the name Jesus. Those were the times when I knew the prayers of others were carrying me through. The times when, though it felt like a knife was twisting in my heart, I had received the grace to make it one more day. The days when I could feel the comforting presence of the Holy Spirit, sustaining me and bearing me up, when I should have been a bawling mess on the floor.

"I know you will." She stood and began unpacking her bag. "Are you ready for some lasagna? I can't eat it anymore, but I thought you would like it."

"You're still doing the low-carb thing?"

She nodded, looking mournful. "It's so hard."

"I'm proud of you for sticking with it," I said, taking time to notice her for the first time in the last few weeks. "Your face looks thinner."

She brightened. "Do you think so? I've lost almost ten pounds, but you're the first one who's mentioned anything about it. Rob will be so surprised when he sees me! I wish he was going to be here for the fireworks tonight."

Fireworks? Oh, yeah. I had forgotten that today was the Fourth of July. And the town always put on a display in the high school football stadium, well within earshot of my house.

"Well, I'm certainly not going tonight," I said. "In fact, I think I'll dig out my earmuffs. All I need is fireworks to light up my headache."

She stood and hugged me, completely missing my pun as usual. "You can watch the show on PBS tonight where they shoot fireworks off in Washington, D. C. You know, where the National Guard sings and they have all kinds of other famous singers come?"

I was fairly certain the National Guard would not be singing at the annual Independence Day event in D.C, but I let it go. I walked with her to the door. "I think I'll wait for next year."

After Mona left, I lay down on the couch for a while, but I'm not much of a nap person, even though I knew I should be resting. I puttered around the house, watered my indoor plants, did a load of laundry. All the while, I was puzzling over an aspect of this whole thing that I hadn't even had time to think about until now: the envelope that Mona had seen on Aunt Dot's nightstand.

Mona had sent me the picture she had taken that day, and though the envelope was partially covered by the one on top, it sure looked like it could be the same symbol. And likely, then, that it was drawn by the same person.

I mean, really. How many people even knew about Latin symbols? So... what did that mean? The person who had given me The Gift also had a connection to Aunt Dot? I didn't like that thought one bit. Had the symbol been drawn on the letter before Aunt Dot received it? Or had someone drawn it on there after she had received it? If so, why? And who? Would that person have been in her room? I wish I had asked her about it the day Mona and I had been there, but I was already so disconcerted, I guess it hadn't occurred to me then. I thought about calling her, but then I decided maybe it would be better to approach it more casually the next time I saw her instead of calling to ask her. I know she would say that she doesn't worry, but still.

And what about the series of numbers and letters written under the symbol? What if...hmm. I suddenly got a crazy idea. What if the person who sent me the symbol hadn't meant for it to be the *festina lente* symbol? Maybe he didn't even know it was a Latin symbol.

What if I was supposed to be thinking of nautical things? Dolphins, anchors, ships, oceans, letters and numbers. Wait a minute. Didn't all boats have to be registered? I thought about the handful of times I'd been at the marina at nearby Belton Lake with Aunt Dot and Uncle Garth. All the boats had some sort of numbers on them. Proof of registration, I guessed. I didn't know much about such things, but—

"What do you think, girls?" I asked the pugs. They both lifted their heads to stare at me, their wrinkles bunching around their black, half-mushroom noses. I stared back at them thoughtfully. Maybe I was supposed to be finding a certain boat? Or a certain place on the ocean? With dolphins? That could be about a million different places in the world. And was the same person who clobbered me with the rock the same person who gave me The Gift? And did the symbol have anything to do with the "Give it back" message?

Make haste slowly...give it back... I struggled to make any logical connection between the contents of the gift bag, the Latin maxim, and the rock-throwing incident. If there had been something valuable in that gift bag, I could understand someone wanting his or her stuff back. But all of it looked like, as Houston had said, somebody's garage-sale leftovers.

My doorbell chimed, and I opened it to find Houston himself standing on my front step, holding a stuffed pug.

"Mona told me what happened yesterday, Callie." He handed me the fuzzy toy. "I would have wrapped it but I thought you'd gotten enough mysterious packages lately."

"That's for sure." I took the animal from him without quite meeting his eyes. Why did this feel so awkward? "Oohhh, it's so cute, Houston. Thank you."

I wasn't sure how I felt about this. I'm guessing he didn't usually make home deliveries of stuffed animals to everyone who was sick. Or maybe he did. The man was incredibly dedicated to his job, from what I had observed.

I stepped out on the porch with him and shut the door behind me to contain the pugs. "It's not quite as hot out today."

That was lame.

Houston backed off the porch, then stopped. He stared past me for a moment as if to gather his thoughts, then focused on me again.

I sucked in my breath at the look on his face. His eyes seemed to almost be pleading with me. But why?

Surely I had imagined it. I clutched the stuffed animal. "Houston—"

He cleared his throat and the moment was gone. "Well, I wanted you to know I'm thinking of you and praying for you. Call me any time."

I stood staring after him as he meandered down my driveway to his truck. Houston Gregory was a nice man. And not only that, he was a man of the cloth. At some point in my life, I had felt absolutely certain I would grow up one day and marry a preacher. In fact, my mother had assured me that the years of piano lessons I endured were practically a guarantee of it. Piano-playing ability was an unwritten requirement for success in ministry, according to Mom, at least.

Unfortunately for my mother's theory, my meager piano-playing skills had not snagged me a clergyman husband. Not that I would be opposed to the idea, exactly, I thought now as I watched him swing his long frame up into the pickup.

What? Where had that come from?

Ignoring Sherm, who had come out to observe the action, I sank down on the porch steps and waved at Houston as he backed out of my driveway.

That rock must have scrambled my brain more than I thought it had. Would I be willing to enter into another relationship with a man? I had been so disappointed in Kevin...as a man, and as a husband. I hadn't expected him to be perfect, but when I married him, I had thought he was as passionate about serving God as I was. After only a few months, it became painfully clear that though he professed to be a believer, he had either lost that passion, or had perhaps faked it for my benefit. Things had gone downhill after that, for various reasons.

I sighed. I couldn't live in regret about that anymore. It was what it was. And since I was still alive, I knew God had a plan for me. I wasn't sure what that was, but in these last couple of months I was beginning to gain an inkling of God's leading in some new directions, and I was excited to see where that was headed.

Hours later, I pushed myself off the couch from where I had, indeed, succumbed to watching the PBS Fourth of July festivities on television. The U.S. Army Band performed an inspiring rendition of "Stars and Stripes Forever." And on the less inspiring side of things, Smokey Robinson and Kenny Loggins looked the same as they had twenty years ago. Scary.

I let the dogs out of the back door, and stood listening to the booms and cheers coming from the high school football field a couple of blocks away while I watched the pugs amble around the darkened yard. They didn't seem to be upset by the fireworks, but I attributed this not to their bravery, but to their somewhat low intelligence. Pugs were lovey, but they were not the sharpest nails in the box, by any stretch of the imagination. Still, they were sweet little dogs and I loved them dearly.

They were taking their time, so I sank down in the wicker rocking chair I had placed outside for that purpose. I wished I had a back porch. Maybe someday I'd build one. It might not look like it would if my dad built it, but that would be okay because then it would fit right in with all of the other unusual features of my cozy cottage. I don't know who had designed this house way back when, but it was a little quirky. The attic steps looked like they had been on the outside of the house at some point, but Uncle Garth had enclosed them, so now there was a little mudroom kind of entrance from the backyard and the stairs went up from there. At least there was a door in between the living room and the mudroom/stairs.

The mudroom made a great space to confine the dogs if I needed to. They had a comfy rug in there, and though Intarsia, especially, did not like to spend much time in there, it was nice to have the option if I had guests who were not dog people.

The pugs had wandered back to my feet, but it was nice out here tonight. Humid as usual, of course, but with a gentle breeze that at least gave the illusion of coolness. The fireworks show must have ended, since all I could hear was the owl that lived in the thicket behind the house, and once in a while the donkeys that lived at the Okie Dokie Donkey place just across the backfield. Texans liked miniature donkeys, I had found out. All in all, I loved my life here in sleepy Short Creek—so far. I could feel God healing my heart while I waited on Him to unfold my new life.

I gazed at the sky, marveling as always at how many stars I could see way out here in the country. I had never known there were so many. I traced the outline of the Northern Cross with my eyes and had moved on to searching for the dim constellation of Draco when I heard Sherm's back door scrape open. Light spilled out over a dark-haired young woman before she closed the door behind her and disappeared into the dark yard.

Sherm's granddaughter was still here. Hmm. It seemed she came and went, though sometimes she'd be gone for weeks or months at a time. What was her name? Natalie? Nina? I was pretty sure I remembered it started with an "N".

The meager light from the one streetlight out in front of the house didn't reach this far, but I could see the glow of her phone, then the flare of a lighter somewhere near Sherm's back porch. I wrinkled my nose when the cigarette smoke wafted over to me.

"I can't come back right now, Vic," she whispered. "I need a few more days this time."

I froze. She didn't know I was out here. Or maybe she didn't want Sherm to hear her conversation. Of course, Sherm was so deaf he couldn't have heard her anyway, even if she was right next to him.

"No! I already told you. I need more time."

I heard a thump and she swore softly, the sounds carrying on the humid air along with another cloud of cigarette smoke.

"Can't you give me one more day? I'm trying to figure all of this out without my Gramps—what? No, of course he doesn't know. I'm not that st—"

I sneezed. Loudly.

She swore again, and I could barely make out her profile as she turned toward me.

"Hi there," I called. "Happy Fourth of July!"

She slammed the door.

Well, then.

I herded the girls into the house and locked both the inner and outer doors, noticing again how much hotter and stuffier it was in the mudroom where the air conditioning didn't reach as well. There was a tiny window in the mudroom, but it was stuck fast, like all of the attic windows. And anyway, one does not open windows in July in Central Texas. The muggy night air was oppressive.

Oppressive. Like the feeling in my spirit when I heard Nicole's phone conversation. Something was going on, and it wasn't good.

Many hours later, I awoke to the pugs' low growls. Rolling over to look at my phone, I groaned when I realized it was two o'clock in the morning. I squinted through the dark in the general direction of the pugs' bed.

"Go to sleep," I murmured.

Pugs aren't exactly watchdogs, and sometimes they get overly upset about things they shouldn't. They probably heard a pecan drop onto the roof and roll down. Or maybe the squirrels were working overtime tonight.

The dogs nestled back down together in a little furry knot. I lay in the dark and listened for several minutes, but didn't hear anything besides the pugs' snoring. What if they had heard something for real? What if someone was in the house? I wasn't usually a scaredy-cat, but after the events of the last few days, I was a little on edge.

I began to pray through Psalm 91, imagining angels hovering over my house, protecting me from harm. I loved to think about angels. I had even prayed before that God would let me see one sometime. I imagined huge, snowy wings. A sense of indescribable peace. Joy. A huge—

I was almost asleep again when Purl's bark nearly sent me through the roof. She rarely barked, and when she did, it was usually sort of a low "mwoof." This was not her normal mwoof.

"What is wrong with you two tonight?" I turned on the lamp.

Purl barked again, a short, high bark, and Intarsia joined in, her black hair bristling. Big dogs trapped in small dog bodies. That's what pugs are.

"I don't hear anything scary," I grumbled as I slid out of bed. I might as well use the bathroom if I was awake again.

I came back into my bedroom, where the dogs had settled back into their bed.

"Is it okay now?" I asked.

Two sets of chocolate brown eyes focused on me, and I stroked both of their silky little heads before I climbed into my bed.

"It's time to go to sleep now," I whispered. "You can growl at the pecans and the squirrels more in the morning."

But there was far more to growl about than squirrels. When I opened the door from the living room into the mudroom in the morning, I was shocked to see the back door hanging wide open, the hot Texas sunlight streaming in. The dogs trip-tripped through the open door and out into the yard, while I sank into the rocking chair once again, my knees weak.

I had dead-bolted that door from the inside. I knew I had. And there was no sign of forced entry.

So that meant that...I squeezed my eyes shut, my heart hammering. Dear God. That meant that someone had been up in the attic when I locked the doors last night. And that someone had come down the stairs and snuck out while I was sleeping.

CHAPTER SIX

I sighed as I pulled up to C. Willikers. I sat staring at the arbor, where the Eden roses were starting to cover it beautifully. They didn't have much fragrance, but their huge flowers and delicate colors were breathtaking. A romantic old-rose type, their bunchy blossoms were a lovely cream color with delicate carmine-pink middles. The foliage was dark green and glossy. By this time next year, they would be stunning.

The two enormous Boston ferns flourished in their hanging baskets on either side of the wrap-around porch, lending their own ambiance to the quintessential Southern-garden look I was aiming for. I was making this little store my own, where I was surrounded on a daily basis with the things I loved the best. I considered myself blessed to be able to find joy in the beauty of God's creation, and to share that joy with others.

But there were days when even that didn't matter so much. Days like today, when I felt fragile; somehow more aware of my dependency upon God's mercy and of my desperate, tenacious hold on His strength alone to see me through. Praying with my friends yesterday morning had helped.

But on top of the troubling person-in-the-attic issue, I'd had a nightmare again last night. The first one since I moved down here. I guessed that yesterday's traumatic events had stirred everything up again. And now my soul felt bruised.

"Thank you, Father, that your mercies are new every morning," I murmured out loud. I definitely needed new grace, new insight, new wisdom today. I felt like Jill Pole, one of C.S. Lewis' characters in *The Silver Chair*. Unexpectedly finding herself alone and in a terrible situation, Jill burst into tears and cried and cried. But, once she had dried her tears, she still had to figure out what to do next.

And if I had learned anything so far in life, I had learned *that*, at least. Oh, I had shed my share of tears, no doubt about it. But when morning dawned the day after Kev's funeral, *I* was still alive on this earth. And so there was nothing to do for it, except to live. I still had to take a shower and brush my teeth. I still had to feed the dogs, water the plants and pay the bills. I still had to pray. I still had to put one foot in front of the other, no matter how dark the path. I still had to believe that God's hand was upon me, even now. That He could see me. That He felt my pain. And that He had a plan for my life—for my future. If I didn't believe that, what hope did I have?

I will see the good of the Lord in the land of the living.

I took a deep breath.

"Come on, girls," I said to the pugs. "Let's get to work." I lifted them out of the van one at a time, and they waddled quickly across the burning pavement to the small patch of grass in front of the shop. It was easily 85 degrees out, though only 8:30 in the morning.

Rain would be nice. I purposely turned my mind from introspection. It could take over, if I let it.

"Callie!"

I glanced up to see Houston waving at me from across the church parking lot. I waved back. "Thanks again for stopping by yesterday," I yelled.

He ambled toward me, then stopped and reached for his phone. He listened for a minute, then waved at me. "Sorry, I need to run to the hospital. Can I call you later?"

Could he call me?

"Sure. I'll probably still be puttering around the store."

Hmm. Houston and I had been friends for a while, but I'd never thought of him as more than that. But he gave me a stuffed animal...and now he wanted to call me?

I unlocked the shop door to let the pugs into the air-conditioned building while I stayed outside to water the caladiums that thrived in the shade of the live oak. The forecasters were saying we'd have a pretty good chance for thunderstorms this weekend, but I couldn't count on that.

I had carefully planted the bulbs early this spring after drooling over the many varieties all winter. After an agony of indecision, I had finally settled on the White Christmas variety, with their large white leaves sporting a blush of red at the center and lovely, dark green veins. They contrasted nicely with the Florida Beauty variety that featured multi-toned olive green leaves decorated with pink or purple splotches and were still holding up surprisingly well in the mid-summer heat.

This building had been neglected for a couple of years before I bought it, and I was slowly designing the garden to look like the gorgeous picture I envisioned in my mind's eye. But I had discovered that down here in Central Texas, there is a set timeframe for planting. And July and August are not it. Fall is the best time, to give the plants' roots time to get established for several months before the unrelenting heat of summer was upon them.

Kind of like people, I mused. People need time to set their roots deep, so the storms of life don't destroy them. *Like a tree, planted by streams of water*...I caught myself. I had a tendency to assign some sort of spiritual significance to everything in life, which is usually a good thing, I think. But I could also quickly slide into over-thinking things, which led to self-recrimination or fear or any number of other unpleasant thoughts if I allowed it.

"Callie!"

I jumped and turned quickly, the hose dribbling lukewarm water over my foot. Awesome. At least I was wearing sandals.

Todd Whitney strode up to me. "I'm glad you're up and about. I ran by to check on you."

Really? Did EMS usually provide such personal service?

I looped my hair behind my ear and smiled at him. "Thank you, Todd. That was sweet of you."

"How's your head this morning?" He moved to stand in the shade of the pecan tree.

He had a little bit of dark scruff and his uniform was slightly rumpled, like he was getting off work. He'd probably been on duty this whole time, while I was home sleeping. Or rather, not sleeping. I winced. I probably should report the person-in-the-attic situation. But I did not want to deal with Sheriff Earl again, truth be told.

"Do you want to come in for a minute?" I asked impulsively. "I was going to have a cup of tea." Maybe I could talk to him about the sheriff for a minute. Something was not right about this whole thing.

"Hot tea?" He raised his eyebrows. "It's got to be 100 degrees out."

I shrugged. "But it's not hot inside. I have a few water bottles in the fridge, though, if you want something cold."

"I'm headed home now." He lifted his baseball cap off then resettled it. "But I'll take you up on the water bottle. It's a little bit of a drive."

I turned off the hose, and Todd followed me inside. I winced at the *screeeech-bang* of the screen door. "I've got to get that fixed," I muttered.

The pugs hurried over to greet Todd, yipping and snorting around his feet.

"Hey, who are these little guys?" he asked, bending to pet them.

He liked dogs. That was good.

What? You'd think I was attracted to him or something.

"The fawn is Purl, and the little black one is Intarsia," I said.

"Purl, as in knitting?" He glanced around my store.

I was delighted that he had made the connection. Many people didn't; thinking I meant "Pearl" if they didn't see it spelled out.

"Yes," I said. "And intarsia is a knitting technique, too," I added.

"Very clever." He grinned at me, his warm eyes sparkling.

My heart did a weird flip-flop, and I dropped my gaze from his. What was wrong with me this morning? A rock to the head sure could do strange things to a person.

"Let me get you that water bottle," I murmured, digging in the mini-fridge I kept behind my counter. When I re-emerged, Todd had moved to examine my African violet display.

"You have a beautiful store." He gently fingered a fuzzy leaf of my "Beau" violet. The rare Russian hybrid was in full bloom right now, the flowers a glorious fuchsia with ruffled golden edges. "My mother was a plant-lover, too."

I didn't miss the word *was*, or the wistful tone of his voice. But I barely knew the man.

"Yes, I've always loved to grow plants—especially flowers. At one point, I considered becoming a botanist, but God had other plans for my life, I guess." At least, I hoped He did...

He took a swig of water. "You moved from the Midwest somewhere?"

"Ohio."

"I've been there a couple of times visiting relatives. Been years, though," he said. "What brought you to Short Creek?"

Ah, the inevitable question. I never knew quite how to answer it. *Nothing in life had turned out the way I expected? My husband was killed, and then my career was destroyed? I needed a place to heal? I was desperate to put the past behind me? God led me here?*

All true, but most people didn't truly want to know all of that. So I usually mentioned I had family down here, and then followed that up with a smile and a flippant remark about how I was very tired of shoveling snow. For most folks, that was enough.

But somehow, looking into this pair of intelligent blue eyes, I sensed that Todd Whitney was someone I could trust.

"I needed a place to rest," I offered.

A kindred spirit, someone who had also weathered a few of life's more difficult storms, would immediately recognize my words for what they were—the tiniest crack in the wall around my heart—the barest invitation to engage in something beyond the casual.

His gaze softened, and I knew I had pegged him correctly.

I plucked a yellowing leaf off the philodendron that draped itself over my counter. "My Aunt Dot has been trying to convince me to move down for years, and when she offered me the house, it confirmed what I had been praying about."

"Dot Murray?" he asked, smiling.

He knew my aunt?

Well, of course he did. I guess I wasn't used to a small community yet, where everyone knew everyone else and half the town was related to each other.

I smiled back at him. "Yes, sir."

"She's a real firecracker. I've missed seeing her at church since she had to move to Willowbough."

I could hear his fondness for her in his voice.

"She's learning to 'do technology,' as she calls it," I said. "She told me she's going to email me soon, once the tech guy over there at Willowbough teaches her how."

He laughed out loud. "Really? Somehow, I can picture her doing that. I didn't know they offered technology classes there."

"Yeah, a guy named Brandon is teaching the class. You'll have to come visit her with me sometime." *Oh, dear. I hadn't said that out loud, had I?*

Uh oh. I had definitely spoken out loud, and it was definitely the wrong thing to say because Todd's face had immediately darkened into a scowl.

"Brandon Delacourte? I remember him being a computer geek, but he doesn't seem like the type to work with seniors."

I shrugged. "I don't know his last name. I've never even met him." But I *would*, if Aunt Dot had her way. I sighed inwardly.

"I hope you never do. If Delacourte is back in town, I'd give him a wide berth." He rubbed a hand over his eyes. "I'd better get on my horse, Callie. I've been up for going on twenty-four hours straight."

I walked with him to the door, Intarsia trailing behind us. "Thanks again for coming to check on me."

He bent down to finger Intarsia's black, velvety little ears, then stood and looked me in the eye. "I was hoping maybe we could talk for a minute about the other day, when you are feeling better."

Which other day? The one where I found a dead body, or the one where I almost *was* a dead body?

I gulped.

"I'd like to go over with you again what happened the morning you called about the man and the package." He searched my eyes.

I nodded. I had kind of been expecting to be grilled again, but I thought Sheriff Earl would do that, not Todd. In my experience, EMTs were not sent to do crime investigation. But this was a small town, so maybe a few of the first responders did double-duty jobs.

"Would you mind giving me your cell phone number?" he

asked.

I gave it to him, feeling the adrenaline kick into my system. I wasn't ready to think about the whole situation again, much less talk about it.

He must have seen me starting to tremble, because he pressed me down into the rocking chair by the door and squatted in front of me. He reached for my hand. "I'm sorry to upset you, Callie," he said. "You seemed like you were handling things okay this morning, or I wouldn't have mentioned the case to you today."

I willed my legs to stop shaking, but they wouldn't obey. Ever since Kev's car crash, my body had reacted to sudden anxiety in ways I wouldn't have predicted. I hadn't experienced the nerve twitches in my legs for a long time, not until the other morning.

The morning.

And now, when I was merely *thinking* about having to talk about discovering the body. I closed my eyes for a moment, and clung to Todd's big hand like it was a lifeline. My legs vibrated like I was in one of those dumb massage chairs at the mall.

"It's going to be all right," he whispered.

It's going to be all right.

I took a deep breath. Those were the same words *she* had said to me. I was sitting in the back pew of the church the day of Marleigh's funeral, trying to work up the courage to actually walk up the aisle to where the rest of the preschool staff was sitting. Marleigh had not only been in my care at my preschool; she was a beautiful little person with her whole life in front of her.

I sat in the shadows of the back pew and wept. I couldn't believe I had to endure another funeral for a person I loved. Losing Marleigh wasn't the same as being robbed of my husband, but it was still a deep, aching loss. A tragic death that shouldn't have been.

And it was my fault.

Someone slid into the pew and sat down close beside me. Closer than I would have liked. I scooched away an inch or two, needing space. But the woman's perfume wafted over to me; a light, beautiful scent unlike anything I had experienced before.

It made me think of...of sunlit meadows...of flowers, more beautiful than any I had ever seen or could ever imagine.

It made me think of—Heaven.

My tears slowed, and I blew my nose. After a moment, I turned to see who was next to me. It was a lovely older woman; someone whom I couldn't recall ever meeting before—yet there was something familiar about her. She reached out a soft hand to cup my cheek and smiled into my eyes.

"It's going to be all right," she whispered.

It's going to be all right.

That was all she said, but I nodded, feeling peace flood through me somehow. I closed my eyes for a long moment, simply breathing in the scent of Heaven.

When I opened my eyes, she was gone.

But Todd was still here, squeezing my hand and looking at me anxiously.

I drew in a deep breath. "I'll be okay." I pulled my hand free to dash away an unwanted tear. "Just...pray for me, okay?"

He stood, and it seemed that he towered above me.

"I will, Callie," he said, and I knew he would.

He seemed to start to say something else, then stopped. "I'll be in touch, okay? Make sure you take care of yourself. Maybe an extra cup of tea today with a pug on your lap."

That sounded good to me. My morning cup was long overdue.

I had pulled myself together by the time Lonnie and Jenna arrived to talk wedding flowers. I'm not usually a huggy kind of person, but I didn't step away when Lonnie threw her arms around me.

"Oh, Callie! I've been praying for you. Are you sure you're up to doing this today?"

I nodded. "How much have you heard?"

She glanced at her daughter, who had already gravitated to my big albums of wedding ideas. "We should probably talk later," she said. A frown marred her perfectly made-up face. "Rick says that the sheriff—"

"Mom, look at this!" Jenna called.

We both joined her at the counter, and I peered over her shoulder to see.

"Where did you get these cool old pictures, Callie?" she asked.

"I've collected old wedding pictures for years. Wedding styles are always changing, but the old styles always come back into fashion," I explained. "Some brides like to look at these pictures to get ideas for retro wedding themes."

"Well, I'm not too into that kind of thing." She flipped to the next page. "I'm looking for something simpler than that."

A girl after my own heart.

"Do you already have ideas?" I had found through experience that usually a bride already had an idea of what she wanted, and no amount of suggestion would change that. It was only a matter of her finding the right image to give me a concrete idea.

"The wedding will be at SCCC, of course," Lonnie said, referring to our church. "Would you also be able to handle the decorating for the reception? We've already reserved the Rose Arbor Ranch in Salado."

"How many people?" I couldn't believe I was contemplating saying yes. I was a florist, not a decorator. I could design beautiful arrangements, but I usually left it up to other more creative people to know how to combine my arrangements with all of the other elements it took to create the beautiful display for an entire event.

But truthfully, I could use the money, and besides, I was a smart person. How difficult could it be to find ideas online and then duplicate them?

More difficult than I had thought. A day later, I was up to my chin in raffia, moss, lace and vintage candelabras. And I was definitely not as adept with a hot glue gun as I thought I was.

I called Mona in as emergency help.

"This is so fun!" she said, happily gluing tiny wildflowers onto a bed of moss.

I raised my eyebrows at her. "It's fun if you're making *one* miniature terrarium," I said. "Not twenty-five!"

She laughed at me.

As it turns out, what Jenna had termed as "simple" was actually "a woodsy shabby-chic feel with subtle Marie Antoinette-inspired details," as I read later on the website she had shared with me. I'm not sure I even knew what that meant, but the pictures were gorgeous.

"Any idea where I could find old sheet music?" I asked Mona now as I scraped a dot of solidified glue off the counter.

She wrinkled her forehead. "For what?"

I showed her the pictures of the centerpieces featuring sheet music displayed with various candelabras, bouquets, and lace—on moss of course. "Jenna and her fiancée are both musicians. She wants to have a music theme."

"A music theme? I thought she was having a princess, woodsy thing." Mona dug through the bag of pinecones. "You know, like Snow White or something."

I pictured short, blond, chubby Jenna Jones as Snow White. Nope, not even close. "*Snow White* has music in it," I said.

"What? Like heigh-ho, heigh-ho; off to work we go?" Mona scoffed. "That's not wedding music."

I sighed. *What about "Someday My Prince Will Come"? And how exactly did we get from creating wedding decorations to discussing the Seven Dwarfs?*

"At least she's found her Prince Charming." *Wow.* How had that slipped out?

"What?" Mona snapped to attention like Purl did when she heard the word "treat."

"Nothing," I said. "Keep gluing."

Houston never called. I couldn't decide how I felt about that. Not that I had been hoping he would, exactly, but I was kind of intrigued about him asking if he could. I was even more intrigued when I saw him pull away from Sherm's house that evening with a dark-haired young woman in the passenger seat. Nicole.

I called Mona. "Does Sherm attend Houston's church?"

"Sherm Grant? Nah, not any more. He doesn't go much of anywhere these days, does he?"

"No. Not really."

Sherm did own a beat-up Plymouth that looked like it was about fifty years old, but I hadn't ever seen him drive it. So how did he get groceries? Or visit the doctor? I was embarrassed to think I hadn't thought about it until now.

"Why?"

"Why what?" Why was I so selfishly unobservant? Why was Houston picking up Sherm's drop-dead gorgeous granddaughter? Why—

"Callie. Are you okay?"

I blew out a sigh. "Too many questions right now. I'll tell you later, okay?"

I had decided not to tell Aunt Dot about the rock incident, but it seems she had heard about it anyway.

"Callie," she said as I came through her door that afternoon. "Are you okay, honey?

Something about her looks different, I thought as I plopped into the chair next to her.

"I'm fine, Aunt Dot." I picked some glue off my thumbnail. I should probably tell her about hearing someone in my attic.

But I didn't want her to be any more worried than she already was.

She shook her head and pushed her glasses further up on her nose. "I can't believe you had to go to the hospital and you didn't call me!"

"I didn't want to worry you." I stared at her hair. Maybe that was what was different.

"You know better than that," she said. "I don't worry. I pray." She squinted at me. "There's a difference, darlin'."

I know. But the problem is sometimes my prayers and my worry were all wrapped up together, and I forgot that the Lord told us to *rest* in Him. The resting and the trusting part were hard to come by sometimes.

"I know, Auntie."

"Brandon showed it to me in the *Star*," she said, adjusting her glasses again.

I grimaced. I had hoped she wouldn't see the news article.

"Did you get new glasses, Aunt Dot?"

She looked puzzled. "No. But somehow, they don't feel right today. Things seem a little fuzzier than normal."

"Maybe it's time for an eye exam."

She nodded, but didn't look convinced. "I couldn't see as well to type today," she said. "But Harry said—"

Harry? Oh, the gentleman "down the hall" who sold stuff on Facetwitter. I grinned, taking in my aunt's suddenly rosy cheeks.

"What did Harry say?" I asked innocently.

"Oh, nothing." She studied her fingernails. "How was church on Sunday?"

I laughed to myself. "It was fine. Oh, by the way, Todd Whitney says to say hi to you."

"Todd?" Her face lit up. "He's such a precious young man. Such a shame about his family and all."

I had no idea what she was talking about, but I didn't want to encourage anything that could be construed as gossip. Not that Aunt Dot would gossip, but I preferred to get to know a person without having preconceived ideas.

"Is he still a police officer?" she asked. "I haven't seen him in so long."

A police officer?

"Not that I know of," I answered. "He's the captain of the EMS squad at the fire station, though."

"Well, that's nice." Aunt Dot fluffed her hair. "Any progress on your mysterious box?"

I sighed. Some days I convinced myself someone had sent it to me as some sort of joke that I had yet to understand and maybe never would. Then other days, I felt sure there must be something I was missing. Some clue, some instructions—but to what?

"Do you think there could be a connection between the newspaper the things were wrapped in and the things themselves?" I asked. I had already pored over the newspaper pages and couldn't come up with much, and Dot and I had discussed this angle once before.

The wrinkles in her forehead deepened. "It seems like it couldn't be coincidental that the newspaper was dated the same day as Kevin's accident."

"I know. That part bothers me. Who would know that? And why would that person have saved Short Creek newspapers from that specific day five years ago?"

"I remember what I was doing that day." Dot stared at me. "I had decided it was time to clean out the attic. I was knee-deep in boxes when you called to tell me what had happened. Then I got down on my knees and prayed for you for the longest time."

"I called you?"

Odd.

I had no recollection of that call. I remembered talking to Dot a day or two afterwards, but not that terrible day of the accident. "Are you sure?"

She furrowed her brow. "Of course, dear. You left a message on my machine, and you called me Auntie. No one else calls me that."

I stared at her.

"I prayed right when I heard it, and I kept on praying until ten o'clock that night. I remember what time it was because I had the timer on my lights set to go on then. I hadn't realized it had gotten so dark in the house until the lights popped on."

Oh, boy. I was feeling a little creeped out now. Though the days following the accident were a blur, I remembered the actual day as if it were yesterday. I had *not* called Dot that day.

But I do remember an unexplained peace that had washed over me that night, enabling me to sleep when I didn't think I would have been able to. It was so palpable, so noticeable, that I had glanced at my phone. It had been eleven o'clock my time—the same time Dot said she had finished praying for me that day.

"Don't you remember calling me?" she asked. "I tried to call you back right away but couldn't reach you. Of course, that was understandable under the circumstances."

It wasn't understandable at any other time, though. If Dot wanted to get hold of one, she wouldn't stop calling until said person answered. I knew that from experience.

I shook my head. "I don't remember calling you that day," I said. "But I'm sure I must have. That was a terrible day."

"But look how far God has brought you since then, darlin'," Aunt Dot's voice grew soft. "We never know what our life is going to hold, but we know He already knows. He's already there in our future, and He'll give us the strength we need to endure."

Yes, that much was true. But sometimes the hard part was accepting the things He allowed. I often thought about Hannah Hurnard's book, *Hind's Feet on High Places*, and her main character, Much-Afraid. Much-Afraid was on her way to the "High Places," led along her arduous life path by the good but surprising Shepherd. Early on in Much-Afraid's journey, she discovered an exquisite, resilient little flower named "Acceptance-With-Joy," and determined that she would do her best to let the Shepherd teach her to have that same attitude toward life.

Not only acceptance, but acceptance with *joy*. Joy in the midst of sorrow. Joy in the midst of pain. Joy in the midst of uncertainty.

"Sometimes I still feel like Much-Afraid," I confessed.

Aunt Dot smiled. "Me, too. But we're getting closer to the High Places every day. And the best part is, we're getting to know the Shepherd better as we go."

Yes, the dear Shepherd. How did anyone make it through life without His comforting presence...His life-giving words?

"I miss Uncle Garth," I said. "No one prayed for me like he did." I remembered how he would always pat my cheek whenever he saw me. Then he would hug me and whisper in my ear, "I'm so proud of you, sweetie."

Aunt Dot's eyes glistened. "Yes, he certainly loved you. I think he thought of you as the granddaughter we never had. I know when you were going through your troubles with Kev, Garth spent many hours praying for you. One day, he even told me—"

"What are y'all talking about so serious-like in here?" A big voice boomed through the doorway, preceding a handsome, silver-haired man who matched his own voice in size and energy.

"Harry, this is Callie." Aunt Dot beamed at both of us.

"Calendula!" Harry took my hand. "I've heard so much about you! Such a pleasure to finally meet you, young lady."

I smiled up at him, taking an immediate liking to the man, even if he had called me by my full name. He was dressed to the T in jeans, western boots, an enormous gold ring and a collared shirt. He smelled like he had just gotten out of the shower. I pegged him as a football coach, or maybe a businessman, in his younger days. "So nice to meet you, Mr.—"

"Parsons," he supplied. "But Harry is fine. Shoot, I feel like I know you already, for as much as this pretty lady talks about you." He glanced at Aunt Dot, and I was amused to see her cheeks pinken again.

"How long have you two known each other?"

Harry plopped down in the chair across from me and crossed his booted feet. "Well, let's put it this way," he drawled. "I've had a crush on your aunt since I first laid eyes on her in Mrs. Marsh's second grade class."

"Oh, Harry!" Aunt Dot protested.

I had never seen my aunt so flustered.

Harry grinned at me. "It's true," he said cheerfully. "Then that old rascal, Garth, stole her heart while I was away in the war."

Aunt Dot huffed out a sigh. "That's all water under the bridge now."

"Yes, ma'am." He winked at her. "Now I've got you all to myself again, and you're prettier'n you were back then, by golly."

I laughed out loud. Who would think Aunt Dot would have a beau when she was in her eighties?

"I'm tryin' to get her to go on a date with me tomorrow." He leaned forward. "The Lutheran church is havin' their annual Polka Worship service."

"Now Harry, you know I can't—"

He patted her hand. "I know it's hard for you to get around, sugar. But the preacher said he'd send someone to pick us up, and they have a nice wheelchair ramp."

"Well, I did have my hair done yesterday." Aunt Dot patted her hair. "It was some new gal, though. She wasn't as good as Karen."

Harry must have been able to tell she was weakening. "They're even having a traditional German meal afterwards in the fellowship hall," he coaxed. "With homemade sausage and potato salad."

The potato salad must have sealed the deal, because the next thing I knew, Lonnie had posted a picture of my aunt and Harry to my Facebook page.

Snapped this picture at the German dinner last night, she commented. *Aren't they cute?*

I leaned back in my desk chair with my favorite tea mug in my hand and contemplated my aunt's face smiling at me from my computer screen. Then it hit me. That had been what was bothering me yesterday when I visited Aunt Dot—her glasses. She had kept fiddling with them, like they were uncomfortable. The frames of the ones she had on the other day were larger and darker, but the ones she had on in this picture appeared to be the ones she normally wore. Hmm. I hadn't seen her so happy in a long time. More than happy—she looked radiant. And Harry looked like the proverbial cat that had swallowed the canary as he posed behind her with his hand on her shoulder, his huge class ring prominently displayed.

I smiled, then logged off the computer. It was Monday morning, and I had centerpieces to create and an appointment to talk with Todd Whitney at lunchtime. It had been a good weekend. No bodies, no rocks thrown at me. And I had also once again escaped meeting Aunt Dot's dream-date Brandon.

I hummed along with my favorite Christian radio station as I created the arrangement for the Methodist church. Their new pastor was finally arriving in town today and would be preaching for the first time on Sunday, so apparently, the powers-that-be had decided to spruce up the sanctuary a little bit with live flowers for the occasion. They wanted the arrangement to be in place for when the new pastor first began work tomorrow morning.

The pastor was a *she*, which I found interesting. I hadn't met her yet, but she was coming from somewhere back east. I poked a few white roses in place, idly wondering what she was like. Did she have a family? How old was she?

I added a grouping of fern fronds, then stood back to appraise my creation. The secretary had said "shades of blue with white," so I guess they weren't too picky. I had begun with a number of gorgeous potted hydrangeas, then added ferns and a few barely-opened white roses as accents. By tomorrow, the roses would open more fully and the arrangement would be stunning when Ms. Pastor first saw it in the church sanctuary.

I carried it to the cooler, then headed back to wipe the counter before I started my next project. I started to move the wedding idea albums to the side, then stopped and opened the album that I had made with old wedding photos collected over the years. Most were old family photos; a few I had picked up at garage sales or antique stores. Since I had moved here, I had been gradually going through the boxes that Aunt Dot had left stored in the attic when she had moved into Willowbough. She had told me I could go through them and take whatever "suited my fancy." I smiled.

There wasn't much left in the attic, but Uncle Garth had created an office up there a few years before he passed. Or at least, Aunt Dot had called it his office. Most of the time, he used the space to build his model airplanes or study the Bible for the Sunday school class he had taught for years. I had adored hanging out up there with him on long summer evenings. We shared a love of learning and an appreciation for great literature.

Uncle Garth's desk was still up there, and a couple of antique bookcases full of his beloved books. *I should go through those one of these days*, I mused. Maybe I could get Rob over here to help me move one of the bookcases downstairs into my bedroom. I loved old furniture, and I could use another bookcase. My to-be-read pile was turning into the Leaning Tower of Pisa. I'd better turn it into a to-be-read bookcase before it overtook my entire nightstand. And floor.

I sighed and pulled my laptop toward me. I needed to finish up Jenna's table decorations, but I had been puzzling about the *festina lente* symbol thing again this morning when I woke up. I couldn't believe I had forgotten to ask Aunt Dot about the envelope that Mona saw with what we thought was the *festina lente* sign drawn on it.

I know I wasn't being realistic, but I guess I was hoping it wouldn't turn out to be anything. It could have been a doodle, right? And besides, the symbol on the back of the envelope didn't appear to have any numbers or letters with it like the one sent to me.

Letters and numbers. What if it was as easy as plugging those numbers and letters into a search engine?

I tried it.

"Your search did not match any document," I read out loud.

Of course not. I looked up "licensing a boat in Texas".

"Ah ha!" I crowed. Except all of the Texas-issued boat numbers started with a TX. And all of them consisted of four numerals followed by two letters.

Okay, that was a dead end. What else could the letters and numbers stand for?

PSIS58610. Could it be a code? That seemed unlikely. It sounded like something out of a kid's mystery book. Could it be an address? How about a city, state, and zip code? Hmm. I typed the numbers in.

"Telakanava, Finland?" That seemed far-fetched. I was grasping at straws here, obviously.

I dragged out the box of sheet music and ribbon I had assembled for Jenna's wedding reception, deciding I might as well give my brain a rest for a few minutes. Clearly, I wasn't getting anywhere with the letter/number thing. I plugged in my hot glue gun. Whenever I had a spare moment, I worked on the woodsy-shabby-chic feel with musical-theme decorations. I think Jenna alone was supporting the local craft store with the supply of moss, dried flowers, candles, ribbons, and glassware I had purchased.

Glancing out the window, I saw Todd Whitney pull up in his white pickup. I looped my hair over my ear, wishing I had at least put it in a ponytail this morning. I rolled my eyes at my own foolishness. Like the man even cared what I looked like. He was coming to question me about The Morning.

I took a deep breath. I had already prayed this morning that God would calm my spirit and help me to make it through this conversation. Through the main shop window, I could see Todd stroll up my walkway. He was carrying a screwdriver, and he didn't look happy.

A screwdriver?

Resisting my inclination to meet him at the door, I hovered around behind my work counter, as if busier than I really was.

The screen door screeched open.

"Hey Callie," he called. "I'm a few minutes early. Hope that's okay."

"Sure, that's fine," I called back. "I'll be done with this in a sec." I wasn't actually doing anything, but I suddenly felt awkward around him. What had changed since the last time I saw him? I had seen him briefly at church on Sunday. He had been ushering that morning, and flashed a smile my direction when he handed the plate down my row. Then I saw the back of his head when he walked through the parking lot ahead of me after church.

Uh, not much cause for excitement there. Maybe I was anxious about reliving The Morning. Or maybe it was because he was on his hands and knees in front of my screen door.

I sidled over to him, where the pugs were joyfully snorting and snuffing around him. "Did you drop something?"

He grinned up at me and my stomach did the weird flip-flop thing again.

"Nope," he said. "Fixing your door."

Ah, the screwdriver. I nodded. "Thank you so much! I kept thinking I should go online and see what I needed to do to fix it."

He stood. "No worries. Need to adjust the mechanism a little bit." He jammed the screwdriver into his back pocket, and looked me in the eye. "But we do need to talk about Friday."

Friday? Uh oh. My pulse kicked up about ten notches.

"Why didn't you call 911 when you found your back door open? The report didn't come across my desk until this morning." He glared at me. "Someone could have still been in the vicinity, Callie. And after all of the weird things that have been happening to you—"

I shrugged. "I figured whoever it was, was probably long gone. I mean, why would he stick around? And at least I reported it. Just not right then."

He had been shaking his head while I was talking.

"And besides, the sheriff doesn't like it when I talk to him."

"What?"

"Earl doesn't like me very much."

"What do you mean?" Todd's eyebrows were high on his forehead.

I sighed. "He always tells me I'm imagining things or that they aren't what I think they are."

He gritted his teeth. "Can we sit down somewhere?"

I followed him over to the book nook. I took the wingback chair while he perched on the edge of the worn leather couch, looking like he was poised for action.

Was he that upset that I hadn't called old Mr. Grumpy-Pants sheriff?

"Callie." He pinned me with a look that I imagined he usually used on bad guys. After all, he was an ex-cop, wasn't he? Well, according to Aunt Dot, at least. And at this moment, it didn't take much imagination to believe it.

I grimaced, and he relaxed his posture a bit.

"I want you to understand something. Your safety is of utmost importance, and you can't let Earl's imbecilic behavior stop you from doing what it takes to be safe."

Imbecilic? Maybe I wasn't being paranoid about the sheriff after all.

Todd jumped up from the couch to pace. I had already noticed he had on his jeans and boots today instead of his uniform. He looked like a rancher. A rancher-cop. A handsome rancher-cop.

"I wanted to talk to you about the morning you found the body," he said. "We're still waiting on an official report—"

The *body*? Now we were back to it being a body?

"Earl told me he wasn't dead."

"I know." Todd stopped pacing. "Callie—"

The man was trying to tell me something, obviously. Something difficult.

He turned from me to scan the store. "Can you close the shop for a little while? I need you to take a ride with me."

What?

I stared at him, trying to understand the sudden desperation in his voice.

"Please? I know you don't know me very well, but we need to talk. I'll bring you back whenever you're ready, I promise."

I glimpsed the pain in his astute eyes and knew I could trust him. Knew, somehow, that I *must* trust him.

CHAPTER SEVEN

I locked the pugs into their kennel, and hung the "Back Soon" sign on the front door. I loved the homey, small-town feel that still allowed one to leave with only a note on the front door.

Todd opened the passenger door of the pickup and gave me his hand to help me up. The truck was one of those tall jobs with an extended cab. I could have hoisted myself up easily, but it was nice that he was courteous. I had noticed that about the men down here. Even when entering the gas station or the grocery store, most men routinely held the door open for women. I liked that.

His truck smelled of aftershave and horses. I glanced into the backseat to see a rope halter and work gloves. I didn't know much about Todd Whitney, except that he had made his way into my dreams a couple of times recently. And he didn't wear a wedding ring.

Todd slid into the driver's seat. The air conditioning and the radio both blasted me the minute he turned on the ignition. "Sorry about that." He reached over to turn down the radio. "It was a good song."

I accepted the piece of gum he offered me. It had been ages since I'd had a piece of cinnamon gum.

He popped a piece into his own mouth, and turned left to head out of town, rather than right to drive past the volunteer fire department and city offices as I had expected.

"Where are we headed?" I asked casually.

He shrugged. "Just a drive. I need to talk to you about some things, and it feels more private here in the truck."

I tried to calm the butterflies in my stomach. "Worried the pugs will overhear you?" I teased.

He flashed me an amused look, and seemed to relax a little bit. "They're funny little dogs."

I agreed. "Do you have any pets?" I asked. Generally, I wasn't good at small talk, but I assumed pets were a safe topic.

"I have a dog. A German shepherd." He gave me a grin. "Her name is Annie."

I noticed he had said "I" and not "we."

"Would you like to see the ranch?" he said suddenly. "It's a little bit of a drive. Way out near Cameron."

"Sure. It was a pretty slow day so far at the shop anyway." I glanced at my watch. "I'll need to be back by 4:00 or so. My friends are taking me out to dinner for my birthday."

"Is it today?" I could feel him studying me.

I nodded. "My second birthday in Texas already. I arrived here at the beginning of July last year."

"Three years for me. I mean, that's when I came back here to live again."

"Where were you before that?"

He grimaced. "I was in the military. But I grew up here."

Was that a good thing or a bad thing?

He kept his eyes focused on the road for a long moment. I let the silence stretch, enjoying the view as we rolled past miles of cotton fields and cow pastures. "It sure is pretty out here," I said finally.

He glanced at me. "What was your impression that first morning when you saw the victim?"

"It was so overwhelming." I closed my eyes briefly, then drew in a deep sigh. I needed to get this over with. "When I first saw him, I was hoping he was still alive. But then I turned to look at him again, and he looked so bad."

His hands tightened on the steering wheel.

"I didn't think it possible that he could be alive." I pictured again the man's face...the ants... I turned to stare at Todd. "Was he? Was he still alive when you got there?"

Todd didn't answer, but slowed down to turn into a gravel driveway. *TNT Ranch* was lettered in black iron on a tall arch, welcoming us onto the property.

This was Todd's ranch? I gazed at the wooded area on my right, then the cattle grazing on the gently rolling land that spread out to my left. How many acres did he own? He pulled up in front of the house, and a beautiful German shepherd, that I assumed was Annie, came bounding up to my side door.

Kevin and I had often dreamed about getting a German shepherd puppy, but we had never ended up living in a place that was conducive to owning a large dog, so we settled on pugs. Kevin loved those little dogs. In fact, sometimes I had wondered if he loved them more than he loved me.

I sat in the truck cab, my hand on the door latch.

"Are you afraid of large dogs?" Todd asked.

I shook my head. "I love shepherds."

His keen eyes assessed me again. What was he thinking?

"She'll want you to play ball with her," he finally said.

"It's been a long time since I've thrown a ball for a dog, but I'll give it my best shot."

I opened the door and slithered down from the tall truck, much to Annie's delight. She didn't jump on me, but nudged my hand before giving my legs and shoes a very thorough sniffing. She had a fine bone structure; more delicate than shepherds who were bred for working. Her large ears were upright and alert, and her classic tan and black coloring was beautiful. "She's absolutely gorgeous."

He ruffled her ears. "I probably could have shown her, but I only wanted a companion dog."

She loped away from my side, then reappeared with a half-flat basketball in her mouth. She gazed at me and whined. I complied and took the ball from her. I tossed it a few feet out onto the expansive front yard, and the dog grabbed it up and brought it back to me in under ten seconds.

Todd laughed. "It's hard to throw that thing very far, but it's her favorite for some reason."

He seemed more relaxed than he had been at the shop. This wide-open space seemed to fit him well. "Do you live here alone?" I asked.

"Most of the time." He kicked Annie's ball far out over the yard. "Of course, Luke stays here whenever he's not at his mom's. Do you know my son?"

I shook my head. I had seen the boy with him at church a couple of times and noticed how much the two of them looked alike. Same wavy dark hair. Same thick black eyelashes framing startlingly blue eyes.

"He's eleven," Todd said. "I'll introduce you the next time he's with me at church. I wish I could bring him all the time, but his mother—" he stopped, then looked at me. "I'm sorry. I won't bore you with all that. Let's get in out of the heat."

Todd settled me at his kitchen table with a glass of iced tea. "No hot tea at my house today." He grinned at me. "If I'd known you were coming—"

"Iced is fine," I said, taking in the rustic cabinets and granite countertops. "This is a beautiful kitchen."

He glanced around the room, as if trying to see it through my eyes. "I grew up in this house. It's sometimes strange to be living here all by myself now, you know?"

Not really, but I nodded.

He gave me a sad smile, then turned serious. "I know you're new to Short Creek, Callie."

Here it comes. I nodded again.

"This little town is no different than any little town. There's a lot of good folks here."

Yes, that was true. I thought of my new friends and my little church family. Short Creek had been pretty friendly to me so far. What was he getting at?

"I don't think what happened to you was an accident."

"What do you mean?"

"It might have been an accident that the victim ended up on your doorstep instead of someone else's, but it wasn't an accident that that man was killed. And it isn't an accident that Earl is trying to cover it up."

I tried to take in what he was telling me. "The sheriff is trying to cover up the man's death?"

He stood abruptly to pace around the kitchen. "That's all I can figure. When the other guys and I arrived at your shop that morning, the guy was alive. Barely alive. There is no way he could have made it."

"But then—" I felt like a five-year-old trying to understand an algebra problem.

"We did what we could for him at the scene. We loaded him

into the ambulance, and Jake and Vic supposedly drove him to the hospital."

"You didn't go with them?" I thought back to that crazy day. Was it only last week? I remembered seeing the ambulance and at least a couple of fire trucks, not to mention Earl's patrol car.

He shook his head. "We had gotten another call, and besides, it doesn't take three of us to drive a guy to the hospital."

"Then what?"

"I don't know." He leaned against the countertop, his arms crossed. "The next thing I heard, the news reports all said he had survived and was recovering in the hospital. I can't believe that."

"I know. Even Houston said he saw the guy in the hospital the next day." I frowned. None of this made sense. "Soooo—?"

"So, I tried to see him at the hospital the day you ended up there with a lump on your head. Supposedly, he had already been released." He pulled his hand through his hair. "I'm thinking they paid someone to pose as the victim."

Unbelievable. "What about the other EMS guys? The ones who drove him to the hospital?" I asked.

He toyed with Annie's collar. "They're sticking to the story that he somehow revived on the way to the hospital. The same bunk that Earl is spreading around. They even wrote it in their reports."

Then what...? I realized I hadn't even asked the obvious question.

"What happened to him? I mean, you said someone killed him. How did he die? I didn't see any blood." I shuddered.

"We saw evidence that he was tased."

"But that doesn't usually kill someone, does it?"

"It can trigger a massive heart attack. Especially if the person already has a weak heart. Or if the perpetrator overdoes it with the Taser. But I don't think it was just that."

My head was starting to throb. "So...he ended up dying after being tased. That doesn't mean that someone purposely tried to kill him."

"True." He flexed his jaw. "But he presented symptoms that would be consistent with a drug overdose, too."

What?

"You mean he was high *and* someone shot him with a Taser?"

He shook his head. "Other way around. I think someone shot him with a Taser, then pumped him full of heroin while he was down."

Shock spread through my body. *What kind of evil, deranged human being*—Annie laid her chin on my lap, and I stroked her soft head.

"She wants to comfort you." Todd plunked down in the seat across from me. "She can tell you're upset."

It was more than upset. I drew a deep breath. Could I trust Todd with my own suspicions about Earl? He knew the man better than I did. But if I told him about the way Earl had been taunting me, I'd have to tell him the whole story. About Marleigh. About the court case. About my own failures.

I couldn't do it.

Mona picked me up from home for my birthday dinner. She reached over to give me a hug, her plethora of silver bracelets jangling. I breathed through my mouth so I didn't start to sneeze immediately from the perfume. She must have sprayed it on before she came.

"Houston's going to meet us there. Had a late meeting or something," she said.

"Sounds good." I had barely had time to run home, change my clothes and brush my hair after Todd had dropped me off at C. Willikers.

"Where were you all afternoon?" she asked, deftly backing out of my narrow driveway. "I came by to eat lunch with you and you were gone."

I made sure my seat belt was buckled. One could never be too cautious when riding with Mona. "I had to talk to Todd

Whitney about everything."

I knew that wouldn't satisfy her, but I didn't feel like explaining. My relationship with Todd, if there even was such a thing, was still in the infancy stage, and I didn't care to discuss it yet.

"You spent all afternoon at the city office? Man, Callie! If I had to spend that much time in that close of proximation to the sheriff, I wouldn't have any hair left!"

Proximation? I laughed out loud, but didn't correct her assumption that I'd met with Todd at the office. "And to think you're related to our venerable sheriff."

She groaned. "Don't remind me. At least it's only through marriage."

"Where are we going for dinner?" Maybe if I changed the topic quickly enough, she wouldn't notice that I hadn't exactly answered her question.

"T.J.'s in Temple." She quirked her eyebrows at me. "We'll talk about Todd later."

"I'll have the Mediterranean wraps and the tomato bisque soup, please." I handed my menu to the waiter.

"No wonder you're so thin," Mona muttered, peering at the menu through her reading glasses. "It's her birthday, and she orders healthy stuff."

She turned to Houston. "Are you getting healthy stuff, too?"

"No, ma'am," he said solemnly. "And it's not even my birthday." He turned to the waiter and ordered a chocolate shake, an extremely large steak, and home-style fries.

Mona must have felt better after hearing Houston's order. She whipped her readers off, slapped the menu down, and ordered a double-bacon cheeseburger and a "real" Dr. Pepper—with a salad on the side. "It's not my birthday either," she said, "but I've lost twelve-and-a-half pounds. That calls for a celebration."

"Congratulations!" I said, and I meant it. I have always been thin, through no real effort of my own, I might add. Came with my genes, I guess. But I had witnessed my mother's constant struggle with her weight, and I knew it was a very real and unending battle. "Rob will hardly recognize you," I teased my friend gently.

"That man knows what's what." She pulled her fingers through her spiky hair. "I married one very smart dude."

Houston cleared his throat. "I believe the rest of our party is here."

What?

I glanced up to see Lonnie, Rick and Jenna, Celia, and Karen and her husband. The twins-times-two were nowhere in sight, thankfully. Next came Harry, pushing a beaming Aunt Dot in her wheelchair.

"You guys! I can't believe you invited everyone!" No one had ever given me a surprise party before.

Mona's earrings danced. "Are you surprised?"

I was. And touched. I don't cry very easily, so the lump rising in my throat caught me off guard. I rose to give out hugs, then settled back into my seat next to Houston. "Thank you all so much," I said. "And since I'm the birthday girl, I have something to say." I looked around at the faces of those who I had come to love in these last few months. "I want y'all to know that God is using each one of you to help heal my heart. Thank you for being there for me."

Amid the choruses of *ah's,* Aunt Dot caught my eye. Her love for me at that moment felt almost tangible, and I knew her innumerable prayers for me over the years were being answered, one by one.

"And she said 'y'all,'" Mona said delightedly. "You're turning into a true Texan, Callie."

"I wouldn't go quite that far. My Buckeye roots run pretty deep." But I had to admit, it had been a long time since I had felt like I belonged.

We sat around the table for an hour after we finished eating. It felt slightly awkward that Houston had draped his arm across the back of my chair at some point during the conversation.

I leaned forward to see my prayer-group friend Karen down the long table. "I didn't know you were back from your mission trip, Karen." She was the one with two sets of twins—all boys—under the age of six. If I were her, I think a mission trip to build an orphanage in the jungle would feel like a vacation. "How was it?"

"It was amazing." She sighed.

Her young husband nodded in agreement. "We want to go back."

I could imagine.

"But not for a while," her husband put in, glancing at her. "Our parents need at least a year to recover from the twins before they'll let us go again."

We all laughed, and Karen made a face. Then she turned to me. "Callie, I keep forgetting to ask you if you got that bag of stuff I put on your back porch?"

I furrowed my brow. "Bag of stuff?"

"Yeah, I found a box of stuff out by the dumpster at Willowbough one day after work and—" She stopped. "What's wrong?"

Mona and Houston were staring at me.

"Was it some old books and like odds and ends?" I asked.

She nodded. "I know most of it was probably junk, but the books seemed kind of nice. I thought—"

I pulled in a deep breath and exhaled slowly. Karen had given me The Gift?

The table had gone silent.

Karen grimaced. "Am I in trouble?"

My mind was whirling. I was relieved to know where the bag had come from finally, but in a way, things were suddenly even more complicated than they were before.

"I guess no one's filled you in on my excitement since you've been gone."

She looked at me blankly.

"Tell the whole story from the beginning, Callie," Rick asked. "Lonnie has kept me filled in, of course, but I'd like to hear you tell it. I'm still puzzled over parts of it."

I liked Lonnie's husband, who was also the mayor of Short

Creek. Rick Holloway was a thick, heavy-set man, whose keen black eyes and trained-as-a-lawyer mind didn't miss anything that went on in this town. If Rick was still puzzled, then everyone else was, too. I started at the beginning, leaving nothing out. I even told about someone being in my attic on the night of the Fourth of July.

Aunt Dot gasped. "You didn't tell me that part, darlin'."

"I didn't want to worry you."

She gave me her stern look. "I don't worry, I pray. There's a difference."

"I know, Auntie. But still—" I turned to Karen. "But if you found the box by the dumpster, why was it in a birthday bag?" The whole birthday angle had stumped me since the beginning.

Karen looked shaken. "I can't believe I was involved in a murder!"

"Well, you weren't. Only your bag of stuff," Mona said crisply. "And if that yahoo of a sheriff tries to—"

"Like I said from the beginning. Garage sale leftovers, no doubt," Houston crowed. "I was right!"

"Y'all are going to laugh. I didn't even know it was your birthday." Karen shook her head. "And even if I had, I would have given you a real gift. Not a bunch of junk in a bag that was left over from the twins' birthday party." She laughed. "I had to practically go past your shop on my way home, so I dug around in my car to see if I had anything to put the box in because it was kind of flimsy."

I slumped back into my chair and groaned. "I can't believe this." Days of puzzling over this situation, and I could have just asked Karen—except that she had been in darkest Africa for the whole time, blithely building orphanages.

We all stared at each other, then Lonnie started to giggle. Harry joined in with his booming laugh. Soon, we were all wiping tears away.

The waitress refilled tea glasses and cleared away the rest of the dinner plates.

"At least that part of the mystery is solved," I said. "Thank you for the books, Karen. I will appreciate them more, now that I know that no one died to give them to me. But I still don't understand the 'Give it back' incident. Give what to whom?"

"Maybe the ding-dong who left the box by the dumpster decided he wanted it back." Mona shook her head. "But you'd think he'd just ask you for it. Not smash you in the head with a rock."

"That would have been much less painful." I rubbed the still-tender spot on my head.

Aunt Dot wrinkled her forehead. "But...how would he know that Callie had ended up with his stuff?"

"That's what I was wondering." Rick leaned back in his chair and laced his hands over his stomach. "Who all knows about this?"

"Well, besides all of you...I guess Rob. And Todd Whitney." I stopped. "Oh, and the sheriff, of course."

"And there was nothing of real value that you could see in the box?" Rick asked.

"Someone had left it next to a dumpster, Callie. I don't think—" Karen paused. "What if one of the books is super valuable?"

"Yeah, you know. Like how you see something on the Antiques Roadshow that looks like a piece of trash and it's worth fifty million dollars or something." Mona caught her glass with her elbow.

I grabbed it right before Houston was baptized with Dr. Pepper.

"Thanks, Callie."

I shook my head. "I don't think any of those books are worth much, at least to my untrained eye."

"Did any of them have names in them?" Harry asked. "Maybe some ol' boy wanted them back 'cause they belonged to his granddaddy or somethin'."

"One or two had a name in them," I said. "Something like Olsen or Owen, maybe?"

"Callie." Aunt Dot's whisper was strangled.

"What, Auntie?"

"Was one of those books an old copy of Pilgrim's Progress? An antique?"

"Yes. That's the one I put up as a display in my shop window the other day." But Aunt Dot wouldn't have seen the display.

"How would you know there was a Pilgrim's Progress book in there?" I asked.

"When you said Owen, I thought of Owen Thompson. He gave me a copy when—" She stopped and glanced at Harry. "He gave it to me when your Uncle Garth passed."

It couldn't be the same book, could it? And who was Owen Thompson?

"But why would one of your books be in a box of junk at Willowbough? Did you take it with you when you moved there? Or donate it somewhere before you moved?"

Aunt Dot looked relieved. "No, I saved all of my books for you. Maybe it was one that looked like it."

That must be it. "Well, I'll bring it next time I visit you, and you can look at it to make sure."

"Didn't Owen Thompson pass away recently?" Lonnie asked. "I thought I heard something about that."

"Yes," Houston and Harry chorused.

"I did his funeral." Houston sipped his iced tea. "It was, what, a few months ago?"

"Two months," Harry said. His strong voice shook. "He was a good friend."

We were all quiet for a moment as Harry excused himself and headed for the restroom.

"Harry and Owen practically grew up together, Callie." Aunt Dot followed Harry with her eyes. "We were all good friends from way back, but those two were almost like brothers."

"Well, what I want to know is if Karen found this box of stuff by a dumpster, then why was there a message to Callie in it? I mean, who else would understand some kind of Latin thingy?" Mona's abrupt change of subject startled me for a minute.

"That's a very good question." Ack. Karen had provided a couple of answers, but now the new questions were multiplying faster than the squirrels in my yard. If the person who drew the *festina lente* sign and addressed it to me *hadn't* sent me the box of stuff, then what did that mean? And how did that person get the note into the box?

Mona was shaking her head. "I think—"

"Who's the birthday girl?" someone behind me shouted.

I jumped.

Mona pointed at me. "Thirty-six!" she added, loud enough for the entire world to hear.

A waiter who looked like he was all of fifteen materialized at my elbow, joined by three waitresses who clearly would rather be anywhere else than singing the birthday song once again. I groaned.

After the spoon-shaking and loud clapping routine ended, my friends sang a hearty rendition of "Happy Birthday," while the waiter set a humongous piece of chocolate hot fudge cake in front of me. "Thank you, everyone," I said. "Who wants to share?"

"I can't believe you guys planned a surprise party for me." I juggled my purse and my box of leftovers as I slid into Mona's tiny car.

She slanted me a glance as she started the car. "Everybody needs a surprise party sometime in their life. Rob's not going to believe it when I tell—"

"I know. Do you know how much sleep I've lost over that dumb box of stuff?"

"And then it turned out to be nothing." She slowed at an intersection as the light turned yellow. "Hey, isn't that your neighbor's granddaughter? What's her name? Jessica? Hailey?"

"Nicole." I studied the disheveled young woman waiting at the bus stop. She leaned against an enormous rolling suitcase, her black shirt straining over her pregnant belly. She sure looked like Sherm's granddaughter—but not like I'd ever seen her. Her hair hung over her eyes, and ugly blotches marred her complexion.

"She's looking a little rough." Mona glanced at me. "You know her mama died a few years back."

"I don't know her at all," I confessed. "I've been so busy since I moved here getting the store up and running and all."

Nice excuse, Callie.

It's time now, Daughter.

I know, Lord. But—

"Well, looks like she's not sticking around long anyway." Mona glanced in her rearview mirror. "So. What's up with you and Todd?"

Once the Holy Spirit started on me, there was no escaping. We'd talk about it again. Lots.

I sighed. "There is nothing 'up' with Todd and me."

"Right." Mona snorted.

She pulled into my driveway and left the car running, pushing her sunglasses up onto her head to peer at me.

I stared out the windshield at Sherm's rundown yard, somehow not in the mood to banter with Mona like I usually did.

She waited a long minute, then let me off the hook. "Todd is a good man."

I had never heard my friend so serious.

"I barely know him." Like I barely knew my own neighbor. Had I been so self-absorbed these past few months...years...nursing my own wounds that I hadn't even noticed the people around me?

"Todd needs someone like you in his life."

Someone like me? What was that supposed to mean?

"I'm not sure I'm ready for another relationship."

"It's been five years. You have so much love to give."

What had happened to my happy-go-lucky Mona? It was almost like she was begging me. I blew out my breath. "Just pray for me, okay? When I think about my relationship with Kev—"

"That's in the past. You don't live there anymore." Mona grasped my hand and held on until I turned to meet her gaze. "Come on, honey. God's opening new doors for you, but you've got to walk through them. I've watched you bury yourself in your store, in the church, in everything except relationships."

That was my pattern. I had always held a wall of reserve around myself, even before all the junk of the last five years. And now, though some of that had crumbled in the wake of life's hardships, it was still there. Even in my relationship with my parents. I could never unbend fully enough to embrace them as they were. And I didn't know why.

"I don't know how," I whispered.

She drew me into a hug. "Yes, you do. Be willing to let other people in, okay?"

I nodded against her shoulder. It had been a long time since I had rested in someone else's embrace, even that of a girlfriend. "I'll try."

"You do know my boss has a crush on you." She pulled away to grin at me.

Ack.

"I was afraid of that." I pushed my glasses up on my nose. "When he brought me the stuffed pug the other day—"

"He actually bought you a stuffed animal? Houston?"

"Yep. He brought it to the house after you left. On the Fourth of July." I grimaced. "It was fairly awkward."

"Oh, Lord. That poor man." Mona laughed. "He can be so clueless."

"It's not that I don't like him, but—"

"Girlfriend, you don't have to tell me about it. I work with him every day."

We grinned at each other. Houston was handsome, no doubt about it. But he was also plain goofy. In a serious kind of way. It was hard to explain.

I shook my head. "At least I've dodged Aunt Dot so far. She's still after me to meet the tech guy at Willowbough."

Mona made a face. "I'd stick with Todd."

Me, too. I could still see us laughing together, throwing the ball for Annie in his front yard—

"Did she ever email you?"

"Who?"

"Aunt Dot."

"Yep. She told me all about Pastor Brian and the youth group from SCC Church coming and singing for their annual Patriotic Praise and Pasta celebration. She loved it."

"Loved what? The pasta? I wonder what her secret is?" Mona's phone dinged and she glanced at it. "Oh, my gosh! It's getting late and I told Lonnie I'd pick her cat up on the way home. They're going down to the coast for a few days, you know? I gotta run."

I leaned down into the car, balancing my container of leftovers on top of my purse. "Thank you, friend."

"Festina a la rapido to el Todd-o." She blew me a kiss. "Not lente."

I rolled my eyes, but I had to smile. "Yes, ma'am."

CHAPTER EIGHT

I picked up the newspaper from the driveway and let myself into the house amidst the pugs' joyous yipping and snuffling. I had been so busy the last few days that I hadn't paid as much attention to them as usual. Neither had I read the paper, I thought as I added it to the growing pile. And the next few days would be every bit as busy.

Jenna's wedding was quickly approaching, and I still had mounds of moss to glue and candlesticks to adorn. And the human-trafficking seminar at church was tomorrow night, too. I couldn't miss that. I had found the issue more and more on my mind lately, especially since the *Star* was printing a special series of articles on the topic. I knew nothing about it, except what we had learned from the presentation at church a couple of months ago.

I couldn't stop thinking about it. I had started to pray about it, thinking that God was nudging me to get involved somehow. But it seemed so out of my league. And I was no longer in a position to be around teenagers as much as I had been when I worked at the middle school. I couldn't sit in front of the local school and watch for students who might be involved. But neither could I sit by and—

I jumped when my phone vibrated against my leg. I didn't usually carry it in my pocket. My heart leapt at the number on the screen. It was my brother, Jason, calling from the penitentiary.

"Hello?"

I went through the usual rigmarole of pushing buttons, entering my debit card number and generally signing my life away before I heard his voice on the other end of the line.

"Callie?"

"Hi! It's so good to hear from you. How are you?"

I grimaced at my own words. I should know by now not to ask that question.

"I'm good, Sis. Really good."

What? Really?

"That's awesome," I said cautiously. "You sound good. What's going on?"

"I—" His voice caught on a sob. "I've come back to Jesus, Callie."

I sank down onto the kitchen chair. "Thank God! Thank you, Jesus! Oh, Jace. I wish I could be there to give you a hug."

"Me, too." He cleared his throat. "I wanted to thank you for not giving up on me."

The tears spilled over onto my cheeks. Tears of joy this time. After so many years. "Tell me about it! What happened?"

"I finally surrendered, Callie. I guess I got tired of fighting so hard against the Holy Spirit."

"I'm so glad." Glad didn't describe it, but I couldn't seem to get much more out right now.

"The Hound of Heaven finally caught me," he said. "I knew you and Mom and Dad were praying for me. And Aunt Dot. I would lie in my bunk at night and remember everything I had learned growing up. Sometimes I would feel like I was going crazy because I couldn't stop thinking of all of the times I heard the gospel being preached. All of the times we did family devotions."

I was bawling by now. Those were the very things I had prayed for my brother over the years. I had prayed that when he was alone at night, that God would remind Jason of His love for Him. That He would bring scriptures back to his remembrance—even the little Bible songs and stories we had learned together in Sunday school. And now God had answered our prayers.

"And when Aunt Dot sent me the 'Hound of Heaven' poem, that about finished me off," he said.

I knew that poem by Francis Thompson. It had long been one of my favorites, and I had often pictured Jace being "caught" by Him who knew my brother best and loved him the most.

Jason cleared his throat. "Listen to this part. I can barely read it without crying, because this was what I did for so many years!

I fled Him, down the nights and down the days;
I fled Him, down the arches of the years;
I fled Him, down the labyrinthine ways
Of my own mind; and in the mist of tears
I hid from Him, and under running laughter.
Up vistaed hopes I sped;
And shot, precipitated,
Adown Titanic glooms of chasmèd fears,
From those strong Feet that followed, followed after.

We were weeping together now.

"He finally caught me. I'm free."

"Yes, you are. I can hear it in your voice. Thank God!"

"It doesn't matter so much now if I have to spend more years in here. My soul is free. I've been reading my Bible lots and going to the church services."

Wait. This was my brother I was talking to, right? "I can't believe it. We've prayed for you for so long."

An automated voice broke in. "This phone call will end in one minute."

Only one minute to relive a lifetime of pain and now joy. My throat closed.

"I love you, Sis. Will you please send like a Bible study or something? I can't believe I've wasted so much of my life. It's like I finally...like I finally get it, ya know?"

"Yes." It was all I could get out.

"And tell Aunt Dot, okay? I wanted to write to her, but I don't have any more stamps or envelopes left. Tell her I love her and that I—"

I laid the phone down and slipped to my knees on my kitchen floor. God had saved my brother. He had rescued him and redeemed him and given him peace in his heart. I was in awe.

"Auntie!" I burst into Aunt Dot's room. "I just got off the phone with Jason!"

Her hand went to her throat. "Is he okay? What's wrong?"

I wanted to grab her up out of her bed and dance around with her. Instead, I sat in front of her and took both of her hands in mine. I felt my face crumple before I could even get a word out. She and I had shared so many heartbreaking moments and now—

"Is it bad, darlin'?"

I shook my head, but couldn't speak for a long moment. "No, no, it's good, Auntie." I took a deep breath. "Jace surrendered his life to Jesus."

She stared at me as if trying to grasp what I had said, and then her eyes filled. "Oh, Callie. Thank God! Oh, thank God. I was praying it would be soon."

I pulled her to me, and we hugged as if we'd never let go.

"God answers prayer, darlin'," she whispered against my hair. "Don't you ever forget that. He is a good God."

"I know, Auntie." I did know. He had brought me through so much, and He wasn't done yet.

"What did Jason say? How did it happen?"

"We only had a few minutes to talk, but he basically said he was tired of fighting. He also said to tell you he loves you and he wanted to write to you but he's all out of stamps. I'll put some money on his account later so he can get more."

"I can't wait to hear all about it." Her eyes were shining.

"And he said to tell you that the 'Hound of Heaven' poem got to him. Pushed him over the edge, I guess."

She nodded. "I knew He would never let go of our boy, Callie. I prayed I would still be alive to see it."

"What are you talking about, Auntie? You're healthy as ever."

Wasn't she? A twinge of apprehension winged its way into my mind.

"No one is guaranteed tomorrow, honey."

"I know, but—"

She shrugged. "My life is in His hands. And I'm going to use every day He gives me. How about you? Any answers from Mr. Big-pants sheriff?"

I didn't want to think about him right now. "Do you think I should call Mom and Dad?"

"You mean you didn't yet?"

"No, I ran right over here to tell you. Plus, they have like an eight-hour time difference, remember? It's the middle of the night over there."

"I forgot about that." She twisted her wedding ring around her finger. "Well, maybe you can email them. Email is a pretty handy thing, you know."

I stifled a grin. "Yes, it definitely is. I'm sure I'll connect with them as soon as—"

"Hello there, Dot. I didn't know you had a visitor."

Aunt Dot and I turned towards the door.

"Brandon! Come in. This is my granddaughter Callie who I've been telling you about." Aunt Dot beamed at the man as he strode into the room.

Uh oh. I was in for it now.

"Callie! Brandon Delacourte." He strode over to me and stuck out his hand.

I took it, allowing him to hold onto mine for a tad longer than necessary. Wow. Aunt Dot hadn't been kidding about the handsome part. I'd never seen such gorgeous brown eyes. He looked slightly familiar, but—

"I hear you're teaching Aunt Dot how to 'do technology.'" I grinned up at him. Way up.

He laughed. "She hardly needs me anymore. Your aunt is a technology whiz. Have you read her latest—"

"Brandon is going to show me how to do Twitterface next, aren't you, Brandon?"

I pressed my lips together for a second, not daring to meet Brandon's eyes until I got my composure. "Facebook, Auntie," I said, conscious of the smell of his aftershave lingering on my hand.

"Isn't that what I said?" She patted her laptop. "Now all I need is one of those intelligent phones like you all have and I'll be all set."

Set for what?

I raised my eyebrows at Brandon.

He shrugged. "Why not? Lots of people her age know how to text."

"And Harry even knows how to do that gram thing," Aunt Dot said proudly.

Harry was on Instagram? Even I didn't bother with Instagram.

"Who would you call on your smartphone, Aunt Dot?"

Her eyes twinkled. "You'd like to know, wouldn't you, Callie?" Aunt Dot tossed Brandon a smile. "An old woman can still have some secrets."

Wow. Okay, then. Something was definitely going on here. "What—"

"So when are you going to go out with me?"

What? The man sure wasn't shy.

"I, um…I'm super busy this weekend." And I hadn't been on a date in years. I looked at Aunt Dot, but I wasn't going to get any help from that direction.

"No worries. Let's plan for next week. Do you like Chinese?"

I still wasn't quite sure how it happened or how I felt about it, but there it was.

"Somehow, I have a date with Brandon next weekend. At Shanghai Gardens," I told Mona the next day when she popped into my shop.

"What?" Mona made a face. "What about Todd?"

"I don't know. It's not like we're in a relationship or anything." I picked at the moss on one of Jenna's table decorations.

"But…Brandon?"

"What's wrong with him?"

"He's not your type, Callie." She pulled her hand through her spiky hair, and I noticed her fingernails were painted in pink and black checks today. "And I don't think he's a believer."

I frowned. "Aunt Dot would never encourage me to get involved with someone who—"

"Callie, your aunt is eighty years old. Brandon tells her what she wants to hear."

I didn't like what she was insinuating. "But—"

She held up her hand to stop me. "All I'm saying is that I don't trust him. Never have. And why are you so willing to go out on a date now? I mean, I know I told you to start letting people in. But not someone like him."

"I don't know. I guess I do miss having someone to be with."

My phone dinged and I glanced at it to see a text from Todd. Good timing.

"Callie, did you read yesterday's newspaper?" I read the text out loud. "If not, you might want to."

"Ooh, that was romantic. Is that the kind of texts you usually get from Todd?" Mona gave me a sassy grin. "No wonder you're willing to go out with Brandon."

I rolled my eyes. "This is why I don't tell you things."

She smirked at me, but folded her hands in her lap. "I'll be good. Why does he want you to read the paper?"

"Maybe there's some kind of development with the case."

But why would information about the case come out in the newspaper before I had heard about it? Aren't the people involved in a murder case told about these things before the details are released to the public?

I texted Todd back: "I haven't, but I will. Thanks!"

I usually read the newspaper in the evening when I got home from the shop, but I hadn't had time to last night, and now I was curious. "Mona, pull up the *Star* website for me."

"Yes, ma'am." She whipped out her enormous phone. "Yesterday's news, Todd said?"

"Yep." I leaned over her shoulder. "Do you see anything about it?"

She scrolled through. "Hmm, let's see. The Lutheran church will be having their monthly senior adult soup supper tonight. Maybe he's subtly asking you on a date. Ha ha."

Oh, puh-leeze. "Mona—"

"Here's the police report. Hmm. Nothing there about your

case. Wait. Oh my gosh, Callie!"

"What?"

She held up her phone about an inch from my face. "Is this Dot? Your Dot?"

I took the phone and zoomed in. Aunt Dot in the newspaper? I scrolled down. Of all the crazy things—

"I think we discovered Aunt Dot's secret," I told Mona. I handed the phone back to her.

"What?" She looked at the screen and then at me. "'Just Ask Dot'? What is that?"

"I believe my aunt is the new advice columnist for the newspaper." I sank down onto my stool. "So that's what she's been doing all of this time on her laptop. And learning to email and everything."

"Like the person people write to for advice when they're super mad that their daughter-in-law doesn't clean her bathroom as often as she should?"

"I think so. Read that one under the headline that says 'Cat Owner in a Conundrum'."

Mona fingered her pink hooped earring. "Girlfriend, I don't even know what a conundrum is."

Well, I do. And I had a feeling that the one I was in was about to get worse.

CHAPTER NINE

I was right.

First, I went to get my hair trimmed and came back home looking like I had gotten in a fight with Fluffers.

Then, I attended the sex trafficking seminar at church, and God broke my heart. Right there, as I sat weeping next to Todd, I had a suspicion of what was going on with Sherm's granddaughter. The last speaker, a woman whose daughter had been trapped into a sex trafficking ring right here in Central Texas, had given me a new perspective.

I had known, vaguely, that the pimps often used drugs to keep the girls in their control. I had understood that sex trafficking was not a far-away thing that was happening only in third-world countries. But until tonight, I hadn't encountered the personal pain of a family right here in my backyard who had lived the nightmare. The frantic calls in the night for a parent to come rescue. The threats to the family from the pimp. The pregnancy—

Dear God. I didn't know. I sat there in the pew, remembering Nicole's conversation I had overheard on the night of the Fourth of July, how I had felt in my spirit that something was terribly wrong. She had been pleading with someone for a little more time. And I hadn't done anything about it. Not even whispered a prayer for her.

Maybe I was jumping to conclusions, but I knew I had to do something.

"Can you stay afterward for a few minutes?" I whispered to Todd.

He nodded and squeezed my hand for a second.

I'm sure my elderly neighbor didn't have any idea of the life his granddaughter might be leading. And I, a mind-my-own-business and stay-at-a-distance Christian, had never even gone out of my way to pay attention to what was going on right next door to me. I had excused myself for too long. I dropped my head into my hands.

In all fairness, I had gone through more than one traumatic

event in my life. I had needed time to heal and to regain my shaken faith. I had had to wrestle with everything I had ever believed about God and His Word, until I came out of the tunnel on the other side. But I had left the tunnel long ago, and what I had excused as "time to heal" had begun to turn into...apathy? No, that wasn't the right word. It was self-centeredness, if I was brutally honest.

Clearly, God was prodding me to leave my comfort zone and get busy doing Kingdom work again. I knew the prompting of the Holy Spirit and to ignore Him would be disobedience. I sighed. Long ago, I had learned that I might as well surrender at the get-go to, as Elizabeth Goudge called it, "the extraordinary contrariness of God's will." Contrary to my lazy human flesh. Contrary to my introverted comfort zone. Contrary to the illusion that I, and not God, am in control of my own life.

To argue was futile and only prolonged the inevitable. *What would You have me do, Lord? I surrender myself again to Your will, Your calling—*

"Callie?" Todd laid a hand on my shoulder.

I lifted my head, realizing that everyone else was leaving the sanctuary. It was strikingly quiet; the congregation seemingly sobered into silence.

"I'm sorry. I—"

He shook his head. "It's sickening, isn't it?"

"Can you come back to the house for a few minutes?" I asked. "I need to tell you something." Normally, I wouldn't have been so forward, but I had to confide in someone about Nicole, and I knew Todd would understand.

He glanced at his watch, then nodded. "I'll follow you home so I can leave from there," he said. "I've got to pick Luke up at ten."

He followed me as I stopped to say goodbye to Mona, and she pulled me into a silent hug, the handle of her umbrella jabbing into my stomach. "We've got to do something, Callie," she whispered.

I drew back to look into her eyes. Was she feeling what I was? "Let's talk tomorrow, okay?"

Todd and I edged out of the crowded church into the humid night. It had been raining when I entered the church, but now it was only a light, warm drizzle.

I shivered, and Todd squeezed me in a quick side hug.

We walked across the parking lot in silence, then paused as one to look at the night sky. I still consciously delighted in living out here in the country, where I could see more stars than I ever knew existed. And God had lovingly created and named each one.

Exactly like He knew and loved each one of those precious girls who were trapped in—

"I hope your battery isn't dead." Todd strode toward my van. "Looks like your interior light was left on somehow."

I turned to look at the same time Todd yelled.

"Watch out!"

I jumped and kind of fell sideways into the rear end of someone's car, then knocked my head on the bumper on my way down. I landed hard on the pavement. What was going on?

"Callie." Todd's whisper came from my left a few seconds later. "Are you okay?"

I smelled the cinnamon on his breath before I opened my eyes to find him crouched next to me. How had he gotten there without me hearing him? "What happened?"

"Shh." He shook his head. "Someone had been messing with your van. When I got close to it, I heard a gun cock. Thought someone was going to try to take a shot at you."

I stared at him from where I lay frozen to the pavement. Why was he still whispering? Were we in danger?

"Who was it? Is he gone?"

"I don't know. I called Earl."

A lot of good that would do. I'd rather go home and have a cup of tea than talk to Sheriff Earl again. "Can I get up now?"

He glanced around. "Yes, but stay low. We're relatively hidden between these two vehicles and—"

"Callie? Is that you? What are y'all doing under the truck?"

Mona's face appeared in my line of vision, her yellow smiley-face earrings oddly out of place in my world at the moment.

"Shh! Someone was breaking into my van and—"

She straightened up and held her oversized umbrella in attack mode. "Where? I don't see anyone. And where is that lazy sheriff when somebody needs him? Did you call him, Todd?" She peered down at us again.

"Yes, ma'am," he said. "But—"

"Well, here he is. Better late than never. I have a few things to say to that man. All of this crime happening right here in Short Creek, and he's not doing a thing about it that I can tell." She stomped toward the patrol car, heedless of the puddles.

Todd helped me to my feet, but I was glad to hang onto his arm for a minute. My legs wouldn't stop shaking.

An hour later, Todd sat across from me at my tiny kitchen table. Intarsia snuggled on my lap while I nursed a mug of tea.

"I think you need to start at the beginning, Callie."

I wrapped my hands around my mug. I couldn't seem to get warm, even though it was a hot night in July. "I don't think you have enough time in your life for me to start at the beginning."

He smiled at me. "You don't have to cover it all tonight. We have time."

We? I liked the sound of that. I also liked the sound of his voice, and the thick dark lashes around his blue eyes—

"Callie?"

He was smiling again at me, and it was making me feel lightheaded, apparently. Or maybe it was because I had smacked my head on the back of Sister Erma's Buick. I hoped the bump on my forehead didn't look as big as it felt.

Get a grip, Callie.

"I can't think of anything that I've done that would cause someone to try to harm me."

Couldn't I? Yes, actually I could. But so much time had passed. Why would—

"But clearly, someone has something against you."

"Either that or it's a whole string of unrelated incidents."

One could always hope, right?

"No way." Todd had his cop face on now.

I blew out my breath. This was so hard. "You know I moved here from Ohio."

He nodded.

"Okay. Here's the short version. My husband, after suffering from ALS for a couple of years, was killed in a car accident five years ago. His brother was severely injured in the crash and is partially paralyzed." I stroked Intarsia's silky head. "I was too much of a wreck to go back to my job as a school social worker right away, you know?"

He nodded again. "It's a tough profession."

That was an understatement. "So, I got my Preschool Director's Certification. I figured it was still along the lines of my experience, only from a different angle."

"I can definitely see you as a social worker." He took a sip of his iced tea, then set the glass down. "But you don't strike me as a preschool teacher type."

I laughed. "Yeah, well. Like I said, I was kind of a mess. One of my friends suggested it, and it sounded like something doable at the time."

"But?"

But.

But it was harder than I thought. But I should have told. But I waited too long. But I am responsible for a little girl's death. But...God.

Every situation in my life came down to that one thing. *But God.*

I should be lost and without hope. But God.

I should be destitute. But God.

I should be in the nuthouse. But God.

I should be on my way to hell. But God.

I should be...but God. But God.

My life. I owed Him my life.

I heard the air conditioner kick on while I fingered Intarsia's velvety ears.

"Callie?" Todd's voice was soft, encouraging.

A lump rose in my throat, and I swallowed it down. It would

be good for me to tell the story. It had been so long since I'd let myself open up to another person besides Aunt Dot.

"There was a little girl at our preschool named Marleigh. She was a beautiful child, Todd. Not just outwardly beautiful, but she had a gentle, loving little spirit."

I bit my lip, waiting until I could speak again. "I often thought that if I ever had a little girl, I'd want her to be like Marleigh."

Todd scooted his chair around close to mine and took my hand.

I leaned my head against his shoulder, thankful that he cared enough to share in my pain. "As you well know, a preschool director is a mandatory reporter."

I felt him stiffen, and I knew he had guessed the rest of my story. "It was Marleigh's birth father. He...he still had rights to see her for a few hours every week. I started to suspect, but I didn't have proof. I thought I should have proof before I got involved in other people's lives."

I groaned out loud, the grief and the horror flooding over me again. "I can't—"

"Yes, you can." He took my chin in his hand and lifted my face until I looked in his eyes. "Get it out in the light, honey."

I took a deep breath. "He murdered her. He took her and...and...I could have saved her life! I knew in my heart that he was doing terrible things, but I didn't say anything. And then I was the one who f-found her. Oh, God—"

I doubled over, wailing. Like I did on that day so long ago. I couldn't help it. It was like the grief needed to be expressed through this horrible noise forcing itself out of my mouth. It had been a long time since I had floundered under the waves of despair like I was now. "Oh, God, help me. I should have—"

Todd laid a hand on my shoulder, but I jerked away and stood, bracing myself on the edge of the kitchen counter, my back to him. I stared into the darkness outside my kitchen window. *Jesus?*

I am here.

Jesus. Jesus. I pictured myself wrapped in His arms, my head against His chest. It was enough.

No. *He* was enough.

I drew my finger through a cool drop of water on the counter, not ready to look into someone else's eyes yet. "I didn't say anything because I was afraid. I had finally made up my mind to tell, but then...he—I—it was too late. And it's my fault! Because I was *afraid*. God, have mercy on me! God, have mercy—"

"No." Todd turned me around and gathered me to his chest.

I didn't have the strength to push away, but I knew I didn't deserve any comfort.

He held me tight while he whispered against my hair. "You cannot take the blame for what this monster did to his child."

I shook my head. "But I—"

"God saw it all." Todd smoothed my hair down my back. "And one day, He will right all of the wrongs."

"I know. But if I hadn't waited that extra day. If I would have been braver..."

"Listen to me." He pushed me away from him so he could look me in the eye. "Did you do what you knew to do at the time? Did you do your best?"

Did I? I think I did.

I hugged Marleigh often and told her how much I loved her and God loved her. I talked to the other teachers and told them to watch over her and let me know if they saw anything. I talked to Marleigh's mom, but she couldn't—or wouldn't tell me the truth. I talked to Marleigh's grandparents.

I prayed.

I cried.

I lay awake nights.

I decided to make the call.

"Did you, sweetheart? Did you do your best at that time?"

Did I?

"I don't know," I whispered.

"Aww, Callie." He held my face and wiped at my tears with his thumb. "There are always 'what ifs' in life. You might not have done things perfectly. But your heart was right toward that little girl. It was her father who destroyed her. Not you."

"I know. But it's just so hard." I pulled away from him and

fished in my pocket for a tissue. I couldn't find one, so I used the paper napkin from under my tea mug. "I'm sorry, Todd. I'm not usually so emotional."

He shook his head. "There's nothing to be sorry about."

I blew my nose and stroked Intarsia's coat, embarrassed now to meet Todd's eyes. "Not quite what you were expecting to hear, I guess. And I haven't even told you about the court case yet."

"Believe me. In my line of work, I've heard it all." He took my hand again and waited until I looked up at him. "I think you have more to tell me, but it's getting late. May I pray for you before I go?"

How could a girl refuse a question like that?

"Yes, please," I said, giving him a watery smile.

I don't remember exactly what he prayed, but I do know that the peace that passes understanding filled my heart and my soul in a way I could not express in words. When I woke early the next morning, I knew I was free from a burden I had carried for a long, long time. Though I hadn't handled things perfectly, my heart had been right. I didn't have to keep condemning myself or driving myself crazy with what-ifs. God saw all that had happened, and He would be the one to eventually make all things right. I smiled, thinking of the scene from C. S. Lewis', *The Lion, the Witch and the Wardrobe,* where Mr. Beaver encouraged the Pevensie children to look for Aslan's return, knowing He was the only one who could set things right in Narnia.

I felt like Mr. Beaver and the children today, yearning to see my Savior, longing for the day when the power of sin and sorrow was broken forever. "Even so, come quickly, Lord Jesus," I murmured.

All wrong would one day be made right—if not here in this

world, then in Heaven. I could rest in that hope.

But I would not make the same mistake twice, so help me God.

The more I thought and prayed about it, the more I was sure that Sherm's granddaughter Nicole was being trafficked. I remembered seeing her that day at the bus stop with her suitcase, hunched down with her cigarette, waiting. Waiting for what?

I would not sit by and be silent. I called Todd, pushing aside my sudden shyness when I remembered his tenderness from the night before. Most likely, he'd had lots of practice in comforting distraught people. It was part of his job, right?

"Me again," I said, picturing him sitting at his kitchen table with his iced tea, Annie by his side.

"Callie! How are you this morning?"

"I'm okay." I peered at the dark rings around my eyes as I passed my bedroom mirror. "I hadn't intended to tell you all of that last night. I hope—"

"Hey, it's okay. Is Mona going to pick you up this morning?"

My van was still impounded until at least this afternoon. Why Sheriff Earl insisted on such a thorough inspection, I still wasn't sure. "Yes, Saturdays are usually my biggest days so I can't close the store. And besides, I still haven't finished the table decorations for Jenna's wedding."

"Speaking of flowers," he said, "would you be interested in attending an event at the botanical garden in Austin this weekend?"

Was Todd asking me out? I gulped. "The Zilker Botanical Garden? I've been wanting to go but haven't made it down there yet."

"Is that a yes?"

I could hear the smile in his voice. "Um, sure. What time?"

"I have a couple of concert tickets for tomorrow night at the garden. A bluegrass band, I think." He paused. "We could get dinner in Georgetown on the way down, if you're up for that."

I raised my eyebrows at my reflection in the mirror. Was I ready for this?

"Sure. Sounds fun." What would I wear? I hadn't been out on

a date in years and now I had two dates in one—uh oh. What about Brandon?

"So I'll pick you up around 4:30," Todd was saying.

"I'll be ready, thanks." I would figure out the Brandon situation later. "But about why I called you...it's not exactly light conversation. Do you have any time to run by C. Willikers today?

"What happened now, Callie?" His voice was sharp.

"Nothing new. I need to tell you what I planned to tell you last night before I had an emotional meltdown instead."

He blew out a breath. "I thought for a minute there that we were going to have to hire you a full-time bodyguard. I'll stop by after lunch. Try not to get into any trouble before then, please."

"Yes, sir," I said.

What was happening between us? And why did I suddenly have the feeling that somehow Marleigh's case was not as far in my past as I had hoped?

CHAPTER TEN

Mona honked to let me know she was in the driveway.

"Out in a sec," I texted to her. I snapped the girls' leashes on and headed out the door.

"Did you see Dot's newest column?" Mona asked the minute I opened the car door.

I shook my head. "Between last night's deal with my van and dealing with a sick pug this morning, I haven't even picked the paper up off the driveway. Do I want to read it?"

She grinned at me. "Maybe."

"What is that supposed to mean?

"Your auntie is a hoot, Callie. She's got the whole town in an uproar over her advice to 'Floundering in Flat."

Great. Exactly what I needed. Uproar.

Flat was a little town down the highway from ours, and there never would be an end to the jokes about it. "What did she say?"

Mona started backing down my driveway. "Well, this poor dude wrote in and asked for advice about his mother-in-law's obsession with—"

"Mona! Stop!"

Sherm was standing in his doorway, waving at me frantically. I flung the car door open and ran toward him.

"Callie! Call the sheriff!" He yelled. "He's a-comin' to git her!"

Who is coming for whom? Nicole?

I sprinted back toward the car for my phone, but Mona had beat me to it.

"They're on their way!" she yelled.

I turned back to my neighbor's house.

"Call Todd!" I shouted over my shoulder to Mona. "His number is in my phone."

Sherm had disappeared back into his house. I yanked the screen door open. I don't know what I thought I would find, but it wasn't a wild-eyed Sherm clutching a tiny baby in his arms.

"Take this baby, Callie. Hurry! Hide her somewhere quick.

He's a-comin' for Nicole, and he cain't see the ba—"

Without thinking, I grabbed Sherm's big roaster pan from the kitchen counter. I laid the little one inside and put the lid on. The child never even woke up. "I'm going to go out the back door, Sherm. Where's Nicole? Doesn't she want—"

"She's—"

I slipped out the back door as Nicole entered the kitchen, looking like the cover model for Vogue magazine.

She gave Sherm a quick peck on his cheek. "I have to go, Gramps. I'm so sorry."

She didn't look sorry. In fact, she looked—radiant.

"Thanks for the veggies," I said extra loud, in case whoever "he" was, was watching.

I am carrying an infant in a roaster pan across my yard. Jesus, help me.

Mona, out of her car by now, stood holding the pugs' leashes and gaping at me. "Callie?"

"I need to take these into the house and we can go," I said in a singsong kind of voice while trying to motion to Mona with my head. "Get my keys," I hissed.

She unlocked my front door, and I edged past her to set the roaster down carefully on the kitchen table.

"Mona, you're not going to believe this—"

Through my still-open front door, I watched Sheriff Earl's patrol car slam to a halt in front of my house as a late-model BMW slid up to Sherm's.

I pulled my front door closed behind me as I stepped out onto the porch, leaving Mona to discover the contents of the roaster.

"What is the problem now, ma'am?" Sheriff Earl strode up my walkway.

I ignored him, watching in stunned silence, the roaster lid still in my hands, as Nicole waltzed out of the house and down to the BMW, dragging her rolling suitcase behind her.

Beside me, Sheriff Earl turned to see what I was looking at.

Nicole was going back. Back to—that life. Back to—him. And she didn't look sad about it. I couldn't believe it.

The well-dressed driver stepped out of the car to hug her,

threw her suitcase in the trunk, then waved merrily at the rest of us before slamming his door shut behind him.

"Sheriff! I'm so sorry we bothered you." I gave him a big phony smile. "I—we—thought Sherm was having an emergency, but it turned out to be nothing."

"That so." He hooked his thumb in his belt and gave me a once-over before glancing at my neighbor's house. "I think I'll go ask Sherm 'bout it."

"Good idea," I said heartily. "Mona and I were getting ready to head to my shop anyway." I started backing away.

He grunted something under his breath and swaggered toward Sherm's.

"By the way, can I pick up my van this afternoon?" I yelled to his back.

He turned. "Yes, ma'am. I'll have it all ready for you."

I should have been happy about that, but somehow, I felt like there was a double-meaning to his words. Or maybe I was being paranoid.

Or not. Because it wasn't until I had explained the whole weird Sherm-baby-Nicole incident to Mona that I realized the significance of what I had noticed earlier.

"Sheriff Earl knew that guy."

Mona glanced up at me from the newborn who was snuggled against her ample chest. "What?"

"I may not be the most observant person in the world, but I know body language when I see it." I puckered my bottom lip with my fingers. How could things get any more complicated than they already were?

I let go of my lip. "You know that eye-contact-chin-jerk thing men do? The guy who picked up Nicole did that to Earl."

"And so?"

"So, that guy was most likely Nicole's pimp. Or...or owner. Or whatever they call them." I was horrified anew. "And she looked like she was thrilled to be going with him. I thought that—"

Mona shook her head. "Remember what we heard last night? Those monsters have those girls under their control so much that the girls have some kind of sick loyalty to them." She pulled the blanket back from the baby's face. "But this precious little girl is not more than a few days old, Callie. What can Nicole be thinking?"

"And what about Sherm? Do you think he knows?"

If I were a betting woman, I would bet that Sherm still had no idea of the reality of his granddaughter's situation. When Todd got here, I'd ask him to go with me to talk to him. But I was still bothered by the flash of recognition I had seen between the two men.

"Callie!" Todd pounded on my door.

I hurried to open it.

"Are you hurt?"

He grasped my shoulders, and I smelled the familiar cinnamon on his breath. "I'm fine, Todd." I pushed my glasses up. "Everything's under control."

"I heard the call come in over the radio before Mona called me, and I got here as fast as I could, but I was way out near Cameron and—"

He spotted the baby in Mona's arms. "What is going on?"

I shook my head. "This is what I was going to talk to you about later today."

"A baby?"

"No, Nicole."

He squinted at me.

"Nicole Grant. My neighbor Sherm's granddaughter."

The light came on in his gaze. "This is Nicole's baby? Then why do you have her?"

I took a deep breath. "I think Nicole is being trafficked, Todd."

He raised his eyebrows.

"I've seen some things over the last few months that made me kind of wonder, you know? Then when we went to the seminar last night, I think I realized what was going on with her."

"Wow." He rubbed the back of his neck. "Are you sure?"

"Pretty sure. And after what happened this morning—"

"So what *did* happen?"

"And so, we need to talk to Sherm." I rubbed my hand over my forehead, wincing when my fingers made contact with my newest goose egg, the remnants of my meeting with Sister Erma's back bumper. "Will you go with me?"

Todd paced around my kitchen. "You think Earl knew the pimp?"

"Yes. Or at least had a connection."

"Sure enough to act on it?"

My pulse jumped. "As in…?"

"As in reporting—"

"Yoo-hoo!" Mona waved to claim our attention. "Y'all can hash that part out later. What are we going to do with this child?"

I grimaced. "Well, Sherm certainly can't take care of an infant by himself. And I'm hesitant to get Child Protective Services involved until we know what we're dealing with."

We both looked at Todd.

He fingered the baby's tiny hand, an unreadable expression in his eyes. "I'm sure someone from church will be willing to care for the baby for a couple of days if it comes to that," he said. "I suppose we don't know when or if Nicole is returning?"

I slumped into my chair. "I can't believe she'd leave her child and willingly go back to—"

"It's far more complicated than that, Callie. I've worked these cases before and they're not—"

So he was a cop.

"Auntie told me you were in law enforcement."

"Not now." He shrugged.

"But once a cop, always a cop."

The lift of his brows acknowledged the truth, but I could see that the topic was off limits.

Mona, as always, was far less astute. "Good grief, Todd. Why are you playing around being an EMT in Short Creek if you're a police officer?

"It's a long story, Mona. One that I don't care to relive at this moment." He turned to me, and I read the weariness on his face. "Let's go talk to Sherm, Callie."

Sherm wasn't there.

"Maybe he's in there but he can't hear us knocking." I stood on tiptoe to try to see through the tiny window at the top of the door. Nothing.

"Sherm?" Todd tried the knob. "Locked. How much do you want to bet that Earl took him to his office?"

I rolled my eyes. "Probably. But I don't think he'll get much information from him. You can't make someone tell you something they don't know."

Todd blew out a sigh. "Look. You need to get to your store, and I'm going to go see what I can discover at the fire department. I'll be back later, okay?"

I nodded. How had things become so complicated? Again? "I can't believe—"

"Shh." He touched my cheek briefly, then smoothed a strand of my hair behind my ear. "It's going to be okay."

"I hope it's okay soon," I murmured. "I'm sorry to be calling you to come to my rescue all the time." I barely knew the man, and I had already taken up so much of his time in the last few days. "What a way to spend your day off, huh?"

"It's fine. This whole thing has become way bigger than you."

Indeed.

Moments later, I stood on Lonnie's front porch and handed her the baby, while Mona brought up the rear with the formula, bottles, diapers, and wipes that she and I had hastily grabbed at the dollar store in town.

"I hope Rick won't mind you taking her for a few days," I said, sidestepping the cat. "I don't even know how long to tell you. A couple of days? Maybe a week?"

"Oh, Callie." She hugged the little one to her, her eyes bright with unshed tears. "He won't mind. We've been praying and praying—"

"You've been praying for a baby?" Mona's eyebrows shot up.

Lonnie smiled. "Not in particular. We're just...with Jenna getting married soon, we're going to be empty-nesters; you know? And God's blessed us abundantly. We feel we have a lot to give." She smoothed a gentle hand over the baby's head. "We've been asking the Lord to show us what's next for us. To send us people to love on, you know?"

I'm sure my eyebrows matched Mona's. "Well, He definitely answered your prayers. I hope we can help her mama come to her senses."

"We?" Mona's eyebrows had not yet come down to their normal position.

I shrugged. "Somehow I am involved in all of this. And it's not as fun as it seems in the Nancy Drew books." In fact, all I wanted to do right now was curl up in my sunny book nook at C. Willikers with a cup of tea, a pug, and a really thick book. Preferably not a mystery.

Lonnie laughed. "I guess God has decided that you need some excitement in your life."

"Speaking of excitement..." Mona murmured in a low voice. "Don't look now, Callie, but there's a guy watching us from across the street."

I groaned. This was getting ridiculous. "It's probably the mailman or somebody."

"If he is, I want him for my mailman," she said.

CHAPTER ELEVEN

"What?" I made a face at her, then angled my body so I could see the man out of the corner of my eye. I was hoping he wasn't the rock-throwing dude. I'd had enough head injuries for the time being, thank you very much.

I blew out my breath as the man smiled and waved at me. "That's Brandon."

Mona choked.

"Brandon Delacourte?" Lonnie squinted at him. "He's sure changed from the last time I saw him, if that's Brandon."

"What do you mean?"

She shrugged. "He used to be real thin and scruffy looking. And his hair was blond."

Weird. "I suppose this is a good time to tell him I can't go out with him next we—"

"You're not? Why?" Mona's eyebrows were high again.

He had started across the street toward me.

Lonnie backed toward her front door. "I'll see you later, girls." She slipped inside.

Brandon ambled to a stop in front of me. His tight jeans and even tighter t-shirt showed off his muscular build—intentionally, I was sure. And he smelled like he had used an entire bottle of aftershave.

"I thought that was you, Callie. Looking gorgeous as usual," he said. "Hey, Mona. It's been a long time."

She stared him down. "Yes, it has."

I fidgeted at the obvious tension between them. There must be a good deal more to this story than I knew. "So…do you live out here, Brandon?"

"Nah. I'm doing some side work for my uncle. Scholl's Landscaping."

"Oh, okay." I pushed my glasses up. "Um, it was nice seeing you again. Mona and I were just leaving."

He wiped the sweat off his forehead with the back of his arm. "I'll let you go. We're still on for next week, right?"

"Uh, sure. Give me a call to remind me, okay?" Good grief.

Why couldn't I tell the guy I didn't want to go out with him? I was making it worse by dragging it on.

Mona snickered. "She might be too busy, though. She is involved in a murder investigation, after all."

"Yeah, I heard. I'm sure she needs a break from that." Brandon smiled at me. "Right, Callie?" Why did I suddenly feel like a pawn in the middle of someone else's fight? I had always hated it when my parents subtly vied for my allegiance. I glanced at Mona, who had her lips tightly pressed together as if to stem the flow of lava boiling inside. Even her rhinestone-studded, cross-shaped earrings were quivering. "Mona—"

"Ewwraaaaah!" Fluffers erupted from under the boxwood hedge, her orangey tail bristling like I'd never seen. She made a beeline for Brandon, and I watched, fascinated, as he broke into a run.

"I'll call you tomorrow," he yelled over his shoulder.

"Well, that's one way to get rid of someone," I said, watching him disappear down the street. Was the man afraid of cats?

Whatever.

I wheeled to face Mona. "What was that about? With you and Brandon?"

She tossed her head, setting her earrings jingling. "I'm too angry to talk about it right now, Callie. Let's say that there's an awful lot of water over the bridge when it comes to Brandon and me."

Under the bridge. I grinned at her. "Well, I'll take you and Fluffers as my bodyguards any day."

"You'll need one with someone like that jerk," she muttered. "Please tell me you're not going to date him."

I shook my head as I slid into the passenger seat of her car. "What I *am* going to do is finish Jenna's table arrangements today. Want to help?"

She backed out of Lonnie's circular driveway with more vigor than necessary. "Girlfriend, you know I would love to help you glue moss any day. But Rob is coming home tomorrow night and—"

"Say no more." When Rob was home, Mona put everything else in her life on hold. "How long is he home for?"

"Only four days this time," she said. "But Rob loves him some chili, and the chili cook-off is this weekend. Last year he got second place."

Ah, yes. I had quickly learned about the annual "world-famous" fish fry and chili cook-off put on by our very own Short Creek Catfish Association. It still kind of tickled me a little, since that kind of thing was unheard of in suburban Ohio. What does one do in a catfish association anyway? I had never wondered enough to find out. But the cook-off was definitely something not to be missed.

"Is Rob making his world-famous recipe?"

Mona slanted me a sideways glance. "My honey's got a secret ingredient this year. He'll win this time for sure."

"Who won last year?"

"Sister Erma." Her face darkened. "She's won it three times in the last fifteen years. And she puts beans in it! Texas chili is not supposed to have beans."

I nodded in sympathy. Personally, I liked beans in my chili. But then again, I was from the Midwest. I also liked my cornbread sweet and my tea unsweet. I stood out like a sore thumb at every church potluck.

Todd's truck was already parked in front of C. Willikers when Mona and I pulled up.

Mona waved at him. "I love that man. If I wasn't already taken—"

"And twenty years younger..."

She laughed. "I hope you get your table decorations done. Though with that handsome hunk hanging around—"

"'Bye, Mona." I climbed out of the car, then stuck my head back in the door. "Give Rob a hug from me and tell him I'll vote for his chili any day."

She gave me a thumbs-up and floored her little car, narrowly missing Todd's truck door as he climbed out.

"Whoa! Never a dull moment around you." He grinned at

me. "Here, I brought you something."

He handed me a bright blue gift bag.

I studied his face for a moment but couldn't read anything in his expression. Why was he giving me a gift? I pushed the glittery tissue paper aside and pulled out an enormous mug. It was tall and delicate, covered in a colorful floral design. "Looks like my cup of tea," I quipped. "Thank you."

He smiled at me, but his gaze was anxious. "I thought with everything going on, you might need a bigger tea mug than usual. I wish I could figure out who…or what—"

"I know." I could only put everything aside for so long, and then I started trying to piece it all together again. But it never made sense. "I could use a cup of tea right now, actually."

He followed behind me as I unlocked the door to the shop. I hadn't brought the pugs with me today with all of the ruckus over Sherm, Nicole, and the baby.

I sighed as I flicked on the lights and flipped my closed sign to open. "I don't even want to think about all of this right now."

He sprawled on the couch in the book nook while I filled my electric tea kettle. "There must be some details we're not connecting."

I watered the philodendron while I waited for the kettle to boil, then moved on to Aunt Dot's Christmas cactus. She had bequeathed it to me when I moved here, reminding me that it was older than she was and that since I had the green thumb in the family, I was now in charge of keeping it alive. It was looking happier now that I had moved it to the east window.

I poured the boiling water over my tea bag in my new mug. I hadn't noticed the Scripture written on it when I first unwrapped it, but now I read it out loud. "Be still and know that I am God."

"Good advice, huh?" Todd grinned at me across the room.

I joined him in the book nook, mug in hand. I intended to sit in the wingback chair, but he scooted over and patted the couch next to him.

"Yes," I said, concentrating on settling myself without spilling my tea. "But why is it so hard to practice sometimes?"

He leaned back and laced his hands behind his head.

"Because we're human."

"Because we think we're in control."

He nodded. "Because we are impatient."

"Because we're afraid?"

He shifted to look at me. "Are you?"

Am I? I hadn't identified it as fear up until now. "In a way, I guess." I'd have to examine it a little more. If so, what was the specific fear?

"You are a very independent woman, Callie."

I cocked my head to the side. That was true, but it had taken me a long time to recognize it in myself. "Is that a bad thing?"

He shook his head. "No."

"But?"

"But sometimes people who are independent have a harder time asking for or accepting help. Or letting others in."

"Have you been talking to Mona?"

He laughed. "No. My own observation. I don't think you realize how self-sufficient you are compared with other people."

True, again. In fact, this was something the Holy Spirit had been dealing with me about for months now. "I know. It's something I have to fight against, now that I see it."

"How so?"

I shrugged. "It's not only in my relationship with God. Sometimes I find myself feeling impatient with others who are timid or overly self-conscious." I took a sip of my tea. As long as we were having confession time, I might as well lay it out there. "It's pride, Todd. I never wanted to see it as that, but once you see yourself for who you really are in the mirror of God's Word..."

"Ain't that the truth." He took my hand, threading his fingers through mine. "But I didn't mean it in that way. I simply meant that you don't have to deal with all of this yourself. Don't apologize any more for calling me, okay?"

I liked the feel of his big rough hand holding mine. "If you're sure—"

"I'm sure, Callie. I wouldn't have offered if I weren't."

"Thank you." I cleared my throat, feeling like things had

gotten a little heavier than I had expected. But, I might as well go with the flow. "I was reading in Daniel the other day. You know the part where the king asked Daniel to interpret his dream for him?"

He nodded.

"The king was saying to Daniel, 'I've heard all kinds of wonderful things about you and how you know how to interpret dreams and how you do this and do that.' Then Daniel basically said to him, 'It's not me. I serve the God who is the Revealer of mysteries.'" I leaned forward to set my mug on the coffee table. "I need the Revealer of mysteries to intervene."

"I'll agree with you." He clasped my hand tighter and bowed his head.

We sat in holy silence for a couple of minutes. I envisioned myself bowing before the throne of God. "Father God, Your Word says that You alone are the Revealer of mysteries and the Untier of difficult knots. You see all from beginning to end. As your daughter, I ask in the name of Jesus that You give Todd and me divine wisdom and insight. I pray that You will reveal what is hidden, and open our eyes to the truth. Your Word says that You are the defender of the fatherless, so we ask You to please protect Nicole's baby. Watch over Sherm. Convict Earl's heart of any wrongdoing. We ask for Your will to be done in every aspect of this situation."

Todd cleared his throat. "And Lord, I pray a hedge of protection around Callie. She is your child. Please give her clarity of mind and the peace that passes understanding as she waits on You."

I raised my head. "Thank you," I whispered.

The man sitting next to me had no idea what I was thanking him for, I was sure of it. It was much more than the prayer that he had prayed. It was the spiritual kinship I sensed between us. That bond that had been so sorely lacking in my relationship with Kev.

Todd took a swig of my lukewarm tea and made a face. "You are an extraordinary woman, Callie Erickson. Have I already told you that?"

I wasn't quite ready for what I thought I saw in his gaze. "It's probably because I've had my head knocked one too many times lately."

He laughed. "By the way, why did you cut your hair? I liked it better when it was longer."

That was diplomatic. Mona had taken one look at me and said, "Well, at least it will grow out."

Sheesh. "I went to a different hairstylist. And worse, I broke my own rule."

He raised his eyebrows.

"I have this rule that I won't ever get my hair cut by someone I know. Like someone at church. Because then if I don't like it, I don't have to feel awkward about never going back to that person."

I watched him struggle against a smile, his eyes scrunching a little in a way I was beginning to recognize.

"Sounds wise," he said.

Smart man.

"Yes, but I needed to get it cut that day and my usual person was busy. So, I went to Boranda's." Really, the poor guy. I'm sure this was way more information than he needed.

"Boranda Stigler? She cuts hair?"

I nodded glumly. "And she only charges ten dollars. But now it will feel awkward whenever I see her at church if I don't ever go back to her again."

"I'm glad I'm not a woman." He grinned at me. "Can't you just not get it cut and let it keep growing? Then you wouldn't have to worry about it at all."

"Sure, if I wanted to look like Rapunzel." I rolled my eyes.

He did laugh then. "I think you'd be a very beautiful Rapunzel. I'd climb up to the top of the tower to visit you."

Seriously. The man was flirting with me and I couldn't think of anything to say.

After Todd left, I tried to get to work on the dumb table

decorations, but my mind could not stay focused on moss. I ambled over to the bookshelf near the African violet display where I kept my very favorite books ever. I pulled out my vintage copy of *The White Witch* by Elizabeth Goudge, thumbing through the pages until I found the passage that had been running around in my head for the last hour:

> "...she had long accepted the fact that happiness is like swallows in spring. It may come and nest under your eaves or it may not. You cannot command it. When you expect to be happy you are not, when you don't expect to be happy there's suddenly Easter in your soul, though it be midwinter."

Unexpected Easter in my soul. That's what it felt like—this gradual awakening to Todd. To love?

CHAPTER TWELVE

I awoke in the night and couldn't go back to sleep. Something was bothering me about Brandon. I ran back through the scene in front of Lonnie's house. We handed the baby to Lonnie. We stood and chatted a few minutes with her. Mona noticed Brandon and said he was "watching" us.

There. That's what was bothering me. For one thing, he said he was there because he was working for his uncle's landscaping business. But he sure hadn't been digging and planting in those clothes. Of course, I guess he could have been handing out flyers or something. But the other thing was that I knew I had seen him somewhere before I had actually met him that day in Aunt Dot's room at Willowbough.

But where? Short Creek was a small town, so it wouldn't be far-fetched to have seen him at the dollar store or the gas station. But I had a feeling I had seen him in a different place than somewhere here in town. And why had Lonnie and Mona both had such a strong negative reaction to him? And Lonnie said he used to have blond hair?

Wait a minute. I felt the jolt of adrenaline hit my system. I lay rigid on my bed, my heart pounding, my breath coming in short gasps. Could this be the same Brandon? The one that used to be friends with my brother Jason?

Oh, God. Please no.

But if it was him, then why on earth was Aunt Dot encouraging me to go out with him. It didn't make sense. Nothing made sense.

I felt around for my phone in the dark. 2:00 AM. I couldn't call Aunt Dot on her new smartphone until morning without giving her a heart attack.

I texted Todd on the chance he might be awake. "Are you awake?"

"Yes, what's up?"

I resisted the urge to apologize for texting him in the middle of the night. "What do you know about Brandon?"

"Too much to text. Want to talk?"

"If you're up for it. I know it's late—"

My phone rang while I was still texting.

"Hey."

"Is he messing with you?"

I shrugged. "Not exactly. But I think I know him from before."

"What do you mean?"

"Did he grow up here? I mean, here in Short Creek?"

"Yeah. I know he left for a couple of years, though. Moved to the Midwest somewhere, I heard."

I sucked in my breath. "That's what I was afraid you were going to tell me."

"Why?"

"Well, I guess God is answering our prayer for help in unravelling this mystery." I sighed. "You know I've told you that my brother Jason and I would sometimes come and spend summers down here with Aunt Dot? Well, one summer Jason met Brandon. Only he went by Brandon Winters then."

"Yes, that would be right. I think his mom had been married and divorced like six times while he was growing up. Brandon hated all of them and stuck with his real dad's name. But how is he connected to your brother? And why didn't I ever meet you and Jason if you were down here for months at a time? I grew up here, too."

I had wondered that, too. What would my life have been like if I had met Todd as a teenager? Before either of us were saddled with all the baggage we carried around now? Would we have been attracted to each other then? Or was it only because of the individuals we had each become as a product of our life choices that we were drawn to each other now?

"Callie?"

"Sorry, I was just thinking." My arm was falling asleep, so I sat up and switched on the bedside lamp, then gathered the covers around my neck. "I wish I would have met you then."

"Me, too."

I also wished we were sitting together on my couch, not talking on the phone. I could use a good hug right about now. "Unfortunately, Jason met Brandon one summer when we were down here. I think they were both about ten or eleven."

"I can probably guess, can't I?"

"I'm sure. Jason was apparently attracted to the life Brandon lived, though why, I've never figured out. Our family wasn't perfect, but we were raised in a loving Christian home. Jason never lacked for anything." The bitterness welling up in my heart as I spoke took me off guard. I'd thought I'd made peace with the situation a long time ago.

"And so?"

The anger of man does not work the righteousness of God. I know, I know. I shook off my angst until I could deal with it later in private. "None of us realized at first what was going on, and besides, the boys only saw each other in the summer. What we didn't find out until later is that after a few summers, they had worked out a plan for Brandon to move to Ohio."

"He actually moved there and lived with your family?"

"Oh, no. All of this was done secretly because by then, they were both using drugs—which none of us knew at the time."

Todd whooshed out his breath, and I could picture him rubbing the back of his neck.

"We were so naïve, Todd. We were this faithful little Christian family who attended church every time the doors were open. We had family devotions around the dinner table every night and served food at the homeless shelter once a month, you know?" I sighed. "Our parents loved God and raised us the best they knew how. They never dreamed Jason could be involved in drugs. It wasn't even on their radar."

"Wow."

"Yeah. And even when the signs became more obvious, they went into denial. It wasn't until they were on a first-name basis with the local police officers that they truly realized the situation." It still seemed unbelievable now, looking back on that time. "Then they decided we should move across town to try to get him away from the 'bad influences'."

"Too little, too late by then. I've seen it a million times."

"Yep. All that accomplished was to uproot the rest of us from our lives, while Jason went on doing what he was going to do no matter where we lived." Sheer madness.

"Where exactly does Brandon fit into all of this?"

"Well, you have to understand that we didn't have much contact with Brandon. We knew he and Jason were always together, but he rarely came to our home. That's why I didn't recognize him until now...especially since he's changed his appearance so much. And it's been years since I've seen him."

"He's always been such a weasely little liar," Todd said.

"Tell me about it. Anyway, you know that Jason is serving time in prison."

"Yes."

"Brandon should be right there with him. But he somehow pinned all of it on Jason. Has an uncle in law enforcement or something."

"Callie." Todd paused. "Do you not know who Brandon's uncle is?"

"No."

"Earl."

I squeezed my eyes shut tight. Well, that explained a lot. But what reason would either Brandon or Earl have to—

"Where does Dot fit into all of this, Callie?"

"I don't know. She was super excited for me to meet Brandon. Called him a nice young man." I wound a strand of hair around my finger. "I'm sure she must not have any recollection of the history between him and Jason."

"Or maybe she doesn't realize that he's the same Brandon that hung out with your brother?"

"Maybe. Especially since he's going by a different last name now. And he looks so different than the scrawny, acne-faced kid I remember. But back to Earl. What would he and Brandon have to gain by picking at me?"

"What do you mean?"

I squirmed a little bit. I hadn't wanted to tell Todd about Earl's stupid innuendoes, but I might as well bare it all.

"Earl has said a few things to subtly let me know that he is, um, aware of my past," I admitted.

Todd growled, and I could picture him grinding his teeth. "But you weren't charged with anything in the little girl's death, were you?" he asked.

"No. But I testified at the trial. Against the dad."

I listened to the pugs snore for a long minute before Todd spoke.

"I don't like this, Callie."

"I know. But I can't think of any connection..." I sucked in my breath. "What if it's not me?"

"What do you mean?"

"What if it's Aunt Dot? What if Brandon is trying to—"

"Extort her. And you're in the way."

I groaned. "This is getting way too complicated."

"Tell me about it. Has he been harassing you?"

"No." I traced the blue and purple zigzag pattern of the afghan with my finger. "He asked me out."

"Well, that's a new tactic," Todd muttered. "You turned him down, I hope?"

I grimaced. This was the part I hated about relationships. Things got so tricky sometimes. "Not exactly..."

"Callie. You can't seriously—"

"I didn't know it was him, Todd. And it was before you asked me to go to Zilker with you tomorrow...today."

"I'm sorry to hear that. Maybe we should call off our date to Zilker."

My heart sank. Why did he sound so cold all of a sudden?

"It's not like I like the guy, Todd. And especially now—"

"It's late. I'll text you in the morning."

Clearly, the conversation was over.

"Good night, Todd," I whispered. But he had already ended the call.

"And then he hung up," I told Mona. We sat perched on the stools behind my counter at C. Willikers, gluing on the last of the moss, thanks be to God.

She peered at me over her half-glasses. Red with rhinestones today, to match her cowboy boots. "I imagine he's a little touchy when it comes to things like that."

"Why? I thought we were getting along pretty well, and

then—"

"Hasn't he told you about Darla yet?"

Who was Darla? His ex-wife? "No, we've talked mostly about me, I guess."

Mona snorted. "She cheated on him from pretty much day one, as far as I could tell. Bless his heart, he did everything he could to hold the marriage together until that last fling when she divorced him to marry some rich old dude from Dallas. Old. Like, really old." She made a face.

Ack.

"I didn't know." Though I could have guessed, maybe, if I hadn't been so focused on my own issues. I had caught glimpses of his soul over the past couple of weeks, and the depth of empathy he had shown me the other night when I told him about Marleigh should have clued me in that he, too, had wrestled with sorrow.

"How long ago was that?"

"Let me think." Mona poked a pine cone into place at the top of the altar arrangement. "It was around the same time Houston came here to pastor. I remember because Rob had strep throat and he liked to have died of it so he couldn't go to Houston's welcoming party thing. But Todd was there and that's the first time I remembered seeing him back in town. So...three years-ish?"

"Three years since the divorce? Or three years since he's been back here in Short Creek?"

"Both, I think." Mona tapped her fingernails on the counter. "At least he has Luke most of the time. Poor kid."

I pictured Todd's son, Luke. Tall and dark-haired like his dad, he would be a heart-throb one day, but right now he was in that gawky pre-teen stage. I had met him briefly once in the parking lot after church, but that was it. I was suddenly ashamed I had been so self-absorbed in the few short weeks since I had become acquainted with Todd. Now what was I going to say to him?

"I think I need to go talk to Aunt Dot. Oh, and by the way, thanks for taking me to pick my van up the other day. Looks like someone tore it apart and then only half put it back together."

"What?"

"Earl again, I bet. Searching for something, I suppose." I couldn't think about it anymore right now. I pushed myself off the stool. "Want to go with me?"

"Now? I thought the plan was to finish these candelabras today."

I shrugged. "It was. But I've got to get to the bottom of this Brandon situation. And my mom emailed me."

"Oh." Mona apparently knew better than to go there. She stuffed wads of raffia back into the Jenna box. "Does Houston seem okay to you?"

Houston? With everything going on with Todd and the baby, I hadn't given Houston much thought in the last day or two. "I guess so. Why?"

"He seems kinda moody. Or like he doesn't feel good. He didn't even tease me when I said something dumb the other day."

That *was* unusual. "I haven't talked to him in a few days." Not since he asked if he could call me and then didn't. I grabbed my purse and led the way through the door, turning to lock it behind us. I had left the pugs at home today. "Maybe he's dealing with something personal. Are things going okay at First Church?"

"I guess. He usually tells me if there's a big deal going on. Like when Owen Thompson's family decided to sue the church a couple of months ago."

I rolled my eyes. I could live my entire life and not need to know things like that about someone else's church. "Are you going with me or not?"

"I need to head back to work. I'm taking tomorrow off since Rob will be home, and Houston needs me to have the bulletin done before I leave today. Tell Dot I'm going to write in to her column and ask her a question."

I laughed. I still was amused by the idea of my aunt writing the local advice column. "Can't you ask her in person?"

Mona shook her head. "Not this question," she said solemnly.

CHAPTER THIRTEEN

"Good morning, Auntie," I called through her open door. "I came to get advice from the famous newspaper columnist."

She grinned at me over the top of her laptop. "I wondered when you would stop by."

I kissed her cool cheek. "I can't believe my own aunt is the advice columnist for the *Short Creek Star*. How did that happen?"

"Well, Harry has a little grandniece who works at the paper, and she told him the other gal was retiring. He told her I would be the right one for the job." She beamed at me.

Oh, good. Harry. Not Brandon. I hadn't realized I was worrying about that until now. "It seems like you're quite a hit, Auntie. Have you gotten any questions so far that you couldn't answer?"

She wrinkled her brow. "No, of course not, darlin'. I simply pray and ask for wisdom."

Of course. Pray and ask for wisdom. Why did that not seem so easy sometimes in my life?

"What's bothering you, Callie?"

I slumped into the vinyl chair, my heart heavier than it had been lately. "I'm feeling like Much-Afraid again today, I guess. The mountain ahead of me seems too high to climb."

Aunt Dot closed her laptop and sat up straighter. "You've already climbed more in your young life than others I know who are my age or older," she said.

Yes. And I was weary. My heart ached for Nicole and all the girls like her. For Sherm. For that tiny baby girl. For my broken relationship with my parents. For the beginning of a new relationship with my brother Jason. For peace. For resolution to the crazy things happening in my life—the murder, the rock, the attic visitor, Sheriff Earl, Brandon...Todd. It was one of those times when suddenly, my yearning for Heaven threatened to grow stronger than my desire to live on this earth.

"I want to go Home, Auntie," I confessed. "I feel like Mossy and Tangle when they sat on the plain, weeping with longing for the land whence the shadows fell."

That scene from *The Golden Key* by George McDonald had long been one of our favorite topics of discussion. Aunt Dot nodded. "I know, honey. I feel it myself some days. But that's what we do when we're still in the valley. We long for home, but we have to be faithful to what God has called us to do until then."

"I know." But that was part of the problem, I suddenly realized. Since I was a child, I had recognized that God had a special claim on me—something that seemed far beyond that which I observed in the lives of other "ordinary" Christ-followers around me. How long did I think playing around at being a florist would last, when I knew God had been working and preparing me for something much greater—something with much more eternal impact? And how did Todd fit into the picture? And why was I dwelling on that now, when I had come to ask Auntie about Brandon?

I massaged my temples. "I need to talk to you about Brandon."

"That doesn't sound good. I thought y'all were going out on a date."

"Auntie...I don't know how to say this." I grimaced. "Brandon is not who you think he is."

"Why, Callie. What do you mean?"

"He's the same Brandon that was Jason's friend. Brandon Winters."

Aunt Dot's hand flew to her throat. "I didn't know, Callie," she whispered. "Why would he..."

"That's what I'm trying to figure out."

"What are you trying to figure out?" Harry's big voice boomed through the room, and we both jumped.

"Hi Harry," I said, glancing at Aunt Dot. She shook her head.

"Say, I saw Preacher Houston out there in the hallway. Not looking so hot. Do y'all know what's wrong with him?"

I shrugged. "I haven't seen him in a couple of days. How have you been, Harry?"

"Fine as frog's hair, 'specially since this little lady is making me so proud." He winked at me and took Aunt Dot's hand. "You been keeping up with her in the newspaper?"

"I've read most of them. But I've been on the receiving end of her advice my whole life." I smiled. "Oh, and I finally remembered to bring the *Pilgrim's Progress* book from The Gift Bag. Remember, the one you thought at first might be from your friend Owen?"

I pulled the book out of my purse and handed it to my aunt.

She ran a caressing hand over the cover before opening it. "It looks exactly like the one Owen gave me," she murmured. She turned the browned pages with reverence, one at a time. "Oh!"

She looked up at me. "This is the very book Owen gave me, Callie. See? Here's a violet I pressed in this book from the day he gave it to me."

Harry and I both crowded close to look. Sure enough, right on the illustrated page of Christian losing his burden rested a flat, yellowed Johnny-jump-up.

"Owen was so sweet," she said. "I remember him bringing this to the house a few days after Garth passed away. He had picked a little bouquet of violets from somewhere, and handed them to me with the book." She held her hand to her cheek as she had probably done on that day over ten years ago, tears glinting in her eyes now as then. "He didn't even say a word to me, just hugged me and left."

"He was a good man." Harry swiped at the moisture in his own eyes.

"Yes, he was. One more loved one waiting for us in Heaven." She looked at me. "Callie and I were talking about that, weren't we, honey?"

I nodded. It didn't seem the right time to bring up the fact that somehow Aunt Dot's book had gotten from her attic to a box left beside the Willowbough dumpster. I glanced at Harry. Had he picked up on my line of thought?

"*Vulpes pilum mutat, non mores,*" he muttered.

What? *The leopard won't change its spots?* I gaped at Harry. He knew Latin? And what was he telling me?

Aunt Dot glanced up from the book in her lap. "What did

you say, Harry?"

"I was thinking of the old hymn, 'When We All Get to Heaven', darlin'." He winked at me, then sang the verse in a bass voice: "While we walk this pilgrim pathway, clouds will overspread the sky, but when travelling days are over, not a shadow, not a sigh."

Aunt Dot and I joined him on the chorus: "When we all get to heaven, what a day of rejoicing that will be, when we all see Jesus, we'll sing and shout the victory!"

"Amen!" Houston poked his head in the room. "Can I join the choir?"

"Come on in, preacher," Harry boomed. "The more the merrier, right, gals?"

We laughed, but my heart sank when I saw my friend. His face was haggard, and he looked like he hadn't slept in days.

I moved my purse to the floor so he could sit in the chair next to me. "Are you okay?"

He nodded, but didn't meet my eye. "Long last few days. How are you, Dot?"

"Blessed," she said.

My phone rang. It was Todd. I stood and stepped over Houston's outstretched legs. "I'll be right back."

"Hi." I walked out into the hallway. "I'm sorry—"

"Callie. No more apologies, remember? You didn't do anything. It was my fault."

"Okay, but—"

"No, it's over. No worries. But I do need to talk to you. Is this a good time?"

It's over? What's over? Our little misunderstanding from last night? Or our fledgling relationship? My heart sank.

"Um, no, not a good time. I'm at Willowbough with Aunt Dot. So are we—do we still have plans for tonight?"

"If you still want to go."

Oh, so the ball was in my court.

Maybe that was good. Maybe I should stop this relationship before I got in too deep. Before I made the same mistakes that I did with Kev. Before I hurt another man. "I guess I'll pass this time, Todd."

"No problem. But I have information about the case that you need to know. Can I stop by your store tomorrow morning?"

I stared unseeingly at the posters on the hallway bulletin board. "Sure, that will be fine."

"Okay, see you in the morning."

Just like that.

"See? This is what happens when I open my heart up a crack and let someone in, Mona," I whispered. "I mess it up and then my heart hurts again." Or still, as the case may be.

CHAPTER FOURTEEN

I called Lonnie from my shop the next morning. "How's the little one?"

"She's such a beautiful baby, Callie. I hope y'all figure something out soon before we get too attached to her."

"I talked to Sherm last night. He doesn't know when Nicole will be back."

"Did you mention anything about—"

"Not yet. I don't know what she told him before she left, but he thinks she's working as an accountant in Dallas. And that the man who came to get her is her boyfriend."

"Oh, boy."

"Yeah, and I guess Earl didn't help matters any when he questioned Sherm. Totally went along with Nicole's story."

"But what about the baby?"

"I don't know. Sherm isn't quite all there anymore, you know. He keeps talking about the bad guy who was going to take the baby away, but he doesn't seem to remember that he gave the baby to me. Todd was going to go with me to try to talk to him, but that didn't work out."

"Todd would be a good one to talk to him, Callie. You should still try to make that happen."

Believe me, I would if I could. "I'll see if I can get him over there this weekend. He's supposed to drop by the store this morning, anyway."

"Oh, really?"

I could picture her gentle smile. "It's not like that, Lonnie. I mean, I thought maybe it was, but now it isn't."

"Why not?"

"I don't know. We had sort of a little misunderstanding."

"Yes?"

"I'm not good at relationships, Lonnie."

"I don't believe that for one minute. That's the enemy trying to lie to you."

Lonnie always told it like it was, that's for sure. "Maybe. But I know that I wasn't a very good wife."

"Hang on a minute. I need to switch the baby to my other arm."

I heard rustling and settled myself on the old couch in the book nook, brushing away the memories of the last time I had sat there with Todd. Why did I always seem to get into these kinds of conversations when I wanted to get back to my peaceful life?

What peaceful life is that? My own thoughts mocked me.

"Okay, I'm back. Why do you say you weren't a good wife?"

I hesitated. Lonnie was a good friend, but I'd never spoken these thoughts out loud before. Only wallowed in them privately. "I don't know how to explain it. I loved Kevin when I married him, at least as much as a twenty-year-old could love someone whom she'd known for less than a year."

"Yes?"

"But I don't think..." I picked dog hairs off my jeans. "I don't think I loved him enough."

"Like what? Sexually?"

"No, not that. Something was missing from our relationship, like we couldn't ever connect on a deeper level even though we tried. And I never felt for him what I think he felt for me. I'm afraid that—"

"What?"

Should I put it out there? It would sound so...so dramatic, in a pitiful sort of way. I sighed. "It wasn't like I didn't try. I think I *can't*. That I don't have the capacity to love that deeply."

"Oh, Callie. That's not tr—"

"It *is* true." I stood up to pace. "When he died, I grieved for him. But not enough. Not like it should feel when the other half of my soul was ripped out."

"You can't measure your level of grief against someone else's. We all grieve differently."

I leaned my head against the bookcase. "I know. But even when he was alive, I could never feel toward him what I thought I should. He had a lot of faults, but so did I. He tried hard sometimes to make me happy, and it wasn't fair to him."

"You will have to work all of that out with the Lord. But I do know this. God created all of us with a deep capacity to love.

Just because you didn't experience that for whatever reason with your husband doesn't mean you don't have the ability to."

I wasn't convinced. And it wasn't about me anyway, right? That was my problem right now. I was getting too focused on myself, instead of focusing on what God was putting right in front of me to do—help Nicole and others like her.

"I don't know. But when I talk to Todd this morning I'll ask him what we should do about the baby. I suppose we should call CPS, but I'm leery of doing that quite yet."

"Listen to me. You are bearing a burden you should not be carrying. God made you to be a sheep. Sheep don't carry burdens."

"I don't—"

"Whenever you look at those little donkeys that live behind you, you need to remind yourself that you are not a donkey. You are a sheep. And the Shepherd wants to carry your burdens for you."

I smiled at the analogy, but she was right. I needed to leave my burden at the cross. "That's good preaching."

She laughed. "And don't you forget it. Go look up 1 John 4:19."

I didn't have to look it up. I already knew what it said.

But what I didn't know was who had stuck the envelope in my purse while I was at Willowbough yesterday. I had found it when I got home after Todd's phone call. The envelope contained a clipping of one of Aunt Dot's columns, so I assumed she had put it in there for me to read. Must be a good one.

I should be working on the flower arrangements for the annual Czech heritage event, but instead, I spread the article out on the counter to read it again.

"Haunted in Houston." I read the title out loud. "That sounds pretty crazy."

"Hello, Beautiful."

I jumped and turned to find Brandon standing close enough to touch me. I stepped back, trying to catch my breath. How had he gotten that close without me hearing him come in the door?

"Did I surprise you?" He smiled at me. "I thought I'd drop by instead of calling you. Hope you didn't forget about our date."

His aftershave was overpowering again today, but the crazed glint in his eye is what made my senses jump to high alert. How had I ever thought him handsome? And how had I not figured out who he really was the first time I had seen him in Aunt Dot's room?

"I guess we never picked a day and time," I said. I had to keep playing the game. Had to keep him thinking I didn't know his true identity.

"I don't care. I'm hungry now." He stepped closer to me and reached out to touch my hair. "Why don't we head on out to my car and go for a little drive into town?"

His pupils were pinpricks, his face flushed.

Jesus, help me!

"I can't leave my shop in the middle of the day, Brandon. I have customers who—"

His fingers tangled in my hair, pulling it painfully tight. "I thought you'd be more cooperative than this, babe." He yanked me toward himself. "If I can't get it out of Dot, then I'm going to get it out of you."

Aunt Dot? Oh, no.

"You're hurting me, Brandon." I was so close I could see the uneven stubble on his cheeks. *God, please...*

Tell him the truth, Beloved. Get it out in the light.

"I know who you are, Brandon."

He wiped his mouth with his free hand. "Yeah?"

"You let Jason take the rap for it all."

"He wasn't as smart as I was." He leered at me. "Guess that's what happens to dumb suckers like him."

The nerves in my legs were going crazy. I grabbed the counter to steady myself. "Brandon, I—"

"Get away from her, Winters!"

Oh, thank God. I sagged against the counter.

Brandon whirled toward Todd. "You can't order me around, Jack."

"I said get away from her. Now." Todd took a step in my direction, his right hand hovering near his belt.

Brandon's fingers tightened on my hair. "She's coming with me, ain't you, pretty Callie?"

"Not right now, Brandon." I kept my voice low and calm. "Remember, we were going to go out next weekend. Not today."

He cocked his head. "That's right. But I want to go now."

Todd was edging closer.

"I know," I said soothingly. Dear God, I'm trying to reason with a madman. "But we want to be by ourselves, right?"

He let go of my hair to cup my face. "All by ourselves, Callie." He whirled to face Todd. "I'm comin' back for her, and you can't stop me. Not you or a fancy cop like the one that preacher killed."

CHAPTER FIFTEEN

I sank to the floor as Brandon banged out of my shop. "What did he say?"

"Later, Callie." Todd stooped in front of me and grasped my hand. "Did he hurt you?"

"No," I whispered. "But he was so—evil. His eyes..."

"I know, sweetheart." He tugged on my hand to help me up, but my legs wouldn't work, so he sat down beside me and pulled me into his arms. "I'm so sorry."

I rested against his heartbeat for a minute, then pulled away to look at him. "What did he mean about the preacher killing someone? What preacher?" Houston's troubled face popped into my mind, but I couldn't go there. "Who did he mean?"

"I don't know that part." He pushed my hair out of my eyes. "But I did find out who the victim was. He was a private investigator working for the state of Texas. Name's Carlos Ruiz."

"What was he doing in Short Creek?"

Todd winced. "Investigating a sex trafficking ring."

"I knew it! I knew something like that was going on. Is Earl involved?"

"I don't know. But it's common knowledge that Bell County has a significant issue with trafficking since we're so close to a major highway." He pinched the bridge of his nose. "It's likely he wasn't only investigating leads here in Short Creek. Temple, Belton, Killeen—all hotspots, no doubt."

I groaned. "This is such a mess."

And not only the Brandon situation. I snuck a peek at Todd. He was staring across the room, his jaw set, his long legs crossed at the ankles. I wanted so badly to make things better between us. But maybe there hadn't been anything to "make better" to begin with. Maybe I had imagined the spark of attraction—

"I was surprised when you turned me down last night." He still stared straight ahead.

I didn't know what to say.

"I guess I'm kind of rusty with relationships." That was the truth, even if it was lame. I felt my cheeks burning.

"Me, too." He shifted to look me in the eye. "It's been a long time since I've allowed myself to be attracted to a woman."

The air left the room.

"I've always wanted the kind of relationship my parents had," he said, as if musing aloud. "I know that kind of marriage still exists."

Marriage?

I gulped. "Todd, I—"

"You feel it too, don't you? The connection between us?" He didn't touch me, but the intensity in those blue eyes pinned me to the wall.

I nodded, startled when I felt the sting of gathering tears. I wasn't much of a crier, so why now?

"I've made a lot of mistakes in the past. I don't want to repeat those again, and I never want to hurt you. But I'd like to think that I've learned from my errors." He reclaimed my hand, rubbing his thumb over the back of it. "Would you agree to give our relationship a chance?"

Our relationship? My nose was running, and I dug for a tissue in my pocket. The ball was in my court. Again.

"Todd, I'm not...I still have a lot of baggage, I think."

He nodded. "Me, too. As was obvious from my reaction the other night when you mentioned Brandon asking you out."

"I'm still sorry I hadn't given much thought to your, um, previous situation."

"You mean my ex?"

"Yes. Mona filled me in a little. I hope you don't mind."

He shrugged. "Pretty common knowledge. So...?"

Well, as long as he'd already mentioned the "M" word.

"I've already figured out I'm not a very good wife." There. I'd said it.

"Hmm." He arched an eyebrow as if thinking about that, then grinned at me. "Maybe you had the wrong guy."

Oh, boy. This was getting too deep, too fast. "Let's take it slow, okay?"

"Yes, ma'am. I can do slow." He lowered his face to mine and kissed me gently. "I won't hurt you, Callie," he murmured.

No, of course he wouldn't. Not on purpose, anyway. But I was tired of my heart aching. Was it worth it to open up to Todd?

I drove home by myself, shaken.

'Tis better to have loved and lost, than never to have loved at all, Tennyson wrote.

Was it?

I thought back over my relationship with Kev...with Jason...with my parents...with Aunt Dot...with Mona and Houston and Lonnie. It was certainly true that I, at least in part, was who I was today because of our common bond of love. How could I conclude love wasn't worth the pain? Did I imagine that by barricading myself from others that I would protect myself somehow?

Risk. That's what it was, and that's what I was fighting against. I was fighting against it not because I didn't know myself well enough, but because I knew myself too well. I knew if I committed myself to Todd that it would be all or nothing. I would burn my bridges behind me and set my face forward—and open myself up to the pain of betrayal again.

Betrayal? I had never labeled it that before in my mind. But that's what it was—to me, at least. I had married Kev, believing he was a godly man. Not perfect. I had no illusions of that. But I realized after a few months that the man I married was an irresponsible fool. I had racked my brain many a time, trying to remember what I had been thinking while we were dating. How had I not noticed his self-centeredness? His careless expenditure of money? Our lack of communication? Had I even prayed about our relationship? Maybe I was the one who was a fool.

I shook my head and climbed out of my van, only to climb in again. I had forgotten the envelope on the counter at the shop. In all of the commotion with Brandon and then Todd, I hadn't had a chance to show it to him. I wanted him to read Aunt Dot's article.

I pulled up in front of the shop I had left five minutes ago. "Maybe it wasn't Aunt Dot. Maybe Harry stuck the envelope in my purse," I said out loud, trudging up the front stairs of the shop. He was pretty proud of my aunt, after all. Maybe he—

"Callie! Wait!"

I turned to see Houston waving at me across the parking lot. After my phone conversation with Todd at Willowbough yesterday, I hadn't been in the mood for talking to Houston. Or Aunt Dot, for that matter. I guess I owed both of them an apology.

Houston strode toward me, startling me. He usually kind of ambled wherever he went. "Don't open your door," he panted.

"What?" I paused with my key in my hand.

"I saw that guy trying to sneak into your shop when you pulled out a minute ago."

"What guy?"

He rubbed the top of his head, making his sandy hair stick out in crazy ringlets. "The one who's been hanging out around here. I thought you knew him."

"Todd?"

"No, not Todd. Brandon."

Would I have to get a personal bodyguard? If Todd had his way, I would. I should at least take his advice and buy a can of pepper spray. "What do you mean, *trying* to sneak into my shop?"

Houston stuck his finger in the collar of his dress shirt and worked his neck. "He was messing around with the windows in the back. I can see back there from my office, you know."

I sighed. "But you didn't actually see him get in?"

"No, I started over here and he must have seen me, because he took off running."

"You didn't call the sheriff, did you?" That was all I needed today—a confrontational meeting with Ridiculous Earl.

"No. But Callie, I—"

"Thank God. Will you walk in with me?" I unlocked the door. "I'm sure everything is okay if he didn't actually enter the store."

"Okay, but—"

I pushed the door open. Everything looked fine. I'd grab the envelope and newspaper article off the counter...

"They're gone."

"Who is gone?" Houston asked.

"Some papers. He must have taken them."

"But he didn't go through the window, so how could he have taken something?"

He must have grabbed them and taken them with him earlier. At least he hadn't taken *me*, thanks be to God.

"It's a long story. Do you want a cup of tea?"

"I would love a cup of tea. Do you have Earl Grey?"

"Of course. I only drink it in the winter but..." I paused in mid-sentence as I focused on my friend for the first time today. "Are you sick, Houston?"

He slumped down onto a stool. "No."

I made a face at him, then turned to grab two mugs. "Is there something terrible going on at the church?" I hadn't heard anything from Mona, but maybe she just hadn't told me yet.

"No. Everything at church is fine." His voice was weary.

"Houston. Something is wrong."

"There are a lot of things wrong." He held his mug out for me to fill it with boiling water.

"Is this why you were going to call me the other day? To talk about stuff?"

He nodded.

I *was* a fool. Here I'd thought he had romantic intentions, and the poor man was weighed down with life's burdens. "I'm sorry we didn't get a chance to talk then. But I have time now."

"It's Nicole."

Wow. Talk about getting straight to the point.

"Nicole Grant? My neighbor?"

"Yes. I don't know what else to do."

I'd better tread very cautiously here. Did Houston know? Or rather, *what* did he know?

"I wasn't aware you were acquainted with her," I said.

"I've known Nicole for a long time." He stared down at his hands. "We...I..."

We? I studied his face again. Oh.

"You love her."

He met my gaze. "Yes."

I closed my eyes. *God, give me wisdom.* I opened my eyes to meet his again. "Do you know...?"

"I know. I just didn't know you knew." His face was ashen.

"I guessed. I had some suspicions after I went to the seminar at SCCC, but then when she left the baby and I watched that guy come pick her up..."

He nodded.

"Sooo...what? Why?"

He dunked his tea bag up and down in the mug. "I've always loved her, Callie. After her mother died, I asked her to marry me, but she said she didn't want to be a preacher's wife. She left for Dallas shortly after that." He took a swallow of tea. "I'm sure she didn't mean to get trapped into this. She always was one to take risks, though."

"And?"

He looked at me steadily. "She always comes back."

I felt sick.

"Are you saying the baby is yours?"

"No! It's not like that." He jumped up to pace to the door and back. "I've never touched her."

I blew out my breath. "But you said—"

"She always comes back to me for help. Out of all of those men," he grimaced, "she knows in her heart I'm the only one who loves her."

"Oh, Houston." I laid my hand on his. "I'm so, so sorry."

He turned away. "I don't know what to do. She's getting in deeper and deeper. I fear for her life. And now the baby—"

"And you've gone to the authorities?"

He laughed. "You think Earl'd do something about it? He's about the biggest joke for a sheriff I ever saw."

"I agree, but—"

"Besides, you don't know how this thing works. She has begged me over and over not to tell anyone. She is terrified someone will harm Sherm or the baby—or even me if I tell."

"Do you think they would? Or are they only threatening her?"

"Callie." He gave me a gentle shake. "Haven't you watched the news lately? These men are brutal monsters. They treat those girls like cattle, even branding them with tattoos so everyone knows who they belong to. It's sick."

"Yes, but isn't there some way to get her out of it? Somewhere she could go, like a safe house or something?"

He rubbed a hand over his eyes. "Believe me, I've checked into every place I could find. There's starting to be more awareness, which means more people helping, but the scope of this thing is staggering. I found one place in Waco where she could maybe go. Run by a Christian couple."

"But?"

"But she has to want to."

I hated the hopelessness I heard in his voice. "Then let's pray that she wants to," I whispered.

He shook his head. "I can't pray about this anymore, Callie. My prayers are bouncing off the ceiling and echoing in my ears."

"You can't lose your faith over this. God is able to—"

"I'm not sure I had any to begin with. That's part of the problem."

Oh, my dear friend. What could I say to him?

CHAPTER SIXTEEN

I woke bright and early the next morning to the comforting sound of jingling dog tags. Todd had insisted that Annie, his German Shepherd, spend the night at my house from now on. At least until we figured out what to do about Brandon.

"No one would dare come in your house with Annie here unless they were extremely stupid," Todd had said.

Well, Brandon was stupid, I thought, but I *had* witnessed him running away from a cat. So maybe he wasn't stupid enough to confront a German Shepherd. At any rate, I was delighted to have Annie to keep me company. We always had big dogs when I was growing up and lately I was missing having one.

"Come here, girl," I called softly. She padded into the room, hopped up onto my bed and settled on top of Aunt Dot's afghan, as if she had always lived here. I smiled. Pugs were snuggly little dogs, but that's about as far as they went. Annie, I believed, understood pretty much whatever I said to her.

"Ready for the chili cook-off today?" I asked her.

She cocked her head and smiled.

"Todd will be here soon, okay?"

She jumped off the bed and raced toward the front door.

I guess I shouldn't have told her that quite yet. I lay on my back and stretched, not quite ready to get up. It should be fun spending the day with Todd, but my heart ached anew for Houston. I guess even pastors aren't immune to the kind of trials that can shake one to the core.

I reached for my journal and found the page where I had copied down Edward Shillito's poem, "Jesus of the Scars." Written in the aftermath of World War I by an English minister, it had resonated deeply with me when I had first read it a couple of years ago.

If we have never sought, we seek Thee now;
Thine eyes burn through the dark, our only stars;

We must have sight of thorn-pricks on Thy brow,
We must have Thee, O Jesus of the Scars.

The heavens frighten us; they are too calm;
In all the universe we have no place.
Our wounds are hurting us; where is the balm?
Lord Jesus, by Thy Scars, we claim Thy grace.

If, when the doors are shut, Thou drawest near,
Only reveal those hands, that side of Thine;
We know to-day what wounds are, have no fear,
Show us Thy Scars, we know the countersign.

The other gods were strong; but Thou wast weak;
They rode, but Thou didst stumble to a throne;
But to our wounds only God's wounds can speak,
And not a god has wounds, but Thou alone.

I would write it out and give it to Houston. Only our God—our Saviour, Jesus Christ—suffered wounds to pay for our sin. Wounds that *we* inflicted. He alone carried the weight of the terrible grief—the agony and pain of Nicole's situation magnified billions of times over. He alone understood the weight of Houston's despair. And He alone could comfort and mend it.

"Holy Spirit, please be very near to Houston right now," I prayed. "Have mercy on him, Jesus. Let Your comforting presence surround him. Send ministering angels to sing songs of hope and deliverance to him and to Nicole. God, I pray that You will bring Nicole to her senses in the name of Jesus. Give her a way of escape. Put a protective hedge around her and deliver her from the evil one. Thank You, Lord. Thank You for Your mercy. Thank You. Your will be done, Father God."

An hour had slipped by before I knew it, and now Todd would be here any minute. I brushed my hair, then quickly put on a little mascara and my Ohio State baseball cap. I guess the man would see me at my worst sooner rather than later.

"Hello, Gorgeous." Todd stood on my front porch, and Annie joyfully launched herself at him.

"Are you talking to me or her?" I surprised myself by acting normal with him. I thought I would feel more awkward after yesterday's brief kiss.

He laughed. "Both. You ready to go?"

"Yep. Let me put the pugs in the mudroom. Purl's not been feeling well, and I don't want to clean up any messes when I get home."

"We'll take Annie with us. I have her leash in the truck."

"I'm sure Bubbles will love that," I said over my shoulder.

"Bubbles? I'm afraid to ask."

I grabbed my purse and locked the door behind me. "Bubbles is Mona and Rob's teacup poodle. They always take him pretty much everywhere with them when Rob's home. In one of those little dog stroller things."

"Ah." He made a face.

I laughed. "I guess we feel the same way about some breeds which shall not be named. Are you hungry?"

"Always. It's been years since I've been to the chili cook-off."

"This will be my first time. Last year I had recently moved here, and I didn't know anyone."

"My dad won it once." Todd opened the truck door for me. "He made killer chili."

This was one of the first times I had heard him mention his dad. "Why was it so special?"

He chuckled. "He kind of made it up once when we had left-over steak. But it was so good that he started grilling steak on purpose to put in the chili."

We pulled into the fairground parking lot.

"That does sound good. What kind of beans?"

He gave me a hard look. "Beans do not belong in chili, Callie," he said sternly.

"They do where I come from."

"But you live in Texas now, darlin'."

I smiled at his exaggerated drawl. "You can take the girl out of the north, but you—"

"Can't take the north out of the girl," he finished for me. "Is that true?"

I hesitated, because the way he was looking at me made me suddenly think he was asking me about something more serious than beans. "I'm making peace with my past, Todd."

And as I said it, I realized it was true. At least to the extent of being ready to finally move on from Kevin. "My heart is here now."

He reached across the console to squeeze my hand. "I'm glad."

Me, too.

I returned his smile. It was going to be a good day.

I shaded my eyes, scanning the crowded fairground for Mona and Rob. Rows and rows of trailers and pick-up trucks ended where the lines of vendor booths began.

"Mona said she thought the cook-off tent would be next to the corncob chucking contest."

"Wow, that brings back memories." Todd chuckled. "My cousin and I always had a rivalry going. When we were in high school, he won two years in a row. But I was ready for him the next year. My record throw was forty-nine feet, five and a half inches."

"What? You waited until now to tell me you were a corncob-chucking king?"

"I am a man of many talents, Callie Erickson." He tugged at my pathetically short ponytail dangling out of my baseball cap. "You haven't seen anything yet."

Oh, boy. I was liking this man way too much.

I took Annie's leash so I had something to do other than stand there staring at him like a love-struck teenager. "Well, I'd better prepare myself then. Pretty soon I'll find out you are secretly a double-agent. Or a world-famous rodeo star. Or something exciting like that."

He raised his dark eyebrows. "One never knows."

"Seriously, Todd. I feel like I don't know that much about you."

"That's why we need to go—"

"Callie! Todd!"

We turned to see Mona, ladle in hand, flagging us down from a booth a few yards away. She was in full regalia today—red cowboy boots, a wild chili-print apron, and, I saw as we neared her, chili-shaped earrings under her red cowboy hat.

"Wow, you couldn't miss her in a crowd," Todd murmured.

I laughed. "Mona never blends into the crowd. But where's Rob?"

I looked for the lanky Texan, certain he'd be wearing his signature boots and enormous belt buckle. I'd never seen him wear anything else, even to church.

"Hey there, Callie. Good to see ya again, Todd." Rob ambled over from the grill to grip Todd's hand in a hearty handshake. "It's been a while."

Mona beamed at us. "Three of my favorite people under one tent," she said, grabbing her phone. "Here. Stand over there by the tortillas and I'll take your picture. Annie, too."

Leave it to Mona to use tortillas as the background. I smiled for her, suddenly conscious of Todd's arm around my waist as we posed.

"Does this count as a date?" he whispered in my ear.

I leaned into him a little, not caring that Mona was watching. "Only if you buy me some fried pickles," I whispered back.

Annie's low growl was my only warning before she leapt toward Bubbles, almost tearing my arm out of the socket in the process.

"Annie! Down!"

She dropped to the ground and Bubbles, his bravado deeply encouraged, stood up in his doggy stroller to yip at her.

Rob roared at the sight, earning him a doleful look from Mona as she bustled over to lift the tiny dog in her arms.

"I'm sorry, Mona," Todd said. "I think Annie was surprised. I don't think she's ever seen a dog that small before. She probably thought he was a squirrel."

"I'm tellin' her that all the time." Rob grinned at his wife. "He ain't a dog, he's a rodent."

Mona covered the dog's ears. "Don't listen to those mean men, Bubbly-poo," she murmured. "They don't know anything."

The men were teasing, but I could tell her feelings were hurt. I reached to pet Bubbles' head, then drew my hand back. The tiny thing might nip me. "I'm hungry for some of Rob's world-famous chili. Aren't you, Todd?"

I gave him a meaningful look.

He motioned for Annie to lie down by the lawn chairs. "I'm starving. Do we have to wait until after the judges test it to give our verdict?"

"No, sir. I'll dip ya both up some right now. D'ya want cornbread and greens, too?"

Eww. I hadn't quite developed a taste for collard greens in my year down here, but I didn't want to seem rude. "Just a little of each, please."

Mona set the feisty little critter back into his dog bed and sank down into a lawn chair across from me. "Bubbles keeps me company so I don't get so lonely when Rob's gone. He's a good dog."

I looked into my friend's eyes as I sat down. "I know. But men like to tease about stuff. You know that."

"Yeah." She looked away then, but I thought I caught a glint of tears in her eyes.

This had to be about more than Rob making fun of the dog.

"What's wrong, Mona?" I glanced toward the men, but they were in deep conversation by the grill. Had Houston told her about his relationship with Nicole? Maybe she was upset about that.

She twisted her chunky red bracelet around her arm. "I don't think Rob loves me anymore," she whispered.

"What? Why, what happened?"

She shrugged. "He's been gone for weeks, Callie. And I've been working so hard on my diet. I lost six and a half pounds, and he didn't even notice."

Oh, dear. "That doesn't mean he doesn't love you, Mona. Sometimes men don't notice things."

"That's what I told myself," she said, sniffing. "But then he started talking about all of these new things he's learning for his job and all of the places he's been lately and I feel—"

"Left out?"

She nodded. "He's so smart, Callie. And sometimes when he talks about stuff, like even from the Bible, I feel so dumb. But you know what my life was like before I came to the Lord. Sometimes I wish I could change the first half of my life, you know?"

I did know. I had half-wished the same thing many times. But not really. Because then I would be a different person now. "We all have our own story, Mona." You wouldn't be you without all of the struggles you've been through."

"But maybe I'd be a better me." She looked over at her husband, tears filling her eyes again. "Rob deserves someone better than me. I'm fat and dumb."

"Mona, that's not true. Rob loves you for who you are."

She swiped at her eyes and sat up straighter. "Well, I hope so, 'cause he's stuck with me."

That sounded more like the Mona I knew. "That's right. And you're stuck with him. For better or for worse, right?"

"The only problem is I'm usually the 'worse,' and he's the 'better,'" she said.

I shook my head. "Nope, it doesn't work that way. It takes two to tango."

She took a deep breath. "I told him I want to go with him on the road."

"Really? What did he say?

"He's always wanted me to."

Was that the hint of a smile I saw?

"That could be great for you guys." I leaned back in my chair, eyeing her. "But somehow, I can't see you as a trucker woman," I teased gently. "You'll need to get a do-rag and a leather vest. You can collect patches for your vest from each state."

She rolled her eyes. "I'm not going to be a biker."

"What? You're not going to be a biker?" Rob bent his tall self over the back of Mona's chair to give her a peck on the cheek. "I thought that's what we agreed on, sugar. We'll sell the house and buy us a couple of Harley's."

Mona reached up to grasp his hand that lay on her shoulder, shaking her head. "What am I going to do with this man?"

I grinned at the two of them. Rob was still obviously smitten with his wife. "I think he's a keeper, Mona."

Todd sat down next to me, balancing two bowls of chili. "Do you want the one with or without onions on top?"

"Either. What were you guys talking about for so long?"

Rob dropped into the seat on the other side of me, stretching out his long legs in front of him. "He was filling me in on your case. I wish you didn't have to be involved in this."

"You and me both." I held my hair up off my neck. Man, it was hot out here today.

"Rob was telling me that the truckers have seen a major increase in trafficking within the Texas Triangle." Todd slathered butter on his cornbread.

"And especially near here, up and down I-35," Rob added. "It's heartbreaking."

"Have you had any girls approach you?"

"Not too often. I'm a pretty old dude." He stroked his beard. "But you can tell who they are. I wish we could do more to stop it. It rips my heart out to see those young girls—"

"How young?" Mona asked.

"Fifteen, sixteen." He grimaced. "Every once in a while I see one who's younger than that. I always want to grab her and take her home to her mama."

"Couldn't you? I mean, if the girl wanted to?" I poked my spoon into my chili.

Todd shook his head. "He could, but those girls are watched. Tracked. His life would be in danger."

"And not only in the state where it happened," Rob added. "Some of these guys have extensive networks that can extend over state boundaries."

"We need to get a big ol' bunch of us to do something about

it. We could have a march or...or a fundraiser." Mona sat up straighter. "We could call the governor. Or sit in front of Earl's office until he did something."

"I think Earl's already doing more than he should," Rob muttered.

CHAPTER SEVENTEEN

Todd and I glanced at each other.

"Why do you say that, Rob?" I asked.

He cracked his knuckles. "I have my suspicions, Callie. I've never trusted the man, and occasionally I hear chatter over the radio that makes me wonder."

"Like what?" Todd crumbled a cracker into his bean-less chili.

"That it's pretty easy to get away with certain things along a particular stretch of I-35." He raised his eyebrows meaningfully.

Really. I thought back to that day when I rescued the baby. The day that Nicole's pimp came to pick her up and Earl had—

"I still say he knows him," I said.

"Who knows who, Callie?" Rob squinted at me.

"Sheriff Earl. I could have sworn that he knew the guy who came to pick Nicole up from Sherm's."

The men's gaze met over my head.

"And then there's Houston."

Uh oh. Why had I let that slip out?

Three pairs of eyes fastened on me.

"What about Houston?" Mona asked.

"I mean that he knows Nicole, too." I squirmed a little bit.

"But the question is, does he know what's going on with her?" Todd asked.

Mona fingered her earring. "Maybe he does. Maybe that's why he's been so grumpy lately."

And he would have to be the one to tell Mona. I fed my last bite of cornbread to Annie and stood up. Todd followed my lead and unfolded himself from the low camp chair.

"Todd tells me he is a champion corncob chucker." I smiled at him.

"Back in the day, I could chuck one pretty far," Rob said.

"My honey won the blue ribbon for it at his high school field day, didn't you, sweetie?" Mona patted his knee. "Rob went to school here right in Short Creek."

"Speaking of blue ribbons, when is the cook-off winner announced?" I asked. "I can't believe anyone's could be better than yours."

"They'll announce it at the beginning of the concert tonight. Are y'all stayin' for that?"

I looked up at Todd, but he was not paying attention. His body was taut as he focused on something or someone I couldn't see.

"What is it, Todd?"

"I thought I saw—" He turned to Rob. "Do you know Vic? Earl's deputy?"

Rob nodded.

"He's over there talking to Brandon."

Rob shrugged. "Prob'ly knows him from high school. Besides, aren't deputies supposed to kind of mill around at these kinds of things so everyone feels comfortable around them?"

Todd was still staring into the crowd. "I wouldn't say Vic usually has good vibes as his main goal. I don't like the feel of it somehow."

"Maybe it was someone who looked like Brandon?" I stood on tiptoe, trying to follow the direction of Todd's gaze.

He shook his head. "Let's go take a little stroll over there, Callie."

He grabbed Annie's lead in one hand and held his other out to me. "We'll stop back by before we leave," he said to Rob.

I took Todd's hand, and Mona squealed.

"Y'all look so cute together, don't they, Rob?"

Rob hooked his arm around her shoulder and winked at Todd. "If you say so, Baby Doll."

Todd was pulling on my hand as Mona whipped her phone out.

"You can take a picture later, Mona." I followed Todd as he plunged into the crowd. Ordinarily, I hated crowds. But with Todd's firm grip on my hand, I didn't mind so much.

Until I saw Vic.

I stopped, staring at him. *Something about him...*

"Todd, wait." I pulled him behind the cotton candy booth.

"I've never seen Vic before when he was not in his uniform."

I closed my eyes for a minute, trying to think.

"What is it?"

I opened my eyes again and studied Vic from my hiding spot. What was it that was setting off warning bells in my head?

The tattoo.

The same tattoo I had seen on Nicole's neck.

"His tattoo. The one on his forearm," I whispered.

Todd flipped his sunglasses up on top of his head and took another long look at Vic, then at me. "Yeah?"

"Nicole has that same one on her neck."

"Are you sure?"

"Positive. Remember when someone threw a rock at me and you made me go to the hospital in the ambulance? Vic was the one who rode with me. I was feeling kind of woozy, but I remember staring at that tattoo on his arm, trying not to pass out again."

"Okay. But when have you been close enough to Nicole to see her tattoos?"

"She was sunbathing in Sherm's yard one day. I had my binoculars out because I use them to look at the birds, you know? I had just seen a female cardinal and I was trying to—"

"Shh, I get it." He pulled me deeper into the shadow at the back of the booth. "Let's watch him for a little bit. We can talk it all out later."

We never did see Brandon again. But we did watch Vic long enough to tell that he was working the crowd—and not in an official capacity.

I leaned my head against the headrest as Todd drove me home. He seemed especially quiet. "What are you thinking about?"

He darted me a quick glance before staring at the road again. "I can't quite put all of the pieces together. But I know we're on to something."

My phone dinged. It was Mona.

I smiled and read it out loud to Todd. "'My honey took FIRST PLACE in the cook-off.' Five exclamation points, two pairs of clapping hands, and three smiley faces. Oh, and she sent a picture of him with his trophy and all five grandkids."

"Guess we missed out on that action," Todd said. "Good for him. That'll give him decent bragging rights at church tomorrow."

"That's for sure." Except that it would likely be Mona doing most of the bragging.

We rode in comfortable silence for a few minutes.

"Oh, I forgot to tell you the latest." I glanced at him out of the corner of my eye. "Harry knows Latin."

"He does?"

"Yep. He came in when I was visiting Aunt Dot the other day, and we were talking about...something. I can't remember what we were talking about, when he dropped this Latin phrase into the conversation."

"What was it?"

"'*Vulpes pilum mutat, non mores.*' It means 'The leopard won't change its spots.'"

Todd wrinkled his brow. "What is that supposed to mean?"

"I'm not sure. I mean, I know what it means but I'm not sure who he was talking about."

"It would help if you could remember the context in which he said it. And does that mean that he's the one who sent you the first Latin message? The one that was in the mystery gift?"

I pulled my fingers through my ponytail. "I would assume so. I mean, he practically told me that the other day by letting me know he knows Latin."

"That was super confusing." He grinned at me.

"You know what I meant. And then when I got home, I found an envelope in my purse with one of Aunt Dot's articles in it."

Todd jerked the truck from the road and pulled to a stop under a towering pecan tree. He turned in his seat to face me. "Why are you just now telling me this?"

I shrugged, feeling suddenly flustered. "I kind of forgot

about it because all of that stuff happened with Brandon. And then he took it. I think."

"Who took what?"

"Brandon. He took the article off my counter in the shop. Or at least I think he did because it wasn't there where I had left it when I went back to get it a few minutes later."

He groaned. "Callie—"

"I know. I should have told you. But..."

Todd grasped my shoulders. "You have to tell me every little thing. Somehow all of this fits together, and we need every tiny piece of the puzzle for it to make sense. Do you remember the article? There must be something important in it. Who do you think put it in your purse?"

"Probably Auntie. I think it was called 'Haunted in Houston' or something like that." I peeked up at him. Was he angry with me? I didn't know him well enough yet to know if—

He dropped his hands from my shoulders, touching my cheek gently. "Don't look at me like that," he said. "I'm not upset with you. I keep feeling like we're on the verge of figuring things out and then something else comes up."

"I know." I folded my hands in my lap. "Maybe we need to leave it alone for tonight. I get weary of talking about it so much. I'll ask Aunt Dot tomorrow morning when I pick her up for church and double-check that she was the one who put it in my purse."

He pulled back out onto the highway. "Okay. But at least read the article online tonight. And if somehow someone other than Dot put it in there, then what?"

"I don't know. And why this article in particular?"

CHAPTER EIGHTEEN

The next morning, I used my van to pick up Aunt Dot for church, knowing Todd had promised to save us a place if we ran late.

"The mystery has been solved," Aunt Dot announced as I pulled away from Willowbough.

If only. "Which mystery is that?"

"The mystery of my glasses, of course. Remember when you visited me the other day and something seemed strange about my glasses?"

I had forgotten all about that. I slanted a glance at her. "Your glasses seemed fine when I saw the picture of your date with Harry at the polka service a couple of days later."

"Callie!" She blushed.

I smiled, keeping my eyes fixed on the road. I shouldn't tease her, but she and Harry were so cute together.

"Well, anyway, remember when Karen was gone on the mission trip? And some other woman came to Willowbough to do our hair?"

I nodded.

"That woman had us all in the chairs in the salon, you know? And she collected everyone's glasses before she started and then she mixed them up and gave us the wrong ones afterwards. Can you believe that? No wonder I couldn't see that day. She had given me Inez's glasses. And Beulah was wearing mine. Can you believe it?"

I laughed, picturing the scene. "All I can say is that I hope Karen doesn't go out of the country again for a long time. She has a way of leaving mysteries behind her."

"You can say that again. I'd like to never have gotten my eyesight straightened out after wearing Inez's glasses for two days."

I was still chuckling when we pulled into the church parking lot.

Aunt Dot's arrival at Short Creek Community Church caused quite a stir. It took ten minutes to get to the front door, because everyone wanted to hug her and exclaim over her new hat.

"Wow, Auntie. You're kind of a celebrity around here." I leaned over and handed her Bible to her.

She craned her neck to look up at me. "No, this is my family, Callie. I walked through the doors of this church every week of my life until I moved to Willowbough."

Rick Holloway, Lonnie's husband, held the door open so I could push Aunt Dot through. "It's good to see you, Mrs. Murray. I've been missing your smile around here." He bent to kiss her cheek.

"Thank you, Ricky," she said. "I'm so thankful I could come today."

I grinned at Rick. "I've heard you called a lot of things, Mayor, but—"

"She was my second-grade teacher. What can I say?" He handed me a bulletin. "Todd's been looking for you. Things are heating up a little bit, I hear."

In more ways than one. "Yes, seems that way. I hope—"

The organist boomed out the prelude, cutting off our conversation. I wheeled Aunt Dot through the double doors of the sanctuary and searched for Todd. He and Luke were already settled in their usual pew on the right side toward the front, directly across the aisle from where Mona and Rob usually sat.

He turned around and I waved.

"Dorrie!" Sister Erma squealed, grasping Aunt Dot's hand. "I didn't know you were coming this morning!"

Aunt Dot grinned. "I thought I'd surprise you. Did you get my email the other day?"

"Ladies, I hate to interrupt, but the service is starting." Todd grasped the handles of the wheelchair. "Y'all can visit after church."

I followed as he pushed Aunt Dot, then parked her chair next to the pew. He motioned for me to slide into the pew next to Luke then scooted in after me, squeezing my hand for a second under the cover of my purse.

"Hey, Miss Callie." Luke looked up from staring at the floor and gave me a self-conscious smile.

"Good morning, Luke," I whispered. My years working in the middle school had taught me a little bit about pre-teen boys, and Luke seemed like a pretty decent kid.

"Good morning!" Pastor Chad, our worship leader, brought us to attention. "It's a beautiful day to be in the house of the Lord. Let's all stand and sing together."

Jenna Holloway and a couple of other singers stood with him on the platform, and I couldn't help but notice how beautiful Jenna looked. She was one of those people who radiated the joy of the Lord. Every minute spent gluing moss would be worth it when the big wedding day finally arrived, I decided.

I studied the young minister as he strapped on his guitar. He not only led worship, but he was the youth pastor as well. I had never seen a more energetic guy. But I sure didn't envy him his job as head of our growing youth group at SCCC.

We began with one of my favorite worship songs, and I closed my eyes. I raised my heart in praise along with my voice, my heart suddenly overwhelmed with how much God had blessed me. I had felt alone for so long. But now, I was surrounded by friends, family and my new church family. Despite all the craziness going on in my life, I knew God had a plan. He had brought me here, halfway across the country, for a purpose.

Mona and I exchanged smiles across the aisle as I resumed my seat. I glanced at today's sermon title in the bulletin. "What is God's Will?"

"Well, that's appropriate," I muttered out loud.

Todd glanced at me, and I pointed to the words in the bulletin.

He nodded, laying his arm along the back of the pew behind my shoulders.

Pastor Brian took the pulpit. "I can't tell you how many people over the years have asked me, 'Brian, how do I know what God's will is for my life?' I'd like to tell you this morning that that's the wrong question." He paused and looked out over the congregation.

"The right question is, 'What is God's will?' Period. And what is God's will? God's will is that His kingdom come and His will be done. His will is that the message of the gospel is preached. His will is that sinners come to salvation."

I blew out my breath. Was this God's direction to me that I should give up my shop and—

"I am not saying that God is calling all of you to be missionaries in China. I am not saying you should all quit your jobs and work at the church. But what I am saying is that it's not all about us. In fact, it's not about us at all. And if we are blood-bought children of God, then He has a right to do with our lives as He chooses and for His glory."

Wow. Was the message especially strong this morning or was it only me? I didn't glance around, but I'm sure I wasn't the only one squirming by the end of the message.

"So I'll close with this quote from Henry Blackaby: 'The Father will always relate to you out of the context of His love for a lost world. Have you been learning obedience through what you have been suffering? If you have, God may choose to make you a source of salvation to others even as He did with His Son.'"

Pastor Brian closed his Bible. "It's not about us, folks. It's about Him. And, as Jesus said in John 4:34, 'My food is to do the will of him who sent me and to accomplish his work.' That's our work, too. To do the will of God."

God will always relate to you out of the context of His love for a lost world. The thought wouldn't let me go. It was Monday morning, the faint red glow of the sunrise barely blushing the edge of the horizon. I loved praying here in my little office in the predawn dark, before the cares of the day pressed in on me. Sitting in His presence, listening for His voice.

God will always relate to you out of the context of His love for a lost world.

It was not a coincidence that I was involved in Nicole's situation. God had placed her in my path, and I had been moaning and groaning about the inconvenience of it. *God, forgive me. Help me. Use me.* I softly hummed, then sang, the words of the old song.

> Spirit of the Living God,
> Fall afresh on me.
> Melt me, mold me,
> Fill me, use me,
> Spirit of the Living God,
> Fall afresh on me.

As I prayed for Nicole, I sensed an urgent need to pray for Houston. I knew he was carrying a heavy burden—shepherding a church while grieving over Nicole. Wrestling with fear and helplessness. But somehow, I felt there was more to it. That day he had told me about Nicole, I had glimpsed something in his eyes that gave me pause. He had more to confess, I was sure. Maybe not to me, but I hoped to someone.

On my knees, I interceded for my friend. I would take him the "Jesus of the Scars" poem when I went to the shop today and see how he was doing. But first, I had something else to do.

While I was praying, the answer to the *festina lente* number/letter thing had come to me. Why hadn't I thought of it before? It wasn't "PSIS58610." It was: "P.S. Isaiah 58:6-10".

As in the P.S. of a letter? Or a note? Maybe I was missing the first part of the message. Maybe that's why none of it made sense. But maybe there was a clue in the passage itself.

I was familiar with Isaiah 58, but couldn't remember what verse six said, exactly. I flipped to it and caught my breath:

> "Is not this the kind of fasting I have chosen:
> to loose the chains of injustice
> and untie the cords of the yoke,
> to set the oppressed free
> and break every yoke?"

Wow. Maybe Houston had been right that first day we opened the box and found the note. Maybe this truly was a message from God. I quickly scanned the rest of the verses until I got to verse 10:

> "...if you spend yourselves in behalf of the hungry
> and satisfy the needs of the oppressed,
> then your light will rise in the darkness,
> and your night will become like the noonday."

Okay. I blew out my breath. I might never figure out who sent me this message, but one thing was clear: God was directly calling me to be more involved with the whole Nicole/sex trafficking deal. I couldn't read it as anything else. It was time to take up my shield of faith. To buckle the belt of truth around my waist. To pray like I never had before.

I knew Mona wouldn't be in the church office today, because she always took Mondays off. I wasn't sure if Houston would be there either, especially this early in the morning, but his pickup was in its usual spot under the pecan trees.

I decided to park in front of my shop and walk over to the church since the heat hadn't cranked up too much yet.

"You stay here for a minute, Annie." I left the van running with the air conditioning on so she wouldn't get overheated while I ran over to the church for five minutes. "I'll be right back, and then we'll go in the shop, okay?"

I grabbed the envelope with the poem in it, leaving my purse and everything else in the van. It was hotter outside than I thought, and I was a sweaty mess by the time I had walked the fifty yards or so to the church. I knew Houston preferred to use the side door during the week instead of leaving the main doors of the church unlocked. I started to reach for the doorknob when I heard voices. Angry voices.

"You think you're going to get away with this because you're a preacher, don't you?"

Was that Brandon's voice?

I backed away from the door.

I could hear Houston's voice reply, but couldn't make out what he said.

Was Brandon threatening him? Should I call someone? I edged into the small space between the hawthorn bush and the outside wall of the church. Why had I left my purse in the car?

"I'll tell you one thing, preacher man, I'm not going to take the rap for this. I'm finally going somewhere in life, and I'm not going to let you ruin it."

I heard a crash and a series of thumps. Houston screaming something.

Dear God, what was happening in there? I pressed myself flat between the bush and the wall.

Brandon came barreling out of the door, swearing.

I held my breath.

He looked wildly around the parking lot, then took off toward my van.

Oh, no. I was stuck. I couldn't let Brandon see me, but what if he tried to steal my van? And what if he had injured Houston?

I had to check on Houston. What if he was in there bleeding or...or worse? Besides, Annie would never let Brandon in the vehicle. I could hear her frenzied barking even from here.

I edged toward the church door, keeping my eye on Brandon. No telling what he would do, especially if he was high. *God, please send someone to help us. We need you. Be our shield—*

Crash! The front window of my shop shattered.

"That's what happens to liars!" Brandon screamed. He heaved another rock through the opening, then took off running down the sidewalk.

I gaped at him, too stunned to do anything else, as he veered crazily off the sidewalk and across the street in front of an oncoming UPS truck.

There was no way the driver would have time to—

"Stop!" I yelled. But even as the words were ripped out of my mouth, I watched Brandon's body fly through the air.

He landed in a crumpled heap on the pavement.

Dear God.

I couldn't breathe. Couldn't run—but I had to. Had to find help. I lunged out from behind the bushes, the branches tearing at my clothes. I had to get to my phone. Had to call 911.

I was halfway across the parking lot when the driver of the truck got out, his phone in his hand.

Oh, thank God. Brandon would be cared for.

I had to check on Houston.

CHAPTER NINETEEN

"Houston!" I staggered into the church. "Where are you?"

"In here." His voice was weak.

I followed the sound to his study and found him sitting at his desk, his head in his hands. A sour smell lingered in the room.

"Are you okay? Brandon—"

He raised his bruised face to look at me and groaned. "Go away, Callie—"

"No! Brandon is—I think he's dead, Houston." My legs started to shake, and I grabbed the edge of his desk. "He—it was an accident. A rock. He threw a rock and—"

I was babbling about a rock. Again. But this time the rock hadn't hit my head. It had shattered my—

Houston braced his hands on his desk and pushed his chair away from it. "What are you—"

The sirens began to wail.

"Outside." I gulped. "He ran across the street and a truck...oh, dear God. Jesus, please help us."

Horror filled Houston's eyes. He pushed to his feet to look out of his office window at the scene, then sagged against the window frame. "No. Please no," he whispered.

The flashing lights bouncing off the window added to the surreal feeling. I couldn't believe this was happening.

Todd was on duty today. Todd would help.

"We have to go see what's happening."

"Oh, God." Houston sank down onto the floor. "I can't, Callie."

"I have to." *I have to. I have to see Todd. I have to tell my brother Jason. I have to get my phone. I have to make Annie stop barking.* Was Brandon dead?

I stood on the sidewalk amidst the shattered glass of my shop window, watching as the ambulance pulled away.

Todd put his arm around me. "He was dead on impact, Callie. Never had a chance."

I burrowed into his chest, his badge pressing painfully into my cheek. "I can't believe this. I can't believe it."

"I'm so sorry you had to witness it." Todd stroked my back. "He must have been high."

I pulled away and ran a shaky hand over my hair. "I don't know. When I saw him come out of the church—"

"You already told Earl, I assume? He took your official eyewitness description?"

"Yes." But I didn't tell him about Houston and Brandon's argument. After all, I hadn't *seen* anything happen.

"Then let's get you out of here. You don't need to be involved in this anymore right now." He scraped up some glass with the side of his boot. "I'll get someone out here to clean this up and board up your window."

I nodded, feeling like I was in shock.

"You can tell me the whole thing later, okay?" He cupped my cheek. "I wish I could stay with you right now, sweetheart, but I'm on duty until this evening."

"Okay."

"Hang in there with me." He took my wrist and felt my pulse for a few seconds. "Do you feel lightheaded?"

Sort of. Maybe. "I want to go home, I think."

"I can take a minute to follow you home. Or do you want to hang out at Mona's for a while?"

Aunt Dot. I needed to see my aunt.

"I want to go see Aunt Dot. But what about Houston?"

Todd glanced in the direction of the church. "What about him?"

"It looked like he and Brandon had a fight. But it's not that. It's...something's wrong with Houston, Todd."

"What do you mean?"

"I know he has been upset about Nicole. But there's more than that. And Brandon was accusing him of...something."

I sucked in my breath, remembering. Brandon, threatening me in my shop. Brandon, screaming at Todd that same day, going off like a crazy person about—

Oh, no. It couldn't be, could it?

I clutched Todd's arm. "Do you remember when Brandon was in my shop, and he screamed something about a preacher shooting someone? Do you think—?"

Todd shook his head. "Brandon wasn't in his right mind. I've heard people spouting all kinds of delusional things when they're off their rocker."

"Do you think he saw whoever Tased the guy that I found on my steps that morning?"

"Brandon? Maybe." Todd edged me over to my van. "He was probably involved in way more stuff than we'll ever know."

I climbed in the driver's seat, then turned to look at him. "So you don't think—"

Todd sighed. "No. I don't think Houston is involved in this in any way. Why would he be, for one thing? Houston doesn't exactly strike me as a murderer."

I winced. Me neither. But still…

"I'm going to follow you over to Willowbough. You need a cup of tea and a nice long visit with your aunt. Promise me you'll stay there with her until I'm off. I don't think you should go home by yourself right now."

"I will."

Annie leapt up into the van with me. I stroked her soft head, then gave her a hug, burying my face in her fluffy neck until I could regroup. I pulled back finally to meet Todd's gaze, feeling cold and shaky even though it was 100 degrees out. "Thank you for letting Annie stay with me for the past few days."

I turned away to hide the tears that had suddenly welled up, but Todd didn't miss much.

"Aww, Callie." He smoothed a strand of hair back behind my ear. "It's going to be all right, sweetheart. We'll get through this. Would it help for Annie to stay with you tonight?"

"Yes."

"Okay. I'll take her with me now and then I'll swing by and bring her to you after I get off."

"It's like a nightmare, Auntie." I sat in Aunt Dot's room, feeling like I'd been the one hit by a truck.

"I don't understand," she said. "I thought he was such a sweet young man. And when you told me the other day who he really was, I started praying for him because I thought to myself, 'Dot, if there's ever been a young man who needed prayers more than Jason, it's that young man.'"

I felt sick. "He slipped into eternity today, Auntie. Just like that."

She shook her head. "I can hardly fathom it."

I stared at the floor.

"You know, Callie, I used to be pretty hard-nosed about things. But see this?" She waited until I looked up, then picked her crocheting up off her lap. "To someone who doesn't know how to crochet, this looks hopelessly difficult. Where does it begin and end? And how do you make all of those loops?"

She crocheted a round or two.

I waited.

"Can you tell what I'm making, darlin'?"

"Looks like the beginning of a pot holder. Or maybe a baby blanket." I'd made enough of those myself to recognize what they looked like in the beginning stages.

She nodded. "But only I know the finished product I have in mind. The exact colors, the size, the types of stitches, the patterns."

I knew my aunt well enough to predict where she was going with this.

"I think our lives are like this, only God is the one holding the crochet hook. He fashions our lives according to the design He has in mind." She pulled her glasses down to peer at me over the top of them. "And now that I've lived longer and seen more, I think that God is much more merciful in His dealings with us than we think."

I pondered that. "So, you think Brandon—"

"I don't know. But I do know that he heard the gospel at

least once. Because I told him myself."

I raised my eyebrows.

"One night when y'all were down here for the summer, he and Jason came over to my house one evening. Your Uncle Garth was still alive then, and we all sat around the table talking."

"I don't remember that."

"No, you weren't there. You had gone to a sleepover or something." She clasped her hands together in her lap on top of her crochet work. "Anyway, I think it was before the boys had gotten into any serious scrapes, but I could sense in my spirit that Brandon was a troubled young man."

Leave it to Aunt Dot to have compassion on a scoundrel, even then.

"Garth had taken the boys up to the attic to move some boxes around for him. I think that's when he was clearing it out to make his space for doing his model airplanes."

I nodded.

"Anyway, after they came back down, we had dinner, and I remember I had made oatmeal cookies for dessert. Brandon had never had homemade cookies, and I thought he was going to eat them all."

Against my will, sympathy for the life Brandon had lived as a child crept in to replace the disgust I had been feeling.

"Garth and Jason headed out to the yard after a while, but Brandon sat at my table, eating cookies and pouring his heart out." She gazed out past me, as if picturing the scene. "I shared the hope of the gospel with him that night."

What should I say to that?

"I'm going to have to tell Jason what happened." I blew out my breath.

"Oh, no. That will be so hard for him."

CHAPTER TWENTY

I couldn't call Jason, so I had to wait until he called me.

I wasn't sure where my brother was in his relationship with Brandon. After all, Brandon had ratted him out and then somehow gotten out of the same sentence Jason was serving.

Jason usually called on the weekend if he could, but he hadn't called and it was Monday night.

"Please, Lord," I prayed. "Have Jason call me soon."

I didn't know why I was feeling such urgency to talk to Jason about Brandon's death, but somehow, I knew I had to.

"Come on, Annie," I said, putting my phone in my pocket. "You, too, pugs. Let's go outside."

Annie bolted past me out the front door, probably eager to find her new friend Sherm. In the few days she'd stayed with me, she had taken a liking to my elderly neighbor. The pugs waddled through the door behind me, snuffling and puffing their excitement.

I smiled, watching Annie trying to gain Sherm's undivided attention. He was using some sort of tool to pick up the green pecans that had blown off the trees earlier. Annie circled him, then repeatedly pawed at his pecan picker-upper until he laughed and laid it aside to ruffle her ears.

"Beautiful evenin'," he called to me.

I nodded, taking a deep breath. It was a gorgeous evening. The earlier wind had blown away most of the humidity, and the sun was setting in glorious streaks of pink and blue. Even after living down here for a year, I never tired of the pink beauty of the sky on a summer evening. Ohio sunsets could be spectacular, but nothing like these fiery golden and mauve displays. My theory was that the sun looked bigger because we were closer to the equator, but since I didn't know much about stuff like that, it was only my fanciful thinking, I guess. I felt myself relaxing for the first time since I left home this morning. Enjoying the beauty of God's creation always helped to bring me peace, to regain focus—to quiet my soul enough to hear the still, small voice.

I turned the hose on and watered the pots on the porch. The lantana and the blue daze were about the only flowers still thriving in the heat of mid-July, but the asparagus ferns in the hanging baskets on the shady end of the porch were still looking decent. And of course, the roses were blooming non-stop.

I dragged the hose behind me across the yard to water the ferns under the pecan trees. I grabbed one of Annie's tennis balls and lobbed it toward her and Sherm.

"Have you heard anything from Nicole?" I yelled.

"What's that?" He cupped his ear.

I laid the hose down at the base of the wisteria, and ambled closer to him. "Nicole. Have you heard from Nicole?"

He shook his head sadly. "No. Not since she left t'other day. And I don't know where the baby went."

"The baby is safe, Sherm." I had told him this before, but he couldn't remember. "Lonnie is taking care of the baby."

"Is that right? Lonnie Holloway?" He beamed. "She's a good girl. I knowed her since she's jest knee-high to a grasshopper."

"Yes, sir. She's taking good care of that baby for Nicole."

Annie dropped her ball on Sherm's foot, and he bent gingerly to pick it up. "This here sure is a nice dog ya got, Callie."

"She's not mine. She's Todd's. Todd Whitney."

"Say again?"

"She belongs to Todd Whitney."

He stared hard at me. "Whitney, you say?"

"Yes, Todd Whitney."

"Whitney? Well, I'll be darned. Ain't he th' one who was mixed up in all that hullaballoo 'bout that kidnapping a while back?"

What?

"I don't know, Sherm," I said, suddenly weary. I couldn't go there. Couldn't think about one more "what if" right now. "Do you need me to take you into town for groceries tomorrow?"

"No, ma'am, but I 'preciate you askin'. That preacher—Gregory, is it?"

I nodded.

"I cain't keep straight if that's his'n first name or last name. He was goin' to bring me some this week. He's a good man, that one."

Yes. Yes, he is.

When I got back into the house, I called Houston.

He didn't answer, so I tried again. I didn't want to bother him if he was resting, but it was only early evening and I had to see how he was doing.

Still no answer. It was only then that I realized I had never given him the envelope with the poem in it. I had had it in my hand when I walked over there, but then what? I couldn't remember what I had done with it. Maybe I had dropped it in the hawthorn bushes?

The bushes...the shattering glass...the squeal of brakes, the sickening thud as the truck made impact with Brandon's body...the sight of Houston's tortured face...

I had to stop thinking about it. Todd had made me promise I'd try to relax tonight. But I was too restless.

I herded the dogs back into the house. I'd try to call Houston again a little later. Maybe I wasn't ready to talk to him yet, anyway. I sank down on the couch with my laptop and pulled up the Star website. It still made me shake my head to think that Aunt Dot was writing an advice column, but really, who better than someone with her amount of well-earned wisdom? I pulled up the archives of her column from the last week or so.

What was the name of the article? Something about hunted or haunted—there it was: "Haunted in Houston." I shook my head. How did people come up with this stuff?

Dear Dot,

I've always heard that "the end justifies the means," but now I'm not so sure. I did something to help someone else, but it didn't help very much and now people are suffering because of what I did—including me. I can't stop thinking about it, and it's driving me crazy. I think I need to tell someone what I did, even if I get in trouble for it. Please help me.

Haunted in Houston

Wow. This letter seemed a little heavier than the ones Aunt Dot usually answered. I scrolled down to her response.

Dear Haunted,

Whoever said that the end justifies the means was wrong. If you have done something that harmed someone else, even with good intentions, you must make it right or you will never have any peace. If you have been untruthful, you must tell the truth.

As noted theologian Albert Schweitzer once said, "Truth has no special time of its own. Its hour is now—always."

If you can go directly to those you hurt, that would be best. I would also advise you to seek the counsel of a pastor or some other trusted advisor and possibly a lawyer if the "trouble" you referred to is of the legal sort.

I knew Aunt Dot probably had restrictions about using scripture in her column, but she had managed to still squeeze in biblical principles. Good for her. My smile faded as I leaned back on the couch. Why would she want me to read this column in particular? I was trying to seek the truth deliberately—in a *festina lente* kind of way. Was she urging me to hurry? Telling me that now was the time for the truth to be revealed?

Annie joined me on the couch, resting her chin on my lap.

"You're such a sweet girl," I murmured. "I bet Todd misses you."

I laid the computer aside and picked up my knitting. I needed to stop thinking about everything for a little while. I always kept a couple of different knitting projects going on—simple, no-thinking-required projects like the baby blanket for days like today, and for the days when I had the energy to focus, an intricate lace shawl pattern that left me cross-eyed after an hour or so.

I turned on praise music and started in on the baby blanket. I had begun knitting it a few weeks ago because it looked like a fun pattern and the pastel rainbow colors made me happy. But now I thought of Nicole's little one. Who else would knit a blanket for her? She had no grandmother. No mommy. No—

I blinked back hot tears and concentrated on the feel of the delicate yarn in my hands. I had the simple pattern memorized, and it was satisfying to see the lacy design take shape in my hands. Exactly like Aunt Dot's illustration of God's hand upon our lives. I smiled at the thought of God with a crochet hook in His hand, my thoughts drifting back to Jason. I was still amazed at how God had finally broken through to my brother. Our family had prayed many times for God to do what it would take in Jason's life to bring him to Himself. I hated that it took being in prison for Jason to finally surrender to God, but Jason himself told me that it was worth it.

"I need to talk to you, Jace," I whispered. Before he had gotten mixed up with Brandon, Jason and I had been close. And somehow, even through everything, we'd managed to hold on to our relationship.

My phone dinged. I snatched it up, hoping it was Houston, but it was only Mona.

"Are you OK?????" she texted.

I texted back: "Hi, yes. But I don't know if Houston is. Have you heard from him?"

She called me.

"How are you holding up, girlfriend?"

I sighed. "I still can't believe all of this."

"Well, I can. Once you start doin' the Lord's work, the devil is gonna try to make you quit."

I made a face. I didn't doubt that was true, but I wasn't convinced that was what was going on with today's situation. "Have you talked to Houston? I tried to call him a couple of times earlier."

"Nope. And I'm supposed to leave in the morning with Rob.

We're going on a three-day trip to Louisiana and back."

Poor Houston. It sure seemed like bad timing for his secretary to leave for three days.

"Do you have someone covering for you at the church while you're gone this week?"

"Yep. Jenna had extra time, and said she'd do it. She might even want to do it full time if I decide I like the trucking life and quit. I still can't understand what happened with Brandon this morning. And why did he throw a rock at your shop window?"

"I don't know, Mona. The whole thing is so sad."

My phone beeped, and I saw the number from the prison. "Jason is trying to call. Text me tomorrow, okay?"

I waited for the security message to play, then heard Jason's voice.

"Hey, Sis!"

"Jason, I'm so glad you called."

"What's wrong?"

"I... Did you know that Brandon had come back here to Short Creek?"

Silence. "Brandon Winters?"

"Yes."

"Yeah, I knew that."

I couldn't tell from his voice what he was thinking.

"I guess this is none of my business, really, but did you have any contact with him after...after the trial and everything?"

He was quiet for so long that I thought our call had dropped. "Jace?"

"Sorry. It's so weird that you're asking me this now."

"Why?"

"I've hated him for so long. I blamed everything on him, you know? Even the stuff that I knew in my heart wasn't his fault."

I could imagine.

"But once the Lord started working on me, I realized I couldn't be a follower of Christ and continue to hate Brandon. I...I wrote him a letter, Callie."

Oh, no.

"I wanted to tell him that I forgave him. And that God would forgive him, too. I told him how God had changed my life so much in the last few weeks and that now I had peace."

Dear God. I swallowed against the lump in my throat.

"When did you send the letter?"

"Like a week ago, probably. Why?"

"Jason..." I cleared my throat. "Brandon was killed this morning. He was hit by a truck and died instantly."

I heard his swift intake of breath.

"Do you think he got my letter in time?" His voice broke.

"This call will end in one minute."

I wanted to scream. Why did we have to be restricted at a time like this? It wasn't fair. Nothing was fair. If only Jason hadn't ever gotten in trouble in the first place—I took a deep breath, then blew it out.

"God is merciful, Jason," I whispered. "That's all I know."

"I'm proof of that," he said. "Remember Dad always quoting Psalm 103, Callie? 'He knows our frame; he remembers we are dust.' And then Mom would say—"

The call ended.

And then Mom would say verses 17 and 18, "But the steadfast love of the LORD is from everlasting to everlasting on those who fear him, and his righteousness to children's children, to those who keep his covenant and remember to do his commandments."

I leaned my head back and closed my eyes. "I'm feeling pretty dusty today, Lord. I need your strength. Please, Father, I'm asking again that you bring breakthrough in all of these situations. Brandon's situation. Nicole and the baby. Sherm. Earl. Vic. The private investigator. Houston.

"Shine the spotlight of the Holy Spirit on those things that are hidden, and bring the truth to light. Lord, Your Word says that it is the truth that sets us free. Show me the truth, Lord God. Make my thoughts conducive to Your agenda. Lead Todd and me in the paths of righteousness for Your name's sake. Your will be done, and Your Kingdom come in all aspects of my life."

CHAPTER TWENTY-ONE

I tried to call Houston again. He still didn't answer, so I called the church. No answer there, either. I was getting a little worried. If he didn't answer soon, I would have to run over there and see if he was okay. Yesterday had been a traumatic day for both of us, and I know I was still feeling the effects of it.

Why had Brandon been there talking to him, anyway? Especially that early in the morning? Had they agreed to meet? Or had Brandon unexpectedly shown up at the church and barged into Houston's office? Or maybe Brandon had broken into the church and Houston had surprised him and they fought?

That didn't seem very far-fetched, except that I was having trouble picturing the gentlemanly Houston taking a swing at someone, even Brandon. In fact, I couldn't imagine Houston ever hurting anyone, which is why it seemed so strange to see a gun lying under the papers on his desk yesterday.

I gulped.

Why hadn't I remembered that until now?

I thought back. I had rushed into Houston's office in a daze, barely registering the chaos in his always-neat office. The lamp was overturned, papers were strewn across the floor and scattered on his desk. The black handle of a gun stuck out from under the stack nearest the edge of the desk.

"It's not unreasonable that he would have a gun," I said out loud. Purl lifted her head to stare at me. "This is Texas, after all."

I knew Rob carried one in the cab of his truck all the time. And I even knew several women who had their concealed-carry permit. But still. Houston kept a gun in his office? At the church?

Todd knocked on the door, setting off a flurry of joyful barking, yipping and tail wagging.

"Wow. That was quite a welcome." He brushed dog hair off his t-shirt. "Are you happy to see me too?"

"I am." I grinned at him. "If I had a tail, I would wag it."

He pulled me into a light embrace, then kissed my cheek lightly. "Did you rest?"

I nodded, relaxing against his chest for a moment. "But I thought of something else. Two somethings, actually."

He pulled away to look in my eyes. "I'm listening."

"I..." My brain felt suddenly foggy. Here I was, standing in my own living room, but it had been Aunt Dot's living room first. I remembered the hot summer night many years ago that Jason and Brandon and Uncle Garth—I sucked in my breath. Another piece of the puzzle fell into place.

"What is it, Callie?"

"I know why Brandon was in my attic."

"Wait. What?"

"Well, I figured out yesterday that he's the one who threw the rock at my head. I think he thought I was on to him."

"You lost me, Callie." He tugged me toward the kitchen. "Let's go sit."

I settled at the table with my tea mug, the corny-looking Texas mug from The Gift. "When I went into Houston's office yesterday morning after the accident, I was all upset and tried to tell him what had happened. I started babbling about the rock Brandon threw through my shop window, but then I suddenly realized that he had to have been the one to throw the rock at my head, too, because there was the same smell in Houston's office that I smelled that day I got clobbered with the rock."

"A smell?"

"Yes. I can't describe it. Almost like vinegar."

Todd squinted at me. "Okay. We can talk about that again later. Why do you think he was the one in your attic?"

"That's what I remembered when we were standing out there in the living room. Did you ever know my Uncle Garth?"

Todd shook his head. "I saw him around town when I was growing up, but never knew him."

"He was a big jokester. He loved to tell stories, and he was good at it." I smiled. "Aunt Dot would scold him for exaggerating the details, but he would wink at her and say, 'Sugar, I'm just speakin' *evangelastically*.'"

Todd laughed.

"Anyway, he had Jason and Brandon going one night, telling them his stories of his days in the Navy and how he and Owen—"

"Owen Thompson?"

"Uh huh...how he and Owen found pirate's treasure and brought it home with them to Short Creek. Uncle Garth convinced the boys that he had hidden it all over the place around town."

"And they believed him?"

"Well, they were still pretty young. He even told them he had made a map and that it was hidden in the house somewhere so after he died, Aunt Dot could find the money and have enough to live on for the rest of her life."

"You don't think—"

I nodded. "I think Brandon must have still believed that. I'm sure Jason didn't, especially once he grew a little older, because he knew his Uncle Garth pretty well, but—"

"So that's why he freaked out when he saw the *Pilgrim's Progress* book in your shop window. He thought you had realized that he had stolen it from Aunt Dot's attic and were on to him."

"But in reality, I had no idea at the time that it came from my—Aunt Dot's attic. But that would also explain why all of the things were wrapped in newspaper from the day of my husband's car accident. Auntie told me herself that she remembers that on the day that Kevin died, she had been in the attic sorting through things and wrapping them."

Todd gave a low whistle. "That's crazy. So Brandon had probably been stealing a box from your attic here and there, hoping you wouldn't notice. And if he didn't find what he was looking for, he simply got rid of it."

"Yes. He probably dug through the box with the books and other stuff in it, didn't find what he was looking for and left it by the dumpster at Willowbough. Then Karen found it and gave it to me. "

"Wow."

We stared at each other.

"It's almost too strange to be true," Todd finally said. "But it makes sense in a weird kind of way."

"I know." I sighed. "And I talked to Jason a little while before you got here. You'll never believe this, either. He said that he mailed Brandon a letter last week. Telling him he forgave him and that God would forgive him, too."

Todd raised his eyebrows. "I wonder if Brandon got it before—"

"I hope so."

We looked at each other.

I cupped my hands around my mug. "Aunt Dot told me that she shared the gospel with him when he was a kid."

"Really. She remembers him being at her house?"

I nodded. "He was over here and there with Jason. I had forgotten about that until today. But Todd, there's something that's been bothering me about this whole thing. It's the trials."

"What trials?"

"Jason's and Brandon's. The whole deal is kind of a blur, because it was such an emotional time. Jason's trial was first, and I was so devastated that he was sentenced to prison that I can't remember much about Brandon's trial."

"Did you go to it?"

I nodded. "My parents bailed—I mean, moved, shortly after Jason's but before Brandon's. Almost like they didn't even want to know."

"I'm sorry, Callie."

That was a conversation for another day.

"Anyway, I'm going to see if I can find the information online. We may never know how many strings Earl pulled to get Brandon off the hook, but I feel like I need to revisit it."

Todd nodded. "It might shed light on the whole mess. Oh, and by the way, we got the toxicology report back on Brandon. He didn't have any illegal drugs in his system the day he died."

"What?" I had been sure that he was high. "Why else would

he be acting like a madman?"

"I don't know. Sometimes people just snap."

"Like he committed suicide?" This was getting crazier by the minute.

"We might never know that." Todd sighed wearily. "There's a lot of ugliness in this world."

"That's for sure. Don't you want to be done with all of this and go to Heaven some days?"

"Every day, sweetheart. Not only some days." He pulled me into his arms and rested his chin on the top of my head.

We stood in silence, drawing strength from each other's closeness.

"He gives strength to the weary—"

"....and increases the power of the weak." Todd finished the verse for me. "That pretty much sums us up, doesn't it?"

"For sure. But I know God is going to give us answers. I keep praying..." I pulled away to look up at him. "Oh, I forgot to tell you that I read the 'Just Ask' article from the person in Houston. I didn't get how it's connected to anything."

"Did you 'Just ask Dot'?"

I laughed. "Mmm-hmm. She said she hadn't put it in my purse, but she was glad I enjoyed reading it."

Todd made a face.

"Who else would have put it in there? And why?"

I hadn't been able to answer that question, but maybe I could answer another one. I stayed up far too late that night, poring over the records of both Jason and Brandon's court cases. The cases had wrapped up shortly before Kev and I had gotten married, and I was surprised at the path my thoughts took now as I relived those days.

I found myself seeing Kevin through a different lens than when I first moved here a year ago. My heart had healed enough, I think, to view him with more compassion than I had in a very long time. I hadn't realized how much bitterness I had been holding in my heart toward him. He hadn't lived up to my expectations, and all my efforts to change him had only resulted in resentment between us. I sighed. How much better our life together might have been had I given him over to the Lord and taken my hands off.

In fact, Aunt Dot had given me that advice right at the get-go. I remember a particular family gathering—our first Thanksgiving, if I was correct. Aunt Dot must have sensed the tension between Kev and me. She wrapped her arm around my waist—tight—and whispered in my ear. "Remember, Callie. You are not Kevin's mother. Nor are you the Holy Spirit."

I smiled through my tears. How like Aunt Dot. And how sad of a young, immature me not to heed her advice. "You were right, Auntie. But I didn't get it. I was too busy feeling sorry for myself."

Turning off the monitor, I pushed away from my desk. It was almost midnight, and tomorrow morning I would regret—

I jumped when my phone rang. Who would be calling me this late?

Houston.

"Hey, Houston! I've been trying to get a hold of you. Are you okay?"

"No. Callie, I—"

I clutched the phone tighter at the tone of his voice. "What's wrong?"

"I'm going crazy, Callie." His voice broke, and I could hear him take a deep breath and blow it out.

"I've got to talk to someone. Can you meet me somewhere?"

"Of course." My mind raced. Should I call Todd?

"I could drop by, but..."

"No, no. No worries. Why don't you meet me at my shop?" I never went to the shop this late, but I knew we were both trying to avoid the appearance of anything that could be misconstrued as immoral. "I'll head over there in about ten minutes if that's all right?"

"Sure. Just—don't tell Todd right now, okay?"

I felt a little weird about agreeing to his request, but this was Houston, after all. My friend. A pastor. Not a murderer.

At least I hoped not.

CHAPTER TWENTY-TWO

My shop looked different at night than it did in the sunlight. The corners were deeper, the shadows longer. And it didn't help that the front window was still boarded up from when Brandon threw the rock.

I had the electric tea kettle going by the time Houston shuffled through the door fifteen minutes later. I started when I saw him. He had aged ten years in the past day. His eyes were swollen, his skin ashen.

Dear God. Please give me wisdom. Whatever it is that Houston needs to talk about—

"You don't look very good." I handed him the Colorado mug. "Have you gotten any sleep?"

He reached out a trembling hand to take the tea, then slumped onto one of the stools, shaking his head.

"Let's sit in the book nook." I led the way, curling up in the wingback chair next to the C.S. Lewis display. "It's comfier over here."

He perched on the edge of the worn leather loveseat, staring at the floor.

I waited. I heard the train jolting by, its lonesome whistle loud in the silent room.

Houston lifted his eyes to mine, then lowered them again. "I read that poem, Callie."

"Oh, I'm so glad. I couldn't remember what I had done with it since things were so—crazy that day." I watched a bead of sweat trickle down his face.

He mopped his forehead with a tissue. "I found it in the hawthorn bush by the side door. I read it."

Was he sick? Or just nervous? I waited, quite sure he had come to discuss more than this.

"No matter what that poem says, I don't believe Jesus could understand what I've done." He fixed his eyes on a point above my head.

"Oh, Houston..."

He shook his head, then dropped his gaze to his feet again. "I don't know where to start," he whispered.

"I'm not in a hurry," I said softly. What could he have done that was so terrible? Was Nicole's baby his after all? Is that what he had to get off his chest?

"I'm not fit to be a preacher anymore." The hoarse whisper carried with it the pain of a thousand regrets.

I waited. *Holy Spirit, comfort Houston's heart. Only You can set him free. Only You can deliver him—*

He lifted his haunted gaze to mine. "I killed him, Callie."

Sweat prickled in my armpits. I stared at him.

"He came to my office, and I—"

"That's all I needed to hear, Preacher-man." The soft voice from somewhere behind my chair was pure evil.

I froze at the look on Houston's face. *Who was behind me?*

"I'm havin' some good luck tonight, gettin' you both at once. Kinda like a two fer one at the fair."

The man's laugh sent chills down my spine.

I had to see who it was, if it was the last thing I did. I knew it wasn't Earl. Or Vic. I turned my head ever so slightly, stunned when my cheek touched cold metal.

"Hold it right there, babe," the voice said. "We can do this the easy way or the hard way, okay?"

I glanced at Houston. His eyes were glazed, his face flushed.

Dear God. I'm sitting here with a gun to my head and Houston is keeling over.

"I think something is wrong with him," I said loudly, not moving my head. "Will you let me—"

"Shut up! There ain't nothing wrong with him. He's just a stinkin' coward."

I squeezed my eyes closed, then opened them in time to see Houston do a face-plant onto the floor. He lay there, unmoving.

I jumped up, only to be shoved back down. "You ain't goin' anywhere, sister."

"But—"

"Shut up, I said!" He tied a stiff bandana around my eyes. "I'm not takin' any chances," he muttered. "You sit there now while I get him, ya hear?"

I nodded. Why hadn't I brought Annie with me tonight?

God, please send someone to help us.

Maybe someone would drive by and see the light. My heart sank as I remembered the boarded-up front window. The only way someone would see the light is if they were on the side of the...

Wait. Had Houston actually said that he murdered someone? Who? The only body I knew of was the one I found under the crepe myrtle tree—the one that Houston had said was alive—the one who Houston had said he visited in the hospital—the bile rose to my throat.

Oh, Houston. My heart broke for my friend. *Why, Houston?*

It had to be Nicole.

Houston had seen the man following Nicole around and thought he was going to harm her—

I sucked in my breath. Aunt Dot's advice column. *Haunted in Houston.* Haunted wasn't *in* Houston. Haunted *was* Houston who had written in, confessing that he had done something that hurt others. He had put the clipping of it in my purse that day when we sang about Heaven with Aunt Dot and Harry in Aunt Dot's room at Willowbough. He must have been hoping that I would read it. That I would understand. That I would forgive him.

My hot tears soaked the bandana. *My dear friend. How could you?*

And how could you carry the burden so long by yourself? Why didn't you tell us? Why didn't you beg God to stop you before you gave way to hatred and violence?

I clutched the armrests of the chair. *God, please help us.*

What was the man doing to Houston? I bit my lip to still its trembling, listening. Judging from the grunts and shuffling sounds, I guessed he was tying Houston up. At least that's what I hoped he was doing instead of something worse.

The soggy bandana started to slip. I pushed it back into place. Did I dare lift it the teensiest bit so I could—

"Don't even think about it."

The man's breath was hot on my ear. I jumped away, screaming and clawing at my blindfold.

He clapped his hand over my mouth, yanking me back

against his chest. He reeked of cheap dollar-store aftershave.

"Your life is over if you see me, babe," he whispered. "So why don't you sit there all nice until I'm gone."

I stilled, then tried to nod. Not easy to nod when one is in a headlock. I clenched my teeth. It wouldn't help Houston at all for me to make a fuss. I'd have a better chance of helping my friend if I cooperated, right? And I still had my phone. Maybe I could manage to call 911 when he wasn't looking.

"Don't move. And don't make a sound or you'll regret it." He released the pressure on my mouth slowly, as if making sure I wasn't going to try to pull a fast one.

"Okay." I folded my hands together in my lap so he wouldn't see them shaking, and strained to see out of the gap at the bottom of the bandana.

Black dress shoes. Shiny.

I let out my breath when I sensed him move away from me. My lips were hot and swollen from his fierce grip on my mouth, and I needed to go to the bathroom. My phone vibrated in my pocket, and I froze. Thank God it was on silent.

I strained to hear any sound from across the small room. Was Houston still alive? He had almost looked like he was having a seizure or something. I'd seen one of my students experience something like that before. Her eyes had kind of gone out of focus for a minute or two, then she had collapsed on my office floor. I racked my brain. What was it called? I couldn't remember.

I heard a scrape and a grunt. Was he dragging Houston? *Dear God. Please have mercy. Send your angels to help us. Show me what I can do to—*

I sensed the heat of the man's body near my face again and shrank back into the chair.

How could he move so quietly? And what was he going to do to me?

I listened to his breath coming in short gasps.

Houston groaned.

I heard the click of a gun barrel.

The man swore under his breath. "I should shoot ya both and be done with it."

I willed the nerves in my legs to stay still.

Houston groaned again.

Cold metal pressed on my neck, right under my chin. "I'm going to be watching you, missy. If you tell that cop boyfriend of yours anything, you'll regret it, ya hear?"

I didn't dare nod.

"I said, 'Did ya hear me?'"

I gulped. "Yes."

Maybe if I sat very still and pretended to be compliant, I might have a chance to save Houston somehow. If the crazy dude didn't blow my head off first, that is. *Jesus, I trust You. Jesus, I trust You.*

"Good. Now you jest relax." He pulled the gun away from my throat, and ran a finger lightly down my cheek. His voice gentled into a sensuous tone. "I'm gonna take your friend here for a little while. He and I have some business to take care of."

I shivered.

"You are going to keep your mouth shut, right, babe?" He kissed my neck. "So I don't have to kill you?"

God, help me! Everything in me rebelled against the evil—the blackness of this man. It took all my willpower not to yank the bandana off. The only thing that held me back was Houston.

If the guy killed me, no one would ever know what had happened to Houston. I had to fight by surrendering. At least for the moment. Once the hideous man took his hands off my shoulders, I would—he started rubbing his hands up and down my bare arms.

Oh, God, no. Please no.

I would rather him shoot me than to—

I had to calm down. Figure out how to get away. Was he still holding the gun?

I squinted through the tiny spaces by my nose where the bandana had slipped a little bit. I could make out the black shoes again...a glimpse of his freckled arm. I gritted my teeth as he slid his hand under my hair at the back of my neck.

Where was the gun?

If only I knew for sure he didn't have it within reach, I

could—

Houston coughed, a low, chesty cough.

The man jerked away from me, and I sank back in the chair, my teeth chattering uncontrollably.

Breathe, Callie.

In and out. In and out.

I crossed my arms over my chest, holding myself tight against the tide of vileness, then suddenly breathing in the strong presence of the Holy Spirit.

"Jesus?" I whispered.

I am here, Beloved.

I rested my head against His chest for a moment until I could breathe again. Like I had the day Kevin had died. The moment Jason's prison sentence had been announced. The hour of Marleigh's funeral.

All will be well, Child.

I imagined angels surrounding me—surrounding Houston. More angels. Warrior angels. Some covering Houston with their great wings, some wielding fiery swords on his behalf.

And then I wasn't imagining anymore. I *saw* them. I heard the rustle of their wings. I smelled the scent of—Heaven.

Someone was praying for us. For Houston and me. The prayers were swirling around us through the air, like luminescent streaks of gold and green. The angels formed a circle around Houston, their huge forms glowing brighter with each prayer that hit its mark.

If only I could see what the man was doing. It sounded like he was dragging Houston—or Houston's body—across the floor. Had the angels taken Houston to Heaven?

Dear God.

I heard the front door squeak open, and a series of grunts.

The scent of Heaven disappeared.

I was alone.

CHAPTER TWENTY-THREE

"Todd! Oh, please answer!" I held the phone to my ear while I dead-bolted the front door of the shop. I would spend the night here before I'd try to go home alone.

"Callie. Are you okay?"

Oh, thank God. My hands were trembling so violently I dropped the phone.

"Callie!" Todd's voice was panicked. "Can you hear me? What's going on?"

"I dropped my phone. Oh, God, please help me! Someone came to my shop and he took Houston and I thought that—"

"What? Where are you now? Are you alone?"

"No. I mean, yes. At the shop. I'm alone."

Was I alone?

I glanced around, wishing now that I'd listened to Todd and had at least bought some mace. "He took Houston. And Houston was sick or something and I—"

"Okay. I want you to stay on the phone with me, sweetheart. I'm coming there right now."

I heard his truck door slam.

"Don't hang up. I want you to stay on the phone, okay?"

"Okay," I whispered. "I'm so scared. I thought he was going to...to..." Horror washed over me anew.

"Hang with me, sweetheart. I'll be there in just a few minutes."

My teeth were chattering again.

"Callie?" Todd's voice penetrated the fog that threatened to overtake me.

"Uh-huh." If I stopped moving, I would collapse right there on the floor. I paced from the door to the counter and back, glancing out the side window on each round to see if I could spot Todd's headlights.

"I'm almost there. I'm coming down Main Street. Do you know who the guy was?"

"Uh-uh." *Hurry, Todd. Please.*

"I'm pulling up in front of your store right now. Unlock the door for me, okay?"

I flipped the deadbolt and fell into his arms, weeping.

"Shh. You're safe now."

He held me tight to his body, and I clung to him for long moments. His uniform was soaked and scratchy against my cheek.

"I was so scared."

He loosened his hold a little, then smoothed my hair back from where it was sticking to my face. "It's going to be all right, sweetheart."

"But Houston—"

"I'm putting in a call to my buddies at the Temple PD right now. Hang tight." He pulled away enough to dial his phone, but left his arm around my shoulder."

I leaned against him and took some deep breaths while he talked.

He stuck his phone in his pocket. "They're on it. In fact, a couple of officers are on their way over here, too. You'll have to tell them what happened." He made a face. "Hopefully Earl's not listening to the scanner, or he'll be over here, too."

Thank God he had called the Temple police and not Earl. I didn't think I could deal with him tonight. "At least my prayer was answered."

He cocked an eyebrow.

"My angel prayer."

His eyes widened. "Let's get you inside." He edged me back into the store, and kicked the door shut behind us.

I stood staring at him, exhaustion crashing over me.

"Come sit by me." He tugged me over to the loveseat in the book nook and pulled me down next to him, wrapping his arm around my shoulders. "Now. Tell me everything that happened."

"I came over here to meet Houston because he really wanted to talk, he said." I glanced at Todd. "He told me not to tell you we were going to meet."

Todd frowned.

"He seemed like he was sick. I'd never seen him look so terrible."

"What kind of sick? Like the flu?"

"No. More like—I don't know. He was sweating like crazy and his skin was kind of grey. He seemed like he was about ready to pass out."

"Probably the anxiety from what happened with Brandon yesterday. He was the last one to talk to Brandon before he died."

"True." I had to tell him this before the police got here. "You're not going to believe this. I still can't believe it."

"What?"

"Houston told me tonight that he killed the guy who I found under my bush."

Todd gaped at me. "He just came out and told you that?"

"He looked at me and said, 'I killed him.'"

"Wow." Todd stood up to pace. "That's a game changer."

I took my glasses off and rubbed my eyes. "Why would he do that? Surely it was an accident."

"Are you sure he meant that he killed the guy who was under your bush? The guy who was tased and then drugged?"

I put my glasses back on and stared up at him. "You think he meant he killed someone else?" I couldn't wrap my brain around that idea.

Todd shrugged. "I'm trying to come up with all possible scenarios."

"So...?"

"Maybe if we can figure out who this clown was tonight, that will give us some clues as to what Houston is mixed up in." Todd strode around the room, examining everything but not touching anything. "The guy must have already been in here before you came."

I hadn't thought of that yet.

My startled gaze met Todd's. Was he thinking the same thing I was thinking?

His grim expression told me he was.

I didn't want to believe it.

"Surely Houston didn't set me up." I rubbed my temple.

"I'm sorry. But we have to consider all—"

"But what would the guy want with me? He said something like it was good for him that he had us both at once. And he took Houston, not me."

"He said that? You didn't tell me that."

"And I was the one who suggested we meet here. How could Houston arrange all that in ten minutes?"

Todd shrugged. "At this point, we have to look at all—"

"I don't believe it, Todd." I pictured Houston's tortured face. "I think he met me here intending to confess the murder."

"But why to you?"

The answer to that question would prove to be the million-dollar winner, I decided over the next couple of days. Brandon was dead. Houston was missing.

And so was Nicole, apparently.

"When did you last hear from her, Sherm?" I stood on his porch, zucchini bread in hand. It had been way too hot to garden lately, so baking was the next best thing to help me get my mind off of everything.

"She always calls me at least once durin' a week," he said. "This time I ain't heard from her since the day she left the baby." He peered at me from under shaggy brows. "I don't know where that baby is."

"She's safe, Sherm. Remember I told you that Lonnie's taking care of her?"

"Is that right? Lonnie Holloway?" He scratched his whiskered chin. "She's a fine gal."

"Yes, sir." We'd had this same conversation five times. Maybe I'd take him over to Lonnie's one day so he could see for himself. But right now, the sick feeling in my stomach was growing. "You haven't heard from Nicole at all?"

He shook his head mournfully. "It's not like that gal to ferget her ol' pawpaw."

"Do you have her phone number?"

"Nah, she allus jest calls me. Says it's easier that way."

Of course.

I handed him the zucchini bread. "I'll do my best to find her, Sherm. Will you let me know if she calls you?"

I was partly down his porch steps when he shuffled back out onto the porch.

"Callie." He swiped at his nose with a crumpled handkerchief. "Do you believe in God?"

I turned back around, looking up at him. "I do, Sherm."

The moment was suddenly holy, and as I looked full into the old man's lined face, I felt faith rise in my heart. "I believe that He knows where Nicole is right now, and that He will help us find her."

He nodded. "I'm ashamed ta say that it's been a right long while since I spoke to the good Lord."

"The Bible says that those who come to Him He will in no wise cast out, Sherm. He's waiting for you to come back."

"That's jest what Preacher done told me, too."

When had Sherm seen Houston?

"You talked to Pastor Houston?"

"Yes'm. He stopped by a coupla days ago lookin' for Nicole." He dabbed his mouth with his handkerchief. "Nah, it was longer than that. Mebbe last week."

"Ah." I blew out my breath. So much for that lead. "I'll be praying for both you and Nicole, Sherm. God is watching over her."

I finally made it over to Willowbough to have a heart-to-heart with Aunt Dot. Houston had been missing for three days with no leads. Earl tried to grill me, but I had already given my report to the detective from the Temple PD, so I kind of blew him off.

"It makes me weary to keep talking about it," I said to Aunt

Dot. "We desperately need God to intervene."

"I've been praying and praying since you called the other day. There's no news at all? What does Todd say?"

I picked a couple of pug hairs off my shorts. "Not much. They're still running the fingerprints and stuff. Doesn't seem to me like that kind of thing should take so long."

"Have you heard from your mother?"

I made a face. What did that have to do with—

"She called me Thursday morning. Said she couldn't get hold of you and wanted to make sure you were okay."

Really? My mom didn't usually seem that concerned about me. "That was nice of her."

Aunt Dot frowned at me. "She said she and your dad were both struck with a very strong impression to pray for you on Wednesday. They understood that you were in some sort of grave danger and even called many of their friends to pray for you."

My face grew hot. My parents?

My parents were the ones who had been praying for me that night. The powerful, swirling prayers that surrounded me and Houston. The angels. The scent of Heaven.

I lowered my face into my hands and wept. God had chosen to call my parents, halfway around the world in Zambia, into prayer for me. And they prayed. And God answered.

But I ignored their calls. What was wrong with me?

"You've got to let go of the unforgiveness, darlin'."

I clasped my hands in a tight knot. "I thought that I had. You don't know how many times I've asked God to help me forgive them. But I never seem to be able to completely let it go."

"I think there's some things y'all need to talk through."

"I know. But it's so hard. I—"

Aunt Dot shook her head. "No excuses. God's Word says if you come to offer something to God, and you remember that someone has something against you, that it is your responsibility to go to that person and try to make it right."

I squirmed a little bit. "I know."

"God will give you the words to say if you ask Him."

"It's not that. It's just that..." So what was it? "I guess it's that

I still feel so hurt. Like they abandoned me."

"I understand. And they kind of did. But y'all don't want to go the rest of your lives with this hurt between you, when God could heal it."

I propped my chin into my hands. "Pray for my heart to be right toward them, Auntie. And for their hearts, too. I haven't told them about Brandon yet. I don't know how they will feel about that."

Aunt Dot leaned back in her chair. "There's still something that's bothering me about all of that."

"Me, too. I went online and was reading over what I could find about the cases. Did you know that part of Brandon's defence was mental illness issues?"

"Hmm. I didn't recall that, but thinking about these last couple of months, it seems plausible."

"At the time, I thought his attorneys were grasping at straws and using whatever they could to get him off the hook. But what if he was mentally unbalanced for real?"

Aunt Dot opened her laptop. "I was reading something about that online the other day. Let me see if I can find it."

"You're getting pretty handy with that computer, Auntie."

"You can find anything on here!" She was typing and clicking furiously. "I was researching the answer for a question someone sent in to my column and—here it is. An article called 'Rethinking Schizophrenia.'"

She handed me her laptop. "I wasn't thinking of Brandon when I read it, but read it and see what you think."

I scrolled through the article. I had had some training in this sort of thing when I was a school social worker, but hadn't had much actual experience dealing with students with the disease. I could recall a handful who had been on meds to help control their symptoms.

I clicked on a link at the bottom of the article. "What in the world? Did you see this article about how doctors can sometimes diagnose a patient by how they smell? Eww."

Aunt Dot laughed. "Sounds pretty gross."

"Listen to this. It says that when people have tuberculosis, their skin smells like fresh-baked bread. And when someone has liver disease, their breath smells like fish."

"Yuck. Don't read me any more of those. I'd rather—"

I sucked in my breath. "It says when people have schizophrenia, their skin smells like vinegar. That's what I smelled that day Brandon threw the rock at my head. And the day that he died. That smell was in Houston's office."

We stared at each other.

"I bet that's why he always used so much aftershave. To cover it up. But on those two days, he hadn't used any."

"Such a shame. For one of God's dear creations to be so tortured in his mind."

I nodded. "But how does Houston tie into all of this? That's the part I can't figure out. Why was Brandon in Houston's office that morning?"

My heart ached for my friend. Was he alive? Or was he being held somewhere? Why was it taking so long to find him? And what about Nicole?

Wait a minute.

"Auntie. Maybe the guy that took Houston has Nicole."

She cocked her head. "Why? That doesn't make sense."

Nothing about this made sense. Especially the part about Houston telling me he had killed someone. But Aunt Dot didn't need to know that piece of information right now.

"You're right." But something about the whole Brandon, Houston, Nicole, dead body thing was niggling at the back of my mind.

"I don't understand why someone would kill a detective to begin with." She shook her head.

Hmm. I guess I hadn't given that much thought. Why indeed? Maybe we were missing something here. Why hadn't I paid more attention to what Todd had said about the P.I.? I wracked my brain. I was sure Todd had said the man was working for the state of Texas. And his name was Hispanic. What was it? Ricardo or Carlos or something like that. Or maybe Carlos Ricardo?

"I'm sure that man had a family, too," Aunt Dot was saying. "The whole thing is so sa—"

"Auntie." I flipped her laptop open again. "I think the P.I.'s name was Carlos something."

She raised her eyebrows.

I hastily revisited the court records I had accessed the night Houston was kidnapped. "There was a detective on Jason and Brandon's cases who was named Carlos. Here it is. Carlos Ruiz."

We stared at each other.

"So...if this Carlos guy was the same guy...and he started snooping around here...Brandon probably thought that the guy was after him." The pieces of the puzzle were coming together.

"But he wasn't? I mean, he wasn't after Brandon at all?"

I shook my head. "Todd said he was investigating a sex-trafficking ring. Unless Brandon...." Oh, no. Was Brandon mixed up in that, too?

"Then it was a coincidence that the same investigator who was on Brandon's case in Ohio is the same one who was killed down here?" Aunt Dot wrinkled her brow.

"It seems crazy, but weirder things have happened. Maybe the guy got a new job and moved here from Ohio. He probably didn't even know Brandon lived down here." My mind was racing. I hated to think it, but what if Houston had been working with Brandon somehow? That would explain Earl's strange behaviour toward me, wouldn't it?

I stared at my aunt. Then it hit me. "Earl thinks I sicced the detective on Brandon."

"Oh my." Aunt Dot twisted her wedding ring around. "What does that mean?"

That means that I had had it all wrong. All of this time, I thought Earl knew about Marleigh's murder case and was planning to pin something on me. How could I have been so wrong? This whole thing had nothing to do with me—or Marleigh—at all, and everything to do with Brandon. And Houston. Yikes.

CHAPTER TWENTY-FOUR

I called Todd early the next morning. First, I told him about the Carlos Ruiz thing. Then, I gave him the real news.

"God gave me a dream last night," I said. This was the breakthrough we had been praying for. I knew it. In fact, I was so sure of it, that I had scribbled down a description of everything in my journal the moment I awoke.

"What do you mean?"

"I saw a place in my dream, Todd. At first it was this huge open space, kind of like a campground, maybe. There was this over-sized wooden sign that looked kind of like a deer head with antlers, but I couldn't read what was written on it. Then behind that there were like some woods or trees." It sounded kind of dumb when I was talking about it out loud.

"Okay."

I wished I could see his face. "I know it might sound stupid, but..."

I had thought maybe he would understand. Todd was a much more spiritual man than Kevin had ever been, and I had hoped—

"It doesn't sound stupid at all. I was only surprised for a minute. Why do you think this dream was from God?"

Maybe he understood after all.

"I can tell. Some dreams are silly, weird dreams, you know? But God shows me things in dreams sometimes."

"I..." He cleared his throat. "My mom had dreams, Callie. What do you think it meant?"

I wanted to pursue the topic of his mom, but that would have to wait. "It was so life-like. I think it's a real place. Like if we could find it and go there, we might find the answers to some of our questions."

"Wow. Okay."

I could picture him running his hand over his jaw, his cop mind clicking into gear.

"Do you think you could draw it?" he asked.

"I'm a terrible artist. Like I can barely manage stick figures, you know?"

He laughed. "Okay. I'm on duty today, so I'll run by your house this evening after I get off. I'm not much of an artist either, but I'm a bit more advanced than stick figures."

How could I wait until tonight to do something about my dream? I pulled up in front of my shop, happy to see that my front window had finally been replaced. I sighed. I had been so distracted with everything going on lately that I was behind with my paperwork. I also had a couple of orders I had to get done today, but it was going to be hard to concentrate.

Todd was going to check up on the Carlos angle, and I couldn't help thinking that maybe we were finally getting close to getting more answers. How could I pay attention to invoices and emails when all I wanted to do was jump in the van and try to find Houston? At least I could pray while I worked. If Houston was still alive—

Stop it, Callie. He had to be alive. Why else would God give me a dream showing me where he was?

I paused outside the front door to water the outside pots. Late July was a tough time for anything to be blooming, but the huge pots of sweet potato vine were still lush. The lime green variety mixed with a couple of the purple spilled out over the terra cotta pots, adding a splash of color next to the blue front door. It made me happy to see them every day when I pulled up.

The marigolds should have been thriving, adding their brilliant orange and yellow hues to the display, but I guess I hadn't gotten the hang of growing marigolds in Texas. When I lived in Ohio, marigolds were one of the easiest flowers to grow, blooming like crazy all summer and into the fall. Here, I'd already managed to kill several plantings of them. I might as well toss this one in the compost heap, too. I picked up the pot and carried it around the side of the shop closest to the church.

I gazed across the church parking lot. Houston's white

pickup was still parked in his spot near the side door. *Oh, Houston.* I wished he was there, in his office writing sermons and making phone calls. I winced, thinking of the last time I had been in his office. Had anyone cleaned it up for him? I knew Jenna had been over there the last few days filling in for Mona.

I dumped the marigold pot onto the compost pile, managing to cover my shoes with dusty potting soil. "I'm going to go over there," I muttered. "Maybe there's something in his office that will give me a clue to what is going on."

But first, I was going to get my purse. I remembered what had happened the last time I left it behind.

I rang the doorbell at the side door, trying not to look at the hawthorn bushes.

Jenna opened the door for me. "Any news?" she asked.

"No." Not anything that I could tell yet, at least.

She fanned herself with a file folder. "The phone's been ringing off the hook with people wanting to know about Pastor Houston. I just tell them to keep praying."

"Good plan. I know God is working." I started down the short hall toward Houston's office. "I thought maybe I'd look around in his office a bit."

"It's still a mess," she called after me. "I wasn't sure if I should touch anything."

"No worries." I slipped inside the office and flipped the light on, closing the door behind me. It looked the same as it had that terrible morning when Brandon—

The gun. It was still there, its butt end sticking out from under a pile of papers. Thank God Brandon hadn't spotted it when he and Houston were arguing and—no, I couldn't go there. I lifted the papers off of it and stared at the ugly weapon. Why would Houston have such a thing?

I had never really been around guns, though with all of the crazy stuff going on, Todd had been after me to take a gun safety course. Was it loaded? Would it go off if I touched it? I remembered Todd saying that guns have safety thingies on them, so probably it was okay to pick it up. Besides, this gun had yellow lines on the muzzle. Maybe it wasn't even a real gun.

I gingerly picked it up, surprised at the weight of it. It had to be real. But what should I do with it? Maybe I'd put it in one of the drawers in his desk—

Was that Sheriff Earl's voice?

Great. Just what I needed—Earl coming in here and finding me snooping around Houston's office with a gun in my hand. What was the sheriff doing here, anyway?

I opened my Vera Bradley purse and laid the gun carefully inside, then zipped up my purse and slung it over my shoulder. I was busily browsing through Houston's shelf of Old Testament commentaries when Earl stepped into the room.

"Fancy meetin' you here, Willie." He hooked his thumb through his belt loop.

"Likewise, Sheriff," I said. "No news on Houston?"

"Seems like you'd know that as soon as me, seein's how ya got your nose in everbody's business these days."

I raised my eyebrows.

"My nephew was a sick man. He didn't mean no harm."

I looked closer at the sheriff, and noticed the bags under his eyes, the weary lines of his face. He looked five years older than when I'd first met him. Maybe the man had some humanity left in him after all. "I'm sorry about Brandon."

He shrugged. "Yeah, me too. That boy had a hard go of it with his mama being so..." He straightened his shoulders. "Look here. I don't know how the preacher was involved in all of this, but he and Brandon had somethin' goin'."

Was Earl asking me for help? Or was he trying to trap me into saying something?

I held my tongue, the gun in my purse weighing down more than my shoulder.

"I don't know, Sheriff." I frowned at him. "I know they knew each other."

He snorted. "It was more'n that, and you know it."

"No, I don't." I stared him down. "All I know is that Brandon accused Houston of shooting that P.I. that I found on my back doorstep."

"Well, if that don't beat all. Are you still goin' on that after I already told you the man didn't die? Even the newspapers said—"

"Don't patronize me, Earl. You and I both know—"

"All right, all right." He glared at me. "Let's jest leave it alone. All I want is to git some answers from the preacher. And you were the last one with him."

I rolled my eyes. "Yeah, until he was kidnapped. What are you doing about that?"

"Well, seein's as your boyfriend decided to git the Temple PD involved, not much."

"I don't know what to tell you. I'm not—"

His radio squawked. He answered it, then swore before stomping toward the door. He turned back to me. "This conversation ain't over. I know you know something and I'm goin' ta find out what it is."

I sank down in Houston's desk chair, praying. I didn't care about Earl at the moment. All I knew is that I needed to find my friend. I also knew I should wait for Todd to come with me, but I couldn't wait to see if I could locate the place I had seen in my dream. But how would I know where to look?

I texted Mona. "Are you coming home today?"

"Just pulled in!!!!! No news about Houston??"

"No. But I have some stuff to tell you."

She called me.

"I'm coming over," she said. She dropped her voice to a whisper. "I don't think Rob believes me, Callie, but I'm pretty sure I saw Nicole at a gas station not long ago on our way home."

"Where?"

"It was near Granger somewhere."

I pictured the tiny town thirty minutes from here. "Would you be able to remember what gas station it was if we drove down there?"

"Hush, Bubbles!" she shouted in my ear. "Sorry about that,

Callie. Yes, for sure. There's only like two, you know. She looked terrible."

I could only imagine. "Did she see you?"

"Nah, I don't think so. We stopped real quick 'cause I had a hankering for one of those cappuccino things and Rob wanted him a corn dog. I picked up a bag of—"

"Meet me at my shop. I'll be there in a sec." I tried to push back in the chair, but the wheels crunched over something. I shoved the chair harder, then bent to pick up the crumpled envelope that had been stuck under a wheel.

I sucked in my breath. That was my brother's handwriting. On an envelope addressed to Brandon.

The letter.

Brandon *had* received Jason's letter. But what was it doing in Houston's office? Maybe Brandon had brought it to show Houston. But why?

I folded it in half and stuck it in my pocket. I could puzzle over that later. Right now, we had Nicole to think about.

CHAPTER TWENTY-FIVE

I texted Todd to let him know what was going on and that Mona and I were on our way to Granger.

He called me right as we pulled away from C. Willikers. "I don't think that's a wise idea."

"We can't lose her again, Todd. If Mona saw her, we need to get down there and—"

He growled. "What do you think you will do if you find her? These are dangerous men."

"I want to see her, Todd. Make sure she's okay."

"I don't like it. Why don't you wait for me, and I'll go with you tomorrow?"

Mona grabbed the phone from me. "Todd Whitney. We can't wait until tomorrow. This girl needs us."

She held the phone up to me. "He says he needs to talk to you. I put him on speaker."

"Promise me you won't do anything stupid. You know she's being watched and if you—"

"I'll be very careful, Todd. I promise." I sped up to pass a semi. "And I'll text you when we get there, okay?"

"Callie—"

Mona ended the call. "Men."

We were almost to Granger when I saw it. I slammed on the brakes.

"Mona! That's the sign that I saw in my dream." I pulled onto the shoulder and backed up until I was in front of the dilapidated sign. "'Hang 'Em High Taxidermy,'" I read out loud.

Mona made a face. "You dreamed about taxidermy?"

"No. In my dream I saw a sign shaped like this, but I couldn't read what it said." I grabbed my phone and got out of the van to look closer at the sign. It was weathered wood, shaped like a deer head with antlers. A faded arrow pointed down a dirt road.

Mona rolled down the window. “Is it the right one?”

“It has to be.” I took a picture of the sign. “What if that’s where Houston is?”

We stared at each other.

At a taxidermist? But that’s where they took dead animals and—

I shuddered.

“What about Nicole?” Mona tapped her fingernails on the window frame.

I was torn.

“Let’s go see if we can find Nicole. Then we can come back by here on our way home.” I started to get into the van, then veered off to walk a few feet down the dirt road. “I can’t even see a building. It must be way back in there.”

Mona honked the horn.

I headed back to the van, dragging my feet. What if we were only a few yards away from Houston? I couldn’t simply drive away.

I yanked Mona’s door open. “We need to at least go see.”

She sighed. “I was afraid you were going to say that. But won’t it be kind of obvious if we drive your C. Willikers van right up to the building?”

“Yes. I’ll park it up the highway a little bit. Then we can walk up the road and see what’s there.”

“How about if I park it and wait there for you in case you need a quick getaway?”

I almost laughed until I realized Mona wasn’t joking. “Um, okay. Head up the highway a mile or so. I’ll look around and then text you when I’m done and you can come get me.”

Seriously. What could happen? I would hike down there a little way to see if I could spot the building, so we would know where to go when we came back.

She maneuvered herself from the passenger’s seat into the driver’s seat, puffing and mumbling. “I want you to know, Nancy Drew, that if you get in trouble with Todd for this, I’m not going to take any blame.”

“I’ll be fine. I’ll even walk through the trees instead of down the road, okay?"

"You'll get a million chigger bites."

"Go park, Mona. I'll text you in a few minutes. Then we'll see if we can find Nicole."

I stuck my phone in the front pocket of my shorts and hiked my oversized purse over my shoulder as she sped away. Why hadn't I left it in the van with Mona? It was like 100 degrees out here, and I was already sweating. I picked my way through the scrubby underbrush until I got to the shade of the trees. It wasn't much cooler, but at least the sun wasn't beating down on my head.

Skirting a big patch of prickly pear cactus, I wound my way through the trees that paralleled the dirt road. Sure didn't seem like good business to have your building so far out in the boonies, I grumbled to myself. I felt ridiculous, slinking through the trees like...like Nancy Drew. Ha. All I needed were my pumps, my string of pearls, and my shiny new roadster.

And a whole bunch of angels.

My little jaunt had suddenly ended at the back of a dilapidated barn from which emanated a horrible smell. Worse, I was looking straight down the barrel of a rifle.

"Hello, Callie. Looking for your friend?"

I knew that voice. Those freckled arms. I raised my eyes to the face of Houston's kidnapper—and Nicole's handsome, red-haired pimp. Of course. Why hadn't I put two and two together before now?

"I'm sure he'd love some company," he continued in a friendly tone, plucking my phone from my front pocket.

My heart sank. At least Mona knew where I was. Sort of.

"Cat got yer tongue?" A grin spread across his handsome face. "I've been watching you."

My throat closed.

He advanced closer. "You weren't supposed to tell your boyfriend about our little time together, sweetheart."

I took a few steps backwards. *Jesus. Please help me.*

"But that doesn't matter now, does it?" He stepped close enough for me to smell the scent of his skin. "You'll forget all about him after I'm done with you."

I gagged. The cruelty emanating from the man was palpable. Dark forms snaked and swirled around me until I felt invisible hands on my throat.

"Jesus!" I screamed.

The man fell to the ground as if stunned.

I staggered backwards, trying to breathe.

What should I do? Surely Houston was here somewhere. I couldn't run. Couldn't leave him to die at the hands of this monster. *God, help me.*

The man struggled to his feet. He pointed the rifle at me again, but this time the tip of it wavered. "Into the barn," he ordered.

I didn't move.

Jesus?

"Now!" He jerked his head toward the barn, but didn't try to touch me.

I edged toward the barn door, hoping to see Mona come flying up in my van any moment. God would not abandon me. Neither would my best friend.

"In there." He pointed with the rifle toward a closed wooden door.

I wanted to vomit. The smell of rotting flesh was overpowering. Flies crawled and hovered everywhere. I opened the door and stared into blackness.

A kick from behind sent me tumbling into the darkness. I landed hard on the dirt floor as the door slammed closed behind me. At least it was cooler in here. And the smell wasn't as bad.

I sat up. I couldn't even see my hand in front of my face. I felt around for my glasses, then froze.

I was not alone in this room.

I could sense the presence of another person. Had I found Houston? Or was there evil waiting in the shadows?

I held my breath, listening.

Jesus?

I am here, Beloved. Do what I sent you to do.

Not daring to move, I strained to see in the dark.

"Houston?" I whispered.

Nothing.

A little louder. "Houston? Houston, it's Callie."

"Callie?"

His voice was raspy, and I bit back a sob. "Yes, it's me. Where are you?"

"Over here. In the corner. I can't—"

I crawled my way toward the sound of his voice, hoping I wouldn't smoosh my glasses on my way. I needed to find them or else I wouldn't be able to—I bumped into Houston's leg and reached out blindly. My hands found the top of his head, and then his face.

"Oh, thank God I found you!" I threw my arms around his neck. "Are you okay?"

He wept then, great racking sobs.

I rocked him as a mother would rock an injured child, holding him until the pain subsided. He was burning with fever.

"I thought God had forsaken me, Callie. I've done such a terrible thing and He is punishing me."

I pulled back from him, wishing I could see his face. "He has not forsaken you, Houston. He sent me here to find you."

"I don't deserve His mercy."

We could discuss that once I was satisfied he was okay. "Let me untie you. Are you hurt?"

"No." He grunted, trying to turn so I could reach his hands behind his back. "Just my wrists and ankles from being tied up. And I have the flu, I think."

"These are some serious knots," I said. "I wish I had a flashlight."

"How did you find me?"

"I told you. The Lord sent me here to find you." I picked at a knot. "Ouch! Broke my fingernail."

"I mean—"

"He gave me a dream. When should I expect our captor to come back?"

"No telling. He usually comes a couple of times a day to give me food and water. I have no idea what he plans to do with me."

"Do you know why he kidnapped you?"

Houston heaved a sigh. "I can guess."

I finally got one of the knots free and started on the next one. "Care to tell me about it?"

"I was planning to tell you that night. That's why I wanted you to meet with me in the first place."

I nodded, then realized he couldn't see me. "Yeah, I gathered there was more to the story than what you told me."

"I still can't believe you found me. Does anyone know you're here?"

"Mona." Surely, she had already alerted Todd. And probably the police, too.

He coughed a painful-sounding cough. "What were you planning to do if you found me? Have a shoot-out with the bad guys?"

I laughed. "No, I was only supposed to see where the building was, then we were going to come back later."

But speaking of a shoot-out—I sat back on my heels, abandoning the knot picking. "Houston. Why did you have a gun in your office?"

He was silent for a long moment. "It's not a gun, gun."

"Sure looks like one."

"It's a Taser. A stun gun."

A Taser. The same weapon that was used on the P.I. Oh, Houston.

"It's a long story. I'm not a gun person. I don't like handling them. But when that guy started harassing Nicole, I decided that I might need to physically protect her at some point."

I braced myself for what he was going to tell me.

He groaned as he worked his arms out from behind himself. "I feel like my shoulders are out of joint."

I took one of his hands in mine, rubbing it to help restore the blood flow. "And so?"

"And so I bought a Taser. I didn't think I could ever bring myself to pull the trigger of a real gun on someone."

I stopped rubbing. "But you told me the other night that you murdered that guy."

CHAPTER TWENTY-SIX

I felt him go still.

I waited, wishing I could see his eyes. What was he thinking?

Finally, he took a deep breath and then blew it out. "I never said I murdered someone. What are you talking about?"

"But you did! You sat right on my couch in my book nook at C. Willikers and said 'I killed him.'"

"I meant Brandon. Not the other guy."

I gulped. Was Houston going nutso? "You didn't kill Brandon. He was hit by a truck."

"I killed him."

A chill ran through me at the terrible finality of those words.

"What do you mean?" I whispered.

"It was my fault he ran out in front of that truck."

I sagged back on the floor in relief. "No, it wasn't. He had schizophrenia and it affected his thinking. That's not your fault."

"It is my fault. He had been coming to me for counseling and I—"

"You were counseling Brandon?"

"Yes. He didn't want anyone to know, so we usually met early in the morning or late at night. I—I think he sincerely wanted help."

The puzzle pieces were starting to fall together in my brain. "And one early morning he saw you—"

"He saw me tase the man."

Whew.

"So you really didn't kill the guy."

"No." He shifted, his foot bumping into my leg. "I didn't know who he was. I thought Vic had hired some new thug to stalk Nicole."

"Vic?" *I knew it.* I knew he was involved in this whole deal in some way.

"I saw the guy slinking around Sherm's house a couple of times. Then that morning, I went to my office extra early, because Brandon wanted to meet at five o'clock. He was super paranoid someone was going to see him going into the church.

"I happened to glance out my window, and I saw the scruffy dude nosing around your shop. That was the last straw. I Tased him that morning, hoping to run him out of town."

"And Brandon saw you."

"Yes. But I didn't know it at the time. Also, I swear to you that the man was not dead. I could see him under your back-porch light. He fell down when I tased him, but then he got up and kind of staggered away."

I couldn't believe this. "Then who—? Could he have died later from it?"

"But I visited him in the hospital the next day, remember? He was a homeless guy named Roger. I'm positive he was the same person I shot. He even confessed to lurking around in your neighborhood. Just trying to get by, I guess."

I thought back to the day I found the body on my back doorstep. I had walked up to the back door of my shop, seen the man with the gift bag in his hand…his expensive clothing...his hair neatly clipped around his ears…his face crawling with fire ants…no way. It couldn't be. But it had to be.

"There were two."

Why hadn't I thought of it before?

"Two what, Callie?"

"Two men." My hair was sticking to the back of my neck. I gathered it into a ponytail and held it there while I put more puzzle pieces together. "The one you tased, and the one someone else killed and put under my crepe myrtle tree."

"I can't believe this."

I let my hair drop down my back again. "It finally makes sense, in a terrible kind of way."

We sat in silence.

"So who killed the other guy?"

"Hmm. Probably Vic or the pimp dude. Do you know what the pimp's name is?"

"No. Or maybe Earl?"

I sat still, thinking. I saw again the grief in the sheriff's eyes over his nephew. Could Earl be capable of murdering someone?

"Nah, I don't think it was Earl. He's a good ol' boy and a cheater, but I don't think he'd kill anyone."

"Brandon?"

"Maybe." Why did everything always come back to Brandon? "Tell me again why you said it's your fault that Brandon was killed."

"I've gone over it and over it. He came to me that morning."

"The morning he died."

"Yes. He came to meet with me. He was all excited to show me the letter he had received from an old friend of his."

My heart skipped a beat.

"This friend told him that God loved him and would forgive him. All the things I had been telling him for months."

"Uh huh."

"He asked me if I believed all of that was true."

I waited, but he didn't go on.

It sounded like he was crying.

"Houston?"

"I'm so ashamed." His voice was tortured.

"It's okay. Take your time."

"I…I had been struggling so much with my own faith. Why does God allow such terrible evil in His world? Why won't Nicole see the trap she is in? Then the baby on top of it." He pounded his fist on the ground. "What chance does that little girl have in this world?"

I felt for his hand, but he thrust me away.

"He came in all happy that morning, but pretty soon he was pushing me again. Accusing me of killing a man, then demanding answers about God. I finally lost it." He groaned out loud. "I shoved him out of my face and screamed at him. Told him I didn't know. That maybe it was all a fairy tale or a big fat lie. That he could only hope that if there was a God, that He would have mercy on him for all of the filthy sins he had committed."

Oh, Houston.

"He—he threw the letter down and ran out the door. I could hear him cussing and raging, but I didn't care." His voice was muffled as if he had dropped his head into his hands. "I'm supposed to be a pastor. The mouthpiece of God. A shepherd. And I didn't care."

"I'm so sor—"

"Don't say it. I don't deserve anyone's sympathy. Brandon was thrust out into eternity without God because of me. I deserve to die in this filthy hole at the hands of a madman."

The sudden steel in his voice scared me.

"No, Houston."

"Yes. And that's what I was going to do until you showed up. I've got to get you out of here."

"No. Only God could know the state of Brandon's soul. You cannot be the judge of that." I grabbed his knee. "Listen to me. If you die in here, that's two lives wasted. Brandon's *and* yours. Do you think that's what God wants?"

"I don't know anymore. I don't even know if I was ever truly a Christian."

"Of course—"

"No. No 'of course.' I've watched your life since you moved here. Saw what you've been through and how you've still genuinely served God. Marvelled at your faith in the power of prayer."

"But it's—"

"No. You and Dot. Todd. Even Mona. You all have something that I don't have. I've never had."

"How could you be a preacher and not—"

His bark of scornful laughter made my heart hurt.

"Believe me, I've asked myself that a million times. I know all the verses. Know all the right stuff to say. Took all the classes. But I never accepted the free gift of salvation that Jesus offers."

I was speechless.

"It's too easy. I can't believe that I don't have to do anything to earn it."

All the more reason for us to get out of here, I thought. I wasn't entirely certain Houston wasn't out of his head after being in a dark hole for three days. We could discuss this again once we were out of this place.

"I've got to find my glasses." I grunted, trying to get onto my hands and knees in the cramped space. "When that guy comes back in here, we need to be ready."

Houston snorted. "Right. Ready for him to bash our heads in, no doubt."

"You can't give up, Houston. 'The worst is not, so long as we can say, "This is the worst," right?"

"Leave it to you to quote Shakespeare at a time like this. What are you doing?"

"I'm trying to find my glasses." And hoping I didn't find a huge spider or a scorpion while I was at it. Or a snake. I froze. Were there snakes in here? What if I put my hand right on top of a huge—

Keep going, Callie. If we didn't get out of this place soon, we'd have a lot more to worry about than snakes. I inched further away from Houston, patting the dirt floor blindly as I went. The closer I crawled toward the door, the more I could smell the stench. "I take it this is a real taxidermy business and not just a front?"

"I would assume so. At least, I hope that those are piles of deer and hog guts out there, not—"

I gagged. "Hush. We need to have a plan. When's the last time you heard from Nicole?"

"A long time. I was afraid he had done something terrible to her. That's partly why I wanted to talk to you that night. I finally heard back from that safe house in Waco and they have a spot for her. I was hoping maybe you could help me talk some sense into her, but then—"

"Mona thinks she saw her this morning."

"What? Where?"

My hand grazed over something. "I found them!" I sat up triumphantly and bonked the back of my head against a beam.

"Where did she see Nicole?"

I rubbed my head. "At a gas station in Granger. Mona and I were on our way there when I saw the sign that was in my dream, so I stopped to try to find you and—"

"Good Lord, Callie!" Houston's voice was horrified. "Why did you stop? You should have gone to rescue her, not me."

"We will find her." Somehow, I knew that in my spirit. "But first we need to get out of here. Do you know if there are other buildings around here besides this one?"

"I don't know. But I hear a lot of coming and going. Car doors slamming; people's voices. It's not exactly hunting season, so I don't think there could be that many people coming here for taxidermy services."

How long had I been here? Surely Todd and the police were on their way by now, but I wasn't willing to sit here in the dark and wait. I stared at the faint outline of light around the wooden door. "I'm going to see if I can see anything."

I stood up and pressed myself against the crack around the door, then jumped back, stumbling over something soft.

"Someone's coming!"

I huddled on the floor, holding my breath.

The door opened slowly.

I gasped.

"Nicole!" Houston's whisper was strangled.

She stood framed in the doorway, a gun in her hand. Her usually perfect hair was dishevelled, her eyes wild. "I have to kill you," she said.

Her voice was dull. Dead.

Dear God.

I scooted backward toward Houston, and in the faint light, I suddenly realized what I had tripped over. My purse.

"Nicole, don't do this." Houston edged toward her. "Think of your baby."

"I have to," she repeated. "He won't love me anymore if I don't."

"Keep talking to her, Houston," I murmured. I only needed a minute.

"But I love you, Nicole." His voice behind me was calm, soothing. "Put the gun down, honey."

"I have to kill you." Her eyes glazed over. "Brandon killed the cop, so I have to kill you. He told me."

I slid the Taser out of my purse, keeping it under my leg. What if I missed? What if she wasn't alone?

God, help me.

"Who told you, Nicole? Who told you to kill me?" Houston inched closer to her.

She was getting flustered. "Vic!" she screamed. "He owns me."

I pulled the trigger.

"Vic owns—" She crumpled in a heap, dropping the pistol as she fell.

I snatched it up and stuck it in the front pocket of my shorts. "Let's get her out of here!"

He gaped at me.

"Now! We've got to take her with us, Houston!" I gave him a push in Nicole's direction, realizing that I had dropped the Taser. I picked it up. "Will this thing fire again?"

He jumped up and grabbed Nicole, throwing her over his shoulder. "I don't know, but we probably don't have much time."

I peeked out of the doorway. "I don't see anyone," I whispered. "If we can get to the trees, we might make it back out to the highway."

We looked at each other.

"God didn't bring us this far to abandon us, Houston."

He nodded. "Let's go, then. We're sitting ducks here. Give me that gun."

I handed him the pistol, then poked my head out of the door. How were we both going to make it across the clearing to the woods?

"Someone just drove up. We need to go now! Go!"

We burst out of the door, Houston right next to me, Nicole flopping over his shoulder.

"Stop!" Someone yelled.

I heard a whizzing sound. I kept running.

"Run, Callie! Run!" Houston was now behind me. What was he doing?

I made it to the trees and crashed over a log. I lay still, panting. I lifted my head in time to see Vic bearing down on Houston, trying to grab Nicole from him.

Was I close enough to tase him?

I had to. It was our only chance. It was either him or us.

A calm descended upon me as I aimed, and I felt an invisible hand on top of mine, steadying me.

Vic and Houston thundered toward me.

Jesus, help me!

I pulled the trigger.

The kickback jerked my arm up, and I screamed.

The next thing I knew, Todd was beside me in the underbrush.

He cradled me in his arms. “Thank God, Callie. I can’t believe—”

“Did I get him?” I struggled to sit up.

“You got him, sweetheart.” He pushed my hair off my face with a trembling hand. “About blew his leg off.”

What? “But I just sh-shot the T-Taser.”

“No way, Callie.”

I couldn’t stop shaking. “Houston.”

“He’s fine. He has Nicole.”

“I know,” I whispered. “God saved us, Todd.”

He hugged me to his chest, smoothing his hand down my back over and over. “That He did, darlin’. That He did.”

CHAPTER TWENTY-SEVEN

A day later, we all sat around my kitchen table. Todd, Aunt Dot, Harry, Houston, Lonnie, Mona, Rob, and I.

"I can't believe it's finally all over." I stroked Annie's head.

Mona's eyes were still red. "I can't believe my best friend almost died." She sniffed loudly, and Rob patted her hand.

"And I can't believe you shot Vic with a pistol." Todd tightened his arm around my shoulders. "You're a brave woman, Callie Erickson."

"I didn't mean to. I thought I had the Taser." I glanced at Houston. "I really thought I handed you the pistol and kept the Taser."

He grimaced. "It's a good thing you didn't miss."

"I still don't understand how everything fits together." Aunt Dot rubbed her bare ring finger. "So it was Brandon who killed the guy who you found on your step, Callie?"

"Yes. But he was apparently just the hit man. Vic is the one who ordered it."

"And Earl helped cover it up." Todd took a swig of his iced tea.

Houston cleared his throat. "And I didn't help matters any by tasing the homeless guy. But I guess Brandon was biding his time to kill the P.I., and when he saw me with the Taser, he figured he could capitalize on that and pin the murder of the detective on me."

"But unfortunately for Brandon and Vic, I arrived on the scene in time to see the P.I., not the homeless guy," I said.

"So what happened to him?" Aunt Dot looked horrified.

Todd winced. "I suspect Vic finished him off once they loaded him up in the ambulance. Probably dumped his body somewhere."

"Then he and Earl talked to Brandon and came up with the story of the homeless guy being the body that I found under my tree."

Rob gave a low whistle. "I always figured Earl was crooked. But I didn't think he'd go that far."

"Brandon was his nephew though, remember?" Mona sighed dramatically. "I guess blood is thinner than water."

That would be "thicker than water."

Todd cleared his throat and I made myself not look at him.

"So sad." Aunt Dot twisted her wedding ring around. "But what about the *festina lente* thing?"

"Uncle Garth."

"What?"

"Last night after I finally got in bed, I couldn't sleep. I kept thinking and thinking about everything, and that was the last piece that didn't fit together. I couldn't believe it was just by chance that that note was in one of the books that originally came from your attic."

Understanding dawned in my aunt's eyes. "You think your Uncle Garth wrote that note to you but never gave it to you?"

I nodded. "You know how he and I always liked to do word puzzles and brain-game kind of things together. I think he must have made that one up for me sometime, then used it as a bookmark and—"

"And then—"

"And then I thought back to that first day Mona and I were at Willowbough telling you about the whole thing. We saw a stack of letters on your nightstand. I assumed they were from your inmate friends."

Mona nodded. "But it freaked us out because it looked like one of the envelopes had the *festine lente* symbol drawn on it."

I took Aunt Dot's hand. "Those were letters from Uncle Garth, weren't they?"

"Yes. I was reading them one last time before I put them away for good." She glanced at Harry and blushed. "Harry and I, you know...well, I had to make peace with my past, too, Callie."

I bent down to hug her. "I'm so happy for you, Auntie."

"Aww." Mona came over and joined the hug, wiping her eyes.

I finally pulled away. "So. There you have it. Mysteries solved."

"You really are Nancy Drew." Todd put his arm around my

shoulder and winked at Mona.

She grinned at me. "Does that mean I'm George?"

I rolled my eyes. "No, I think you'd make a better Bess."

"What exactly are you saying, Nancy? I can be brave when the occasion calls for it." She squared her shoulders.

Rob gave her a loud peck on the cheek. "That's right. My sweetie is a very brave woman. After all, she married me, didn't she?"

Mona snorted, and we laughed.

"What now, Callie?" Aunt Dot asked. "What's happening with Nicole?"

All eyes turned to Houston.

He smiled sadly. "I visited her in the hospital this morning. She agreed to go to detox when they can find her a spot."

"That's a start." My heart went out to him.

"Yes. She was so high yesterday when she—" His voice broke and he lowered his gaze to the table.

Aunt Dot scooted her wheelchair closer to him. "God is going to deliver her, Houston."

He shook his head. "I want so badly to believe that," he whispered. "They destroyed her, Dot. They forced her to use drugs so they could control her. They ravaged her body. They—"

"We can't give up hope." I glanced around the table. "God allowed her to be rescued. And Vic and the pimp and all of the other guys they rounded up this morning are going to go to prison for a very long time."

"And think of the other girls," Todd said. "When they raided the house that was on the property with the barn, they found a couple of other girls, plus the records and information for at least ten or fifteen more. We're going to find those girls and rescue them, too."

"And then what?" Houston raised his head, his eyes blazing. "There's not enough safe houses to help them." He pounded his fist on the table. "I know. I've tried for two years to find places. They will need intensive counselling to even be able to function as human beings again. Where are we going to find that for fifteen girls?"

"We're not going to find it," I said. "We're going to build it."

Everyone turned to look at me.

I sensed the power of the Holy Spirit as He suddenly filled the room.

"Uncle Garth's been in Heaven for more than ten years. But God sent me that message from him when it was His time—our time." I sat up straight in my chair, my hands shaking. "We all sat in that seminar. We all wept over the plight of these girls. We all pledged to pray that God would break the power of the enemy over the Texas Triangle."

Tears flowed down Lonnie's face.

"And He did. He is." I looked around the table. "What happened yesterday was not just for Nicole. How do we call ourselves followers of Christ if He has laid this in our lap to do, and we don't do it?"

Todd grasped my hand. "I'm in."

Aunt Dot nodded and nodded. "We have to do it, Callie. I could write a column about it for the *Star*."

"Let's do this thing." Rob scraped his chair back and stood, his hand on Mona's shoulder.

Houston laid his head on the table, weeping.

Silently, we gathered around him, surrounding him with our love.

"Let's pray," I said.

We bowed our heads and closed our eyes, but no one spoke.

It was a holy moment. The weight, the enormity, settled upon me. How could we, a little group of friends in small-town Texas, accomplish such a huge thing?

Festina lente, *Daughter.*

Make haste slowly.

Go in My power. Loose the chains of injustice. Set the oppressed free.

Festina lente.

Now, a Sneak Peek at Book Two

TO ERR IS HUMAN

CHAPTER ONE

Two things happened at once. My phone rang, and every nerve in my body snapped to attention like weary soldiers who knew the drill.

Middle-of-the-night calls are never good. "Auntie. What's wrong?"

"It's Erma, darlin'. I've been praying for her all night, and now she's not answering her phone. I know it's early, but I need you to check on her." The tone of Aunt Dot's voice brooked no argument.

I flopped back down on my pillow and blew out a long breath. Erma, my aunt's friend. Not my aunt. I glanced at the time. Five-thirty. Okay, so it wasn't exactly the middle of the night. But it was still dark, for crying out loud.

"I didn't know she was sick." In fact, I had sat across from Sister Erma in Sunday School a couple of days ago. She was eighty-three years old—fifty some years older than me—and could run circles around me. "Don't you think I should wait until at least eight?"

"I don't think she's ill, exactly. But I have this urgency in my spirit that something's not right. I haven't slept a bit all night. And you know all about that."

Yes, yes, I did. My Aunt Dot was a hero of the faith, as far as I was concerned. I would probably never know the hours she had spent praying for me over the years. If she said the Lord told her something, who was I to argue? Even if it was my day off.

"Okay." I pushed myself upright with considerable effort. Mornings were not my thing. Especially mornings that started with stressful phone calls before the birds were awake. But Aunt Dot wasn't a worry wart, so if she was concerned, I'd better take it seriously. "I'll head over there in a sec."

"Thank you. I wish I could still drive. I'd just pop on over there by myself."

"No worries. I'll call you once I see her, okay?"

Annie, the German shepherd, padded into the room and nudged my hand as I said goodbye to my aunt.

"Good morning to you, too," I said, rubbing the dog's head. Annie belonged to my boyfriend, Todd, but she was staying with me for a few days while he was in Dallas. "Did you hear me up a little earlier than usual? I have to run an errand for Auntie."

She pricked her ears up at the name and looked toward the door as if she expected Aunt Dot to materialize any second. She and my aunt were mutual fans.

I brushed my teeth, threw on some sweats, and grabbed my purse. I felt a little awkward about showing up at Sister Erma's house at the crack of dawn, but she and Aunt Dot were more than friends. They had grown up together and had lived life together in the same little town for their entire lives. If Aunt Dot said Sister Erma needed me, I'm there.

I'd at least take her a few of the cranberry-orange muffins I'd baked last night. I arranged a half-dozen on my favorite antique plate and headed out the door. Annie stared at me. "You have to stay here this time, Annie-dog."

Sister Erma lived only a few blocks away on Ivy Street. I could have walked, of course, but it was still dark, and February in Central Texas can be cold. I closed the door behind me, noting that my neighbor Sherm's kitchen light was on. That was odd. I knew Sherm was not an early riser, and he certainly didn't leave lights on all night. It was too wasteful.

I'd have to check on him, too, I decided, juggling the plate of muffins as I unlocked my car. But that would have to wait. I drove the short distance to Sister Erma's in the faint glow of dawn and pulled up in her driveway, staring. No worries about saving electricity here. Every light in the house was blazing. For the first time, I experienced a twinge of apprehension. What if I was walking into some kind of emergency?

I guess I didn't have to worry about waking her, at least. I stuffed my phone in the pocket of my hoodie and grabbed the plate of muffins, leaving my purse in the car. I rang the doorbell. No answer. I could see into Sister Erma's kitchen and living room through her front window. Nothing seemed amiss.

I knocked loudly, but still no Sister Erma. I fidgeted. Should I try the door? If something really was wrong...I heard thumps coming from somewhere. Loud, rhythmic thumps. My armpits prickled, my breath shortened. Thump, thump.

Now I wished I had brought Annie. I edged off Sister Erma's porch and peered up her driveway. Her Buick was parked in the carport, and light from behind the house pooled on the driveway. The noises emanated from that direction.

Thump, thump. Thump, thump, thump. Thump. Thump.

I pulled out my phone, my hands shaking. Should I call 911?

Not yet.

I sidled over to the dark shadows at the side of the house. I would work my way up the driveway a little and see if I could tell what was happening.

Thump, thump. Thump, thump, thump.

The sun peeked over the horizon. I edged closer to the clump of Texas sage bushes near the back of the house. Thump, thump.

I didn't hear anyone screaming or anything. In fact, I almost thought I heard...panting.

I parted the bushes, my legs shaking. What was I thinking? If someone was murdering Sister Erma, I sure wasn't keen on being a witness. On the other hand, if she needed help—

Thump, thump.

Okay, Lord. Here goes. I poked my head around the corner.

Thump, thump. Thump, thump, thumpity thump.

I closed my eyes and sagged against the wall.

Not only was Sister Erma *not* being murdered, she was whaling away on her stair-stepper with such vigor that the thing was pounding rhythmically against the wooden deck like...like my delivery van when I drove too fast over the speed bumps on Fourth Street.

I blew out a breath. My knees were still jelly, and I had ditched the plate of muffins somewhere along the way up that long, long driveway in the dark. Maybe I could slink away, back home to my cozy bed—

My ring tone for Todd started blaring out "Holy, holy, holy is the Lord God Almighty, who was and is and is to come..."

I guess I was still shaky, standing there in the shrubbery, because the dumb thing played almost the whole chorus before I could silence it.

The thumps ceased.

I might as well fess up. I brushed past the bushes wearing as big a grin as I could muster. "Good morning, Sister Erma," I said, as if I always appeared in her back yard at the crack of dawn.

"Law, Callie." She blinked at me, still panting. "When I heard that singin' a minute ago, I jest said to myself, 'Erma, this is it. Hallelujah, thank you, Jesus.' I thought my time'd come to go on Home." She looked distinctly disappointed.

"Nope. Guess not. Just me coming to check up on you." I looped my hair over my ear. "I'm sorry I interrupted your workout."

"Thought maybe the Good Lord done sent an angel to escort me on." She seemed puzzled. "He been talkin' to me 'bout it some lately, you know?"

I didn't know. But I nodded. "Aunt Dot sent me over to check on you. She said she was up all night praying."

Sister Erma swiped the sweat off her face with a dishtowel. "Was she now? I reckon the Lord's done told her too."

I wasn't sure what to say. "Anyway, it looks like you're fine today. I brought you a plate of muffins."

"Why, that's right sweet of you. Guess I'll have one after I finish them cookies they brought me by last night."

"Okay, then. Is there anything I can do for you before I head home?" I was itching to call Todd back. And to pick the twigs out of my hair.

She beamed at me. "No, ma'am. Sharlene's comin' by later, and we're gonna work on clearing out those closets upstairs."

"I'll leave the muffins on the front porch. Is that okay?"

"That'll be fine, sugar. You're a sweet one, all right. Dorrie's blessed to have you. She shore was proud when you done moved here and started up that lil' ol' store of yours."

"Yes, ma'am," I said. "I'm so grateful I've been able to live near her these last couple of years. I'll tell her you're fine. She was worried when you didn't answer your phone."

She wiped her glasses on her t-shirt. "I'll ask Sharlene to take a look at it. Silly thing's been dead for a day or two."

I loved how she drew the word "dead" out into two syllables: "day-ed."

What I didn't love was the call I received a day later, alerting me that Sister Erma herself was day-ed.

It was a normal Tuesday morning in February. I opened the blinds in my small den, then knelt in front of my chair. Since moving to Texas and into this house that held so many memories for me, this spot had become my favorite place to pray. Every morning, my gaze fell on the cross-stitched saying that my Uncle Garth had loved and lived by: "Only one life, 'twill soon be past. Only what's done for Christ will last."

I added my praises and petitions now to the many thousands that had been offered from this very same room over the years, and sighed as I felt His presence surround me. I opened my journal and began to write.

Much later, I raised my eyes to the window, watching a faint glow where the sun should have been. The sky was heavy with clouds. We were in for a storm today, for sure.

The branches of the pecan tree swayed, and I spotted a brown, spiky little lizard clinging to the bark of the trunk. *Stubby.* I snickered at the name Todd had given the little creature. I still couldn't believe that Todd and I had been dating for almost six months. Ever since all that crazy stuff with Houston Gregory and the sheriff, Todd and I had been inseparable. And things had finally calmed down. I liked calm.

Annie snuffled at my door. I smiled, happy to have her for a few days while Todd was out of town. I pushed myself up off the floor and opened the door. Annie nudged my hand, then led the way down the hallway to the kitchen, checking over her shoulder to make sure I was following.

"I need to grab my phone," I said, detouring into my bedroom. "I'll be there in a minute." I picked my phone up off my nightstand and frowned at it. How had I missed a call from my friend Karen? She never called this early in the morning.

I called her back, my heart beating a little faster. I prayed that nothing had happened to Justin or the twins. Or to Sister Erma. Sister Erma was Karen's grandmother. "Karen? Is everything okay?"

Karen drew a ragged breath. "Grandma called me a few minutes ago. But she didn't say anything. I'm so scared, Callie!"

"Oh, no. Did you call 911?"

"Yes, they're on their way over. I'm on my way too. Could you come?"

"I'll be there as soon as I can." It wasn't raining yet, and it would probably be faster to jog over there than to drive. "Let's go for a walk, Annie."

She jumped up and beat me to the door. I didn't bother to put her leash on. Todd had trained her well, and I knew she would obey me. She pranced and whined while I took a second to wind my long, mud-brown hair into a messy bun. I stuck a knitting needle through it. That would hold it until we got home. I shoved my phone into my hoodie pocket. "All right, I'm ready."

She burst out the door, then flopped down on the front lawn for her morning roll in the dew.

"Come on, Annie-girl. You can do that later."

Thunder rumbled as we hurried down our street, and I glanced at the sky. Even after living in Texas for a couple of years, I wasn't used to thunderstorms in the morning. In Ohio, where I had grown up and lived most of my adult life, thunderstorms usually occurred in the afternoon or evening. Or during the night. Down here, they came whenever. And often.

The first few raindrops splashed onto my glasses as we turned the corner onto Sister Erma's street. I sucked in my breath. "Oh, no."

An ambulance idled in front of Sister Erma's house, and Karen stood on the driveway, alone. She hugged herself, rubbing her hands up and down her arms. Annie and I reached the driveway right as Pastor Brian pulled up, looking like he'd made a mad dash over from the gym.

Karen shook her head in answer to our unasked question, pushing her dark hair over her shoulder with a shaking hand. "She's gone home to be with Jesus."

What? Just yesterday she was thumping away on her stair stepper. The shock zapped my nerves, and my legs started shaking. I guess I should have kind of expected it, since Sister Erma had more or less told me straight out yesterday morning that she knew her time was soon. But still...something didn't seem quite right.

Annie whined and pushed her head against Karen's leg. Karen stooped and buried her face in Annie's neck.

I exchanged a glance with Pastor Brian. He frowned. Were we thinking the same thing?

Karen rose finally, and I pulled her into a hug. "I'm so sorry."

She returned my embrace, then drew away. The look on her face probably mirrored mine. "I can't believe it. Yesterday she was talking about planting her garden, then today she's gone."

"What happened?" Pastor Brian stuck his hands in his pockets.

Karen shrugged. "The paramedics think probably a heart attack. She called me pretty early this morning, which was unusual to begin with, but when I answered, she didn't say anything. I thought I heard her breathing..." She closed her eyes tightly for a minute, then opened them. "I called 911 and they beat me over here. Said she was already gone by the time they found her."

"What can I do to help?" I asked.

"I don't even know. At least the twins spent the night at my mother-in-law's last night." She shook her head. "Thanks for running over here, Callie. I know you probably need to open the shop. I just needed someone with me and I couldn't get a hold of Justin."

"I'm fine. Annie and I can stay as long as you want us." I had a big order of flower arrangements due to the Methodist church by two tomorrow for their annual Spring Fling, but that could wait. I would figure out a way to accomplish it by the deadline.

"I wish I would have gotten here in time. I'm so sad she was alone when she...when it happened." Karen wiped a raindrop off her cheek.

"It's so hard." Nothing I could say right now would help. *Jesus, please comfort my friend.*

Pastor Brian rested a hand on Karen's shoulder. The ambulance finally pulled away, dragging our gaze with it.

"I still can't believe this. I'll miss her so much." Karen watched the ambulance turn the corner, then slung her purse over her shoulder and straightened her back. I could almost see her mentally regrouping, facing the everyday realities of life even in the midst of her shock. "I've got to rescue Mary Jane from the twins. I'm already late, and she'll be having a fit by now."

Mary Jane, Karen's mother-in-law, could only take the twins—two sets of them—for so long. I could understand. Even one set of twins would finish me off in under an hour.

"Wouldn't she keep them for you a little longer today, given the circumstances?" I asked.

"She probably would. But I need to see them and hug them."

I had never been a parent, but I appreciated her need to hold tight to her loved ones who remained.

Pastor Brian gave Karen and me each a brief side-hug. "Sondra and I will be praying for you and your family, Karen. Do you want me to send out a church-wide email to let everyone know today? Or wait until tomorrow when you've had a little time?"

"I can't even think right now." Her phone beeped, and she pulled it out of her purse. "It's Justin, Pastor. Please just do whatever y'all usually do in situations like this. I need to run."

Justin was Karen's husband. He would step in and take care of things, I knew. I admired Justin Kimbrough. He was the strong, protective, capable husband mine never was. But that was in the past. And this wasn't about me, anyway. My friend needed me.

"I'll check on her later," I said to Pastor Brian.

He nodded, his hand on his car door. "Losing Sister Erma will leave a big hole in our little congregation. You're planning to break the news to Dot?"

My heart sank. "I'll head over there now. I'd rather she hear it from me than through an email." I so wished Todd had not chosen this week to be out of town. I sure could use his steady presence right now.

Annie and I jogged home, ignoring the flashes of lightning. "I wish it would just rain if it's going to." I opened the front door. Annie pushed past me to check on the pugs. They stared up at her groggily as she licked their faces. I couldn't figure out the relationship between the German shepherd and the pugs. Sometimes I thought Annie viewed them as her puppies, but other times she almost seemed to be worried that they were not doing what they were supposed to.

I left the dogs in the kitchen while I went to get ready for the day. I changed out of my sweats, French-braided my hair, and swiped on a little mascara. Done. But what would I tell Aunt Dot? Funny how life can change so dramatically in one day.

I drove the couple of blocks to my shop, C. Willikers, and left a "Back soon" sticky-note on the front door. Nothing like living in a small town. I prayed as I drove the mile or so to Willowbough, the adult retirement center where my auntie lived. My aunt was a spunky gal, as her beau, Harry, liked to say. And sharp. She still wrote a weekly advice column for the *Short Creek Star* newspaper. And she was closer to the Lord than anyone else I had ever known. But I knew how much she loved Sister Erma. This would be hard.

Aunt Dot lived in the nursing-home section of the facility, though if Harry had his way, she would soon marry him and join him in his assisted-living apartment across the campus. I smiled. Who would have thought my aunt would have a boyfriend when she was in her eighties? It was very cute, the way they held hands and flirted with each other like teenagers. I was glad she'd have Harry to lean on in this hard time.

I wandered down the wide hallway to Aunt Dot's room, still trying to think of what to say. When I reached her door, I paused, listening. She was singing one of her favorite hymns, "In the Garden", her sweet, high voice quavering. My throat tightened, and I sank into the vinyl chair outside her room. I could wait while she spent time with Jesus.

Glad for a few minutes to gather myself, I glanced around. The hallway was unusually quiet for this time of day, and the door to the room directly across from me stood open. I wasn't really being nosy, but the last few times I had been here to visit Aunt Dot, that room had been vacant. I could hear the low rumble of a man's voice, and I wondered idly if the new resident was someone I knew. After all, Short Creek was a pretty small town, population 1203, to be exact. A far cry from the huge suburb of Columbus, Ohio, from where I had moved a couple of years ago.

I fidgeted in the chair, wishing I had brought my knitting bag with me. I wanted to talk to Todd, but I knew he was in meetings all day. Some kind of annual training for the sheriff's department. It had only been since last summer, when we had muddled through the thing with Houston, that Todd had decided he was ready to re-join the law enforcement community. I wasn't sure how I felt about that.

I rose and stepped to Aunt Dot's closed door again, listening.

"What do you think you're doing, young lady?"

Author Note

I hope you enjoyed Callie's story as much as I enjoyed writing it. This story has been a long time in the making. I first came up with the idea many years ago, but soon afterward, my life became, well, messy. Like Callie, things in my life gdidn't turn out like I'd thought they would.

As my family and I walked through a series of valleys that seemed to have no end, I arrived at the point where I no longer had the emotional or creative energy to write fiction.

But, God.

Do you remember Callie saying that in the book? That was my cry, too. That's what it came down to. My heart was broken...but God. My dreams were shattered...but God. I had nearly lost hope...but God.

He forced me, sometimes moment by moment, to find hope in Him alone.

My questions were—are—many. Sometimes inarticulate groans, sometimes laser-sharp accusations...but, God.

He's my only hope.

He's your only hope.

He's the only hope for a girl trapped in sex slavery.

He's the only hope for a forty-something woman watching her husband die of cancer.

He's the only hope for a young man in prison.

He's the only hope for an average, middle-class woman trying her best to be a godly woman. To raise her children well. To walk worthy of His calling.

He's the only hope for single moms. He's the only hope for a pastor staggering under the weight of his burden. He's the only hope for widows. For addicts. For sinners. For orphans. For me.

Hope.

That's the message of the gospel, isn't it?

Romans 8:23b-25 says, *"...[we] groan inwardly as we wait eagerly for our adoption to sonship, the redemption of our bodies. For in this hope we were saved. But hope that is seen is no hope at all. Who hopes for what they already have? But if we hope for what we do not yet have, we wait for it patiently."*

If you're in a battle that seems unending, waiting patiently for what you do not have, encourage yourself in the Lord. Remind yourself of His past faithfulness. Ask Him to renew your hope. Rehearse this little list of reasons for hope, then dig in your Bible for more:

1. You can have hope because God promises that He will take even our brokenness and use it to create good.

"And we know that God causes everything to work together for the good of those who love God and are called according to his purpose for them." (Romans 8:28)

2. You can have hope because God is good.

"You, Lord, are forgiving and good, abounding in love to all who call to you." (Psalm 86:5)

"You are good, and what you do is good; teach me your decrees." (Psalm 119:68)

3. You can hope because God is not finished with you yet! It's not over!

"For it is God who is working in you, enabling you both to desire and to work out His good purpose." (Philippians 2:13)

"I am sure of this, that He who started a good work in you will carry it on to completion until the day of Christ Jesus." (Philippians 1:6)

And, my favorite:

4. You can hope because Heaven, not this sinful world, is your true home.

"The Lord will rescue me from every evil work and will bring me safely into His heavenly kingdom. To Him be the glory forever and ever! Amen." (2 Timothy 4:18)

"All praise to God, the Father of our Lord Jesus Christ. It is by his great mercy that we have been born again, because God raised Jesus Christ from the dead. Now we live with great expectation, and we have a priceless inheritance—an inheritance that is kept in heaven for you, pure and undefiled, beyond the reach of change and decay." (I Peter 1:3-4)

So, if you're not familiar with the old hymn that Callie, Aunt Dot and Harry sang that day in Aunt Dot's room at Willowbough, here's the rest of the words, written over 100 years ago. Sing them out loud when the going gets rough, okay? And take heart. You are not alone.

When We All Get to Heaven

Sing the wondrous love of Jesus,
Sing His mercy and His grace;
In the mansions bright and blessed
He'll prepare for us a place.

Refrain:
When we all get to heaven,
What a day of rejoicing that will be!
When we all see Jesus,
We'll sing and shout the victory!

While we walk the pilgrim pathway,
Clouds will overspread the sky;
But when trav'ling days are over,
Not a shadow, not a sigh.

Let us then be true and faithful,
Trusting, serving every day;

Just one glimpse of Him in glory
Will the toils of life repay.

Onward to the prize before us!
Soon His beauty we'll behold;
Soon the pearly gates will open;
We shall tread the streets of gold.

Eliza E. Hewitt, pub.1898

Book Discussion Questions

1. Callie moves to Texas for a new start, but soon realizes that she is still dealing with the same issues as she was before, just in a different location. What is your experience with new starts?

2. When describing her relationship with her parents, Callie says, "It wasn't that there was a problem, exactly, between my parents and me. More like...a wall. One that I didn't know how to break down or didn't care to. Some days I wasn't sure which." What do you think she meant by this? What reasons might she give for not trying to rebuild the relationship? Have you experienced a similar wall or situation? Were you able to overcome it?

3. At one point, Callie realizes that she's been very self-absorbed and wants to change. How does she go about changing? What is God showing you needs to be changed in your life? How will you go about accomplishing that change?

4. In the beginning, Callie is hesitant to begin a new romantic relationship. Why do you think she changes her mind about this as she begins to spend time with Todd?

5. How would you describe Callie's relationship with Aunt Dot? Do you have anyone in your life like Aunt Dot? Is there someone in your life who needs you to be an "Aunt Dot" to them?

6. At the end of the book, Callie and her friends choose to take on a huge task because they believe God is calling them to do so. Is there something in your life that God has been speaking to you about? What, if anything, is keeping you from being obedient to His call?

CPSIA information can be obtained
at www.ICGtesting.com
Printed in the USA
LVHW082327140621
690236LV00024B/740